Ivan is sitting on the throne when the queen walls in with a long dress on and she has her hair out she has the top of dress showing her skin he watches as she shakes her arse when she walks and he gets an instant hardon and stands up then walls towards her she smiles then he kisses her his lips pressed against hers he takes her to the wall then keeps kissing her with open mouth tongue kisses he tilts his head then pashes her he lifts off her dress then takes off his shirt as he feels her breasts she knuckles his pants then he steps out of them and lofts her up into the wall and shoves his cock up her vagina then lunges into the wall with her and slams his cock straight up her vagina as she screams he keeps pumping her up the wall and shoving his girth up her vagina ring as he pins her to the wall kissing her his arms under the back of her knees he spreads her legs open with his arms and slams his body into her groins as his cock triples in hardness he keeps pounding her pussy into the wall and she screams argh then comes he keeps doing upwards strokes with his cock and shoves his tongue down her throat and kisses her she is screaming he pins her throat to the wall in his hands then rams her vagina his body slamming into her inner thighs making loud slapping sounds he heaves his torso upwards as his cock stabs up her vagina and his girth slams into her pussy ring he keeps pounding her pussy into the wall then feels his girth stretch her vagina ring as he keeps pumping his cock deep up into her vagina with hard and fast thrusts that stimulate his cock he keeps drilling his erect pole up her vagina threading her tight vagina he can feel his shafts scraping her vagina ring her whole body tenses as she comes he takes his hands off her throat then she screams as he keeps grating and threading her vagina with hard and fast upwards thrusts he keeps pumping her vagina making loud thuds as he slams her back into the wall she screams argh argh argh with every upwards thrust with each upwards thrust he stiffens his cock and grates her vagina she screams argh then comes he keeps pumping her and thrusts hard and fast upwards getting his erection in deep into her vagina his knob hits her cervix then he shoves his knob up her arse then slides his cock into her arse hole she screams as he shoves his girth into her arse hole ring then pounds her arse up the wall ramming his cock straight up her arse he can feel his knob and shafts tight as they slide up her arse hole and she screams argh then comes he keeps pounding her arse hole ring with his girth then takes her from the wall and shoves his cock up her standing up his hips pumping his erection up her arse hole he feels his cock grate and thread her arse hole ring as he re braces her lifts her up with his arms then plugs his stiff cock up her arse hole then slides his cock back and forth into her arse hole ring she screams argh then comes he keeps pounding her arse hole and does hard and fast upwards thrust that shred and thread her arse hole ring pumping upwards he gets his cock up and up and around up into her arse hole smashing his girth into her tight arse hole ring she keeps screaming as he takes her to the lounge then pins her legs over her head holding the back of her knees then javelins her impaling her with his whole cock he downwards thrusts and pounds her arse hole she screams argh then comes as he is hammering her arse cheeks and arse hole into the lounge he leans forward and kisses her then tilts his head and shoves his tongue on her throat his cock hardens then he lifts his arse up and slams it back down smashing his erection between her arse cheeks and I to her arse hole he keeps spitting and lubricating her arse hole as he slams his girth into her arse hole ring she is screaming as he thrashes her pounding her with hard and fast downwards thrusts he feels his balls slamming into her arse cheeks as he keeps pounding her arse hole ring with his erect cock smashing into her arse hole she is screaming as he keeps pounding her arse hole ring lunging upwards he does a heap of rapid intense thrusts shoving his erection up her arse hole she screams argh then comes he keeps pounding her arse hole ring with his cock then launches upwards and spears her arse hole she screams argh then he lifts her up and throw her into the lounge she lands with her hands on the back of it as he spanks her arse around she screams then he spits on her arse hole then heaves his cock up her arse and keeps pumping her sliding his erection deep up into her tight arse hole he feels his girth stretch her arse hole as he slides his whole cock from knob to girth along her arse hole ring then keeps pumping her and shoving his cock up her arse hole with hard and fast upwards thrusts he grabs her hips then starts to thrash her ramming and smashing her arse hole with upwards heaves and whole body upwards thrust his cock slams her arse hole ring he slides his shaft along her arse hole ring she keeps screaming he keeps his girth slams into her arse hole ring she screams argh then comes he keeps vertically shoving his cock up her arse as she kneels there screaming he slams her arse head and fast and it makes a loud clapping sound as his body slams into hers and his pole slides back and forth along her tight arse hole she screams argh then comes he keeps pumping her arse hole and can see her breasts bouncing underneath her as he rams her she keeps screaming as he slams his body into her muscly arse cheeks his cock slides along her arse hole ring and he shoves his girth into her arse hole he keeps spitting then re braces her hips and rams her from behind pumping her with hard and fast thrusts he hears her screaming as well as the sound of flesh slapping into flesh quick clapping sounds he can feel her muscly arse cheeks as he bounces back off them she is screaming as he does a heap of hard and fast upwards thrusts sliding his cock along her arse hole he steps closer and his body touches hers then he re grabs her hips then pumps vigorously plugging her arse hole with his girth he ploughs her arse hole and stands there thrusting his hips as his erection slides back and forth along her arse hole ring he feels sensations all along his shafts and girth as his cock slides up her arse hole he does a heap of hard and fast thrusts as she screams argh then comes he keeps pumping her and shoving his cock deep into her arse hole she is screaming he grabs her throat in a headlock then pull a her off the lounge she makes a choking sound as he stands up with her neck in a headlock then shoves his cock up her arse hole he can feels his girth sliding deep up her arse hole ring he keeps pumping her arse hole with hard and fast upwards thrusts heaving his cock up her from behind he keeps choking her and thrusting his hips as his pole slides in and out of her arse hole he lunges upwards and keeps shoving his cock up her arse hole then slams her with a heap of upwards hard and fast pumps sliding his cock along her arse hole and shoving his girth into her arse hole ring he keeps thrusting upwards then her whole body tenses as she comes he takes his arm away then she coughs and inhales gasping then straight away screaming he keeps pumping her then he bends her over the lounge spits in her arse hole then shoves his cock up her arse and thrashes her arse hole pumping her and thrusting upwards he slams his cock straight up her arse with a heap of energetic upwards thrusts pounding her arse hole she is screaming as he keeps pumping her and looking down at her round wide arse and curvy figure her whole body shaking with each thrust he keeps pounding her and then re grabs her hips then thrashes her shoving his cock hard and fast upwards and up and into her tight arse hole she screams argh then comes she keeps screaming then he hammers her hard and fast drilling her he thrashes and bangs her arse hole he keeps pumping her and stuffs his cock deep up into her arse she is screaming he slams his erection up her arse hole ring and keeps hammering her arse with his cock he feels his shafts sliding along her arse hole then feels his girth grating her arse hole ring he shoves his whole cock deep up her arse from behind then pulls her hair she screams ouch then he re braces her by the hips and drills her plugging her tight arse hole with his erection he slams his cock up her arse then keeps pumping her thrusting his hips as his cock drives up into her arse hole and his girth plugs her arse hole ring he ouch as her up she fall over the back of the lounge then he gets on the lounge then grabs the back of it and pins her between his hard cock and the back of the lounge she screams he uses the back of the lounge to thrust his cock forward and slam it up her arse hole ring with rapid hard and fast thrust he keeps using the back of the lounge to launch his body forward as his cock slides deep up her arse she screams argh then comes he grabs the back of the lounge then heaves himself forward and smashes into her arse hole pumping her with intense hard and fast thrusts he keeps pounding her arse hole banging into her arse hole ring with his girth he plugs her tight arse hole with his thick girth and stretches her arse hole ring as he keeps throwing his body forward using the back of the lounge and banging her into it making loud clapping sounds as he pumps her arse cheeks she screams he can hear her argh argh argh screamo mg over the back of the lounge in a echoing tone she tries to stand back up then he headlock her and chokes her then keeps pounding her from behind banging her arse hole into the back of the lounge and slamming his girth into her arse hole ring as he keeps choking it goes silent in the sound of his body slapping onto hers he reaches his left hand around then feels her breasts and keeps fondling her breasts sliding his palms over her nipples he squeezes her breasts her whole body tenses as she comes he takes his hands then p have a her back over the lounge she screams as he pumps her arse hole into the top of the lounge and thrashes her arse hole shoving his girth into her arse hole ring from behind as he bends her over the lounge she is screaming argh argh argh as he keeps pumping her and shoving his cock deep into her arse he spits on her arse hole then keeps spitting and then feels his cock slide along her warm wet arse hole ring as he is pumping her he re grabs the back of the lounge then thrashes her and pounds her with hard and fast upwards thrust ramming her arse hole into the lounge she screams argh then comes he is banging her with his whole body thrusting forward and slamming her over the back of the lounge as he comes he plugs his erection deep and hard up her tight arse then grabs the back of the lounge and thrusts upwards using his stiff cock to slam up her arse hole he keeps pumping her and does fast upwards thrusts he heaves his whole body forward using his arms then pins her between his body and the lounge he thrusts forward then shoots his come up her arse and keeps pumping her she screams argh then comes he is slamming his erection straight up her arse hole as he keeps pumping come up her arse he feels his cock stiffening and slamming as he keeps ramming her and pounding her with rapid hard and fast cock slamming up arse thrusts that keep him coming he re grabs the lounge then pumps her after he has come with rough upwards thrusts jamming his girth into her arse hole ring he grabs her right arse cheek and turns her around she he steps off the lounge and he lifts her off it into his arms and he kisses her as she wraps her legs around him he tilts his head and open mouth pashes her and shoves his tongue down her throat then changes side tilting his head he keeps tongue kissing her holding the back of her neck he has one hand under her arse holding her up onto him and the other on the back of her neck pulling her lips onto his in a passionate embrace

Ivan ties the queen up to the top of the bed then blindfolds her he tickles her with a feather duster and tickles her she is laughing and giggling then he tickles under her feet and her toes and she laughs and giggles he gets a paint brush then tickles under her arms then she goes hysterical thrusting and screaming she keeps laughing and he has to get on her and straddle her to stop her from moving and then sits on her waist then keeps doing it he watches as she keeps laughing as he get the inch thick paintbrush then tickles all up and down her underarms the with the feather duster he turns around and does her feet at the same time does under her arms sitting on her she keeps laughing loudly she can't move as he keeps sitting on her she starts to scream as he keeps using both hands to tickle her on the feet and arms he keeps using the paintbrush on her underarms and the feather duster on her feet then runs the feather duster up the inside of her legs and up her groin she keeps screaming and laughing he keeps tickling her vagina and all up and down her legs he stops and she is getting her breath back then ties her legs back to the top of the bed and gets the belt then whack her arse with it he spanks her telling her he going to tickle her he keeps slapping the belt across her are cheeks and she screams ouch argh stop please stop he hears her say bastard then he links it he slaps her using his arm to loft the belt up then slams it into her arse cheek he keeps belting her with hard slaps from the leather belt across her arse cheeks then shortens the belt then slaps her harder and faster all across the arse she screams argh argh it hurts and tries to do with hold her body from him belting her he keeps slapping the belt across her arse cheeks she screams stop it then twists turns and keeps screaming argh argh argh with each belt slap her arse cheek bright pink with rectangles across it from the studded belt he keeps spanking her then goes wild she is screaming and he just nonstop hits her whacking her with the belt she is screaming stop stop he just keeps slapping her pink arse with the belt she screams constantly saying it hurts and stop it it hurts he keeps humming and slapping the leather belt across her arse till it goes red then holds the bedhead while standing on the bed then smashes her with the belt using the bedhead to pull him into the smacks he belts her arse harder she is screaming and thrusting he just keeps slapping her with the belt and she thrusts around screaming he chases her with e dry move he slaps her then slaps her again laying into her with hard and forceful slaps she screams please stop pleeeaasse stop he ignores her then keeps slapping her left and right across the bed as she keeps screaming and thrusting with her whole body tensing after each slap he watches as her eyes widen and her arse and pussy got bright pink he is instantly drawn to her he unties her legs then keeps upwards shoving his erection straight up her vagina and pumping her slamming his cock between her legs he lunges a bright up and his stiff cock threads grates and threads her tight wet vagina she screams as he keeps launching himself upwards and stiffening his cock as his erect pole and knob slide straight up into her vagina his shafts expand then he can feels the sides of his shaft scrape along her vagina ring then his girth stretches her tight vagina ring as he shoves it up her with forceful whole body thrusts upwards he feels he tears her vagina ring with each upwards heave she is screaming he is going wild shoving his girth into her vagina ring with powerful hard and fast upwards thrusts slamming his erect cock straight up her vagina he feels his top shaft grating her vagina ring as he keeps upwards and plugs her vagina with his thick erect cock he lunges upwards then does deep upwards thrusts that have his knob pounding into her cervix as he keeps slamming his cock in her tight vagina as she screams and comes he feels her vagina gush with warm pussy juices that flow around his knob and shaft instantly lubricating his upwards thrusts as he starts to glide up her threading her tight wet vagina with hard and fast upwards thrusts he feels his cock to deeper and further up into her vagina she screams argh then comes he keeps pounding her vagina ring with his erect shaft and girth slamming up into her he keeps upwards and stiffens his cock and the veiny top shaft grates her vagina ring she screams as he smashes his erect cock up between her legs and deep up into her tight vagina he lunges upwards stiffening his cock he feels his girth slam her vagina ring then his shafts threading her vagina he keeps shoving his cock up further and deeper than ever he feels his cock slamming up her vagina as if it can't get any further he maxing it out shoving his whole pole up inside her she keeps screaming as he goes hard and fast pumping her he puts his hands around her hips then drills and hammers his pole between her legs slamming her vagina he can feel his girth threading her vagina ring as he keeps thrusting upwards and slamming her tight pussy with his erect stiff cock he goes on his knees then rubs her breasts at the same time she wraps her legs around him he slides his hands all over her nipples she screams as he rocks his veiny top shaft along her g spot as he is stiffening his cock he is rocking his shaft back and forward pleasuring her special spot as she screams argh then comes he keeps pumping her and shoving his cock deep into her vagina leaping forward he puts his chest on her breasts then slams his cock into her wet tight vagina his girth slams her vagina ring he keeps launching his whole body up her with no hands he thrashes her pussy drilling his cock up her vagina he thrusts and humps her pounding her vagina ring with his girth she is screaming as he keeps up then grabs her throat and chokes her into the bed and shoves his cock up her vagina using his hands around her throat to pivot off he lifts his arse up then slams it back down pounding her tight wet pussy into the bed with hard and fast downwards thrusts he feels his veiny top shaft scrape and thread her upper roof of her vagina then keeps sliding his erection up and down her tight vagina ring she is looking straight at him making a orgasm face and her eyes start to roll back her whole body tightens and she comes he takes his hands off her throat as she sits up and coughs inhaling air he keeps pounding her into the mattress with a heap of hard and fast thrusts she is screaming he keeps pumping her pussy with his cock and slamming his erection into her vagina she screams argh then comes he keeps pumping her then grabs her hips and slams her vagina with hard and fast upwards thrusts he feels his shaft sliding deep up into her vagina then his girth keeps stretching her vagina ring as he lunges up the bed heaving his cock up her vagina she keeps screaming as he pins her hips to the mattress then humps her pumping his cock up I to her vagina he unties her hands then takes off her blindfold she scurries into position with her arms on the bedhead bent over he runs and leaps into her with his erection and slams her vagina with his cock then humps her and pumps her with hard and fast upwards thrusts and heaves ramming her from behind he feels his cock stiffen inside her tight vagina he lunges upwards and shoves his girth into her vagina ring then grabs her hips and thrusts upwards as he thrusts upwards his erection hits her vagina and she screams argh then he shoves his knob into her cervix and keeps slamming his cock up into her tight pussy she screams argh then comes he just keeps pumping her and doing hard and fast upwards thrusts sliding his cock deep up into her vagina re bracing her by the hips and pumping her vagina with rapid upwards thrusts he feels his shafts threading her vagina ring then belts her arse cheek ouch she screams he pumps her harder and faster than does a heap of vertical upwards thrusts she screams argh then comes he keeps pumping her and shoves his cock deep up on her vagina she screams argh argh argh with each upwards thrust he keeps shoving his cock up her vagina and grabbing her hips and thrashing her with intense rapid thrusts he does hard and fast upwards lunges that have his erection drilling her vagina then he re braces her by the hips and does vertical upwards strokes his pole getting shoves straight up into her tight vagina she screams argh then comes he keeps ramming her then feels his cock grate and thread her vagina grabbing her by the hips he kneels there pounding her vagina with rapid upwards heaves he pumps his cock up deep up into her vagina scraping her vagina ring and threading her tight wet pussy he feels his erect pole slide back and forth rapidly along her tight vagina then lunges upwards and slams his girth into her vagina while spanking her she screams ouch he re grabs her by the hips then thrashes her pounding her pussy he keeps slamming his cock up her vagina then whack he belts her again she screams argh he re brash her hips then thrashes her and slides his cock in and out of her vagina his girth stretching her vagina ring as he shoves his cock deep and hard up into her tight wet pussy she keeps screaming as he throws her up and off the bedhead then body slams her onto the bed onto her stomach then quickly straddles her shoves his cock in her arse then slides up wards and shoves his whole cock straight up her tight arse hole she screams he thrashes her plugging her arse hole with his erection he lunges upwards and hears her screaming as his cock slams up and into her tight arse hole he keeps thrusting upwards then gets his girth to stretch her arse hole ring as he lunges upwards she screams argh then comes he keeps pumping her and does upwards thrusts launching his whole body upwards his stiff cock threading her arse hole ring as he keeps doing powerful upwards lunges that have his erection slamming into her arse hole ring as she kneels screaming he pounds her arse hole into the mattress grabbing her hips she is screaming as he holds her there and drill her arse hole in with his pole shoving his cock hard and fast up her arse pounding her arse hole ring with his cock she keeps screaming as he launches upwards and his stiff cock tears her arse hole his girth pounds her arse hole ring and she screams argh then comes he keeps pumping her whack he lets her arse cheek with his hand then re grabs her hips and thrashes her using her arse hole to pleasure his shaft he keeps sliding his cock up her arse hole while grabbing her breasts and gently squeezing them he pumps her arse hole with hard and fast thrusts spitting on her arse he keeps pumping her and shoving his cock deep into her arse hole he feels his girth slam her tight wet arse hole she screams argh then comes he keeps pounding her arse hole into the mattress with hard and fast downwards thrusts he feels his cock harden then slides his whole erection up her arse hole slamming her arse hole ring she screams argh argh argh as he pumps her arse hole with hard and fast upwards thrusts sliding his erect pole up her arse hole he keeps spitting then re braces her by the hips and thrashes her arse hole in with his bonor ramming her arse hole with upwards heaves that make his stiff cock thread and grate her tight arse hole ring as he is thrusting upward and pounding her tight arse hole he gets sensations all around his knob and shafts from slamming them into her tight arse hole he slides his cock hard and fast upwards thrusting his hips as his pole drills her arse hole into the mattress and slams her muscly arse cheeks into the bed he keeps fondling her breasts and nipples sliding his hand and rubbing them as she screams argh then comes he feels his girth stretch her arse hole ring as he slams his cock up her arse hole he does a heap of hard and fast upwards thrusts then shoves his girth up her arse hole she keeps screaming as he slides his cock up her arse hole and slams her arse hole with his cock he keeps thrusting and slamming her arse hole pounding her arse hole ring with his stuff cock slamming her tight arse hole he grabs her hips and throws her up onto all fours argh argh argh she screams as he keeps pumping her arse hole straight away pounding her arse cheeks his cock slams into her arse hole ring as he keeps pumping her and shoving his cock up her arse with rapid hard and fast upwards heaves he feels his cock slam her arse hole then re grabs her hips then keeps slamming her arse hole with his girth he keeps doing upwards thrusts and hard and fast pumps sliding his cock up her arse hole she keeps screaming as he teaches forward and chokes her it goes silent only the sound of his body slapping onto hers making a flesh hitting flesh clapping sound as his cock slides up her arse hole and his cock slams her arse hole her whole body tightens as she comes he takes his hands from her throat and she coughs then inhales gasping for air he keeps pumping her then whack ouch she screams as he belts her arse cheek and pumps her with rapid hard and fast upwards thrusts he keeps pounding her arse hole then whack he spanks her again then re braces her by the hips and rams her arse hole with his cock shoving his whole cock deep up inside her arse hole he keeps grabbing her by the hips and pumping her arse hole with his cock then leaps upwards and tears her arse hole apart with upwards thrusts and hard and fast heaves pounding her arse hole he keeps spitting on her arse then pumping her arse hole shoving his cock hard up her arse hole ring she screams argh then comes he keeps thrashing her and shoving his cock on her tight arse hole then steps off the bed slides her across by the ankles then grabs her hips and pushes her into the edge of the mattress pinning her there he gets his cock then shoves it back up her arse then pumps her with a heap of hard and fast upwards thrust that keep her screaming he pounds her arse hole with his erection then lunges upwards and heaves his cock up her arse she screams argh then comes as he keeps slamming her arse hole into the mattress edge pounding her arse hole he keeps slamming his erection up her arse he lifts her up then throws her on her back then pulls her to the edge of the mattress then holds her by the back of her knees as she slips his cock in her arse then screams as he thrusts forward and shoves his cock up her arse he keeps pounding her then slams his cock deep and hard into her arse hole sliding his erect pole up her arse she screams argh then comes he keeps pounding her arse hole into the bed then puts her legs on his shoulder then keeps pumping her and shoving his cock up her arse hole his girth smashes up her arse hole and she screams she braces her by the hips then thrashes her holding her by the hips he shoves his erection up her arse hole and keeps pounding her arse hole into the mattress with a heap of hard and fast pumps that drills her arse hole and slams her arse hole ring he keeps sliding his cock up her arse she screams argh then comes he dies a heap of hard and fast upwards thrusts then leans right over and with his arm out straight he snatches her throat and chokes her she makes a choking sound then he keeps pounding her arse hole ring and doing hard and fast pumps slamming his cock into her arse hole he keeps sliding his cock into her arse then slams his erection up her arse hole he lunges upwards and his cock slams her arse hole he keeps sliding his cock up her arse then pounds her arse hole into the edge of the mattress she comes then he takes his hands of her throat and she gasps for air coughing he grabs her by the legs then keeps pumping her arse hole she screams then he keeps pounding his cock up her arse hole and bracing her legs up in the air his erection slides up her arse as he keeps pounding her he goes hard and fast then starts to come he grabs the back of her knees pins her down onto the bed then slams his cock deep and hard akin to her arse hole she screams as he thrashes her doing hard down wards thrusts he slams his cock into her arse she screams and comes he keeps pounding her arse slamming his erection into her arse hole he re braces her by the back of the knees and pins her down then smashes her arse hole with upwards thrusts and hard and fast downwards penetration he shoots come in her arse and comes he keeps pounding her then does a heap of powerful downwards thrusts he keeps coming and feels his cock spasm uncontrollably inside her tight arse hole ring as he keeps slamming his cock into her arse hole and shooting come up her arse hole ring his balls slapping against her arse cheek as his whole cock slams back and forth inside and along her tight arse hole ring he takes his hands off her back of her knees then lays on top of her and kisses her tilting his head he open mouth pashes her and shoves his tongue down her throat then lifting her up by the back of her neck he stands back up kissing her as she sits up on the mattress he stands between her legs tongue kissing her as she sits on the bed

Ivan is in the study reading then the queen walls past one of the end of the aisles she stops then walls backwards when she sees him he puts down the books and she says to him blah blah he gets her then pins her up against the bookshelf and kisses her he slides his hand up her dress then pulls down her undies then she kicks them off at the same time he undies his pants his cock goes up and then he lifts her up and slams her with his hips thrusting his cock goes in and on further he feels his top shaft thread her vagina ring as she screams he keeps pumping upwards and shoving his cock up her he slams her into the bookshelf then re braces her lifting her up around her legs he gets up and under her the man drills his cock vertically up and in her vagina she is screaming ah ah ah as he keeps slamming his cock between her legs and up her vagina he keeps pumping her as she screams argh then comes he does hard and fast vertical thrusts shoving his erection straight up into her vagina making her scream he slams her back again into the bookshelf them lifts her back up then keeps pumping her and shoving his girth up into her pussy he re braces her lifting her up by the legs then pumps her and plugs her vagina with his whole pole sliding up into her pussy he feel his knob hitting her cervix then he lets out a groan as she is screaming he keeps slamming her into the bookshelf then does hard and fast upwards thrusts he feels his cock to hitter as her vagina leaks all around his knob feels a gush of hot pussy juice that stimulates and lubricates his erect cock as he thrusts upwards she screams oh my god he keeps pumping her and looking into her eyes she keeps staring at him with a look of fuck me harder on her face her arms around his neck as he keeps pumping her whole body voices up and down of his cock as he keeps sliding his cock up her vagina he feels his cock threading and grating her vagina as it goes both up and down along her vagina walls he van feels the side shafts scraping her vagina ring she screams argh then comes he keeps pounding her pussy and slamming his girth into her pussy he gets a good rhythm going where she is bouncing up and down at the same time he is pumping her with his cock he keeps slamming her back into the bookshelf as she screams he just keeps plugging her vagina with his erect pole he feels his veiny top shaft scraping along the roof of her vagina and his girth slamming her vagina ring she keeps screaming as he thrashes her he slams her into the bookshelf then smashes her pussy with his erection ramming and plugging her with his erect cock he does upwards heaves that shoves his erection deep up into her tight wet pussy she keeps screaming then he pins her to the bookshelf arghh she makes a choking sound and it goes quiet only the sound of his cock slamming up into her vagina as he gets right up and under her then plugs his cock up her vagina he can feel his cock having to squeeze in to fit in her tight pussy as he keeps jamming his erection up her he gets an instant sensation his cock hardens then he feels it grating and threading her vagina he keeps shoving his cock vertically up her vagina and slams her vagina ring she comes he lets go of her throat and she gasps and falls back into his arms as he catches her then shoves her back into the bookshelf she screams as he re braces her legs then pumps her with hard upwards thrusts he feels his side shafts being stimulated as they squeeze into her tight wet pussy he lifts her up off that bookshelf then slams her up against the one behind she screams as he quickly re braces her lifting her up properly up higher then gets up and under her and thrusts upwards he stiffens his cock and he feels his girth slam into her pussy lips he keeps pounding her pussy his arms under the back of her knees his hands on her side he thrusts his hips and his cock drills into her vagina he keeps pumping her and does a heap of rough hard and fast upwards thrusts that make her screams and come he keep pumping her and shoves his cock deeper and harder up further into her tight wet pussy as she screams he keeps lifting her up with powerful upwards thrusts that slam her pussy lips with his girth he runs then leaps onto the lounge with her argh she screams as he lands on top of her impaling her with his erection he downwards thrusts pumping her from above he quickly grabs her by the wrists and pins them behind her head then lifts his arse up and down then keeps kissing her sliding his palms and hands over her breasts at the same time he slams his cock into her pussy then does upwards thrusts as soon as he starts lunging up and tearing her vagina ring she starts screaming louder he keeps launching upwards stiffening his cock as he lunges up his cock scraped and threads her vagina and she screams s argh then comes he is launching upwards and his girth smashes her vagina he feels his knob hitting her cervix then places his hands around her throat and chokes her into the lounge he lunges upwards then feels his top shaft slide along her vagina ring he keeps looking at her as he pumps his cock up her vagina and keeps pounding her vagina ring with his girth he feels his girth slam her vagina ring and he keeps shoving his erect pole up her vagina he uses his whole body to lunge up into her and his erection spears her vagina he keeps heaving his stiff cock up I to her vagina then feels his knob pounding her cervix as he does hard and fast vertical thrusts shoving his pole straight up her vagina he gets he gets his pole to go up and under her then he keeps pounding her pussy into the lounge she comes then he takes his hands off her throat and she gasps for air pant- ing heavily before screaming as he thrashes her he takes his hands off her then pumps her with hard and fast upwards thrusts he keeps pounding her pussy grabbing the sides of the lounge he heaves his pole up her vagina as it hits her cervix she screams argh he keeps pumping her vagina with his erection then lunges upwards and feels his girth slam her vagina ring then thread her inner walls he keeps pounding her pussy into the lounge then with both hands grabs the sides of the lounge then slams his cock up her vagina argh she screams as he keeps using his arms to propel his body upwards and ram his stiff cock between her legs and straight up her tight pussy ah ah ah she is screaming as he pumps her with hard and fast thrusts he feels her vagina leak then as he is sliding his cock up her it becomes more faster and feels good around his shafts he keeps holding grabbing the sides of the lounge and heaves his whole body for- ward his cock plugs her vagina and she screams argh then comes he thrusts upwards then keeps pumping her and uses all his body to thrusts upwards and shape his erection up her tight va- gina she keeps screaming as he grabs the lounge behind her then pounds her pussy and rams her using his arms up and holding the lounge he heaves his erection into her pussy she screams argh then comes he keeps grabbing the lounge and hurling his cock up between her legs and up deep into her wet vagina thrashing her pussy he stiffens his cock at the same time he uses his arms to then his body into her resulting in his erection threading and grating her tight vagina as his cock slams into it he keeps using his arms to launch his body forward and shoves his erect stiff cock up her vagina his veiny top shaft pleasuring her g spot he keeps pumping her as she screams argh then comes he lunges upwards and is pumping her pussy as she screams he gets up off the lounge then turn a her around like one of them plates at a Chinese restaurant she spins then he stops her then using both his hands he holds the back of her knees then whack he does a powerful upwards thrust that slams his erection up her vagina argh she screams he keeps pounding her vagina into the lounge and then drills her with a heap of hard and fast downwards thrusts he slams her her pussy into the lounge then grabs her leg and lifts them back to the back of the lounge then pumps her pussy with hard and fast downwards thrusts pounding her vagina she is screaming as he keeps sliding his cock into her vagina his body slams her arse cheeks making a loud flesh on flesh clapping sound as well as her screaming he can feel his cock going deep into her vagina his girth hitting her vagina ring as his knob pounds her cervix she screams argh then comes he keeps pumping her and looking into her eyes as she looks up at him screaming her arms out to the sides he pounds her pussy into the lounge as she lay almost on her shoulders he has her legs up and over her head pinning her calves to the top of the lounge as he pumps his cock into her pussy he keeps thrusting and shoving his erection into her vagina then slams his cock in deeper and harder she screams argh then comes he drops her legs then chokes her into the lounge then smashes his cock into her vagina pounding her pussy into the lounge he feels his cock slam between her legs and his erect cock tears and threads her tight vagina as he keeps pounding her pussy with hard and fast thrusts ramming her into the lounge he keeps drilling his cock into her pussy and plugging her vagina with his stiff erection he lunges upwards then spears her tight pussy with his pole shoving it deep up into her wet pussy he thrashes her vagina with his stiff cock and slides her whole cock up deep up into her vagina shoving his girth into her pussy lips he feels her vagina leak then goes into ramming speed pumping her and pounding her with rapid intense thrusts her eyes roll back and she comes he lets gi3 of her throat and she gasps and slaps him he kisses her into the lounge and keeps pumping his cock into her vagina she screams he keeps pounding her pussy then does upwards thrusts that slam his knob I to her cervix he lifts her up then throws her into all fours she lands and then braces holding the top of the lounge she turns around arghh she screams as he shoves his cock up her vagina then grabs her by the hips and pumps her with hard and fast thrusts that stimulate his cock he feels sensations all along the sides of his shafts as they scrape into her vagina he throws his hips back and forth and his cock pumps into her wet tight pussy he belts her arse cheek ouch she screams then he keeps pounding her pussy and grabbing her hips and thrashing her with hard and fast upwards thrusts he slams his cock up her vagina his body slams into her arse cheeks making loud banging sounds he keeps pumping her and shoving his cock up her vagina then feels his cock threading grating and scraping her vagina ring as he stiffens his pole it keeps slamming her vagina she screams argh then comes he keeps lunging upwards and his cock nearly lifts her up he gets up and under her and does vertical thrusts spearing her vagina his knob hits her cervix belting her arse cheek she screams ouch he pulls her hair then grabs her hips and thrashes her vagina with wild penetrating upwards thrusts he shoves his cock in deep and hard truth up in her tight wet pussy she screams argh then comes he keeps pumping her then grabs her hips and pound her pussy with deep upwards thrusts he hears her screaming argh argh argh with each thrust he feels her vagina leak then his cock slides along her vagina he keeps pumping her and shoving his deep up her vagina pumping her with rapid hard and fast thrusts slamming his erect pole between her legs and up her vagina she screams then he sees her holding onto the back of the lounge she tenses her body to brace herself as he unleashes a heap of powerful upwards heaves that slam her pussy and make her screams louder and more intense he keeps banging her pussy smashing her arse cheeks his cock slides up deep into her tight vagina he re braces her hips properly then slams his stiff cock up between her legs and deep into her vagina as she screams argh then comes he reaches around and pulls her arms back then grabs her by the arms and pounds her pussy with his erection slamming into her tight wet vagina he feels his cock to in deep as his girth smashes her vagina ring he keeps slamming her she is screaming he feels his girth slamming into her pussy lips she keeps screaming then as he pounds her vagina with a heap of rapid intense pumps she screams argh then comes he keeps pumping her and feels his shafts threading her vagina he lets gi3 of her arms and she crashes s back onto the back of the lounge with her hands he stands there grabbing her hips and pounding her ramming her tight vagina he feels his cock slamming up her vagina as he shoves his cock in deeper and harder she is screaming looking back at him he reaches up and grab her hair by the roots ouch she screams he thrashes her pounding her with hard and fast thrusts that make a loud clapping sound she is screaming then as he re grabs her hips and holds her still her slams her pussy with hard and fast rapid thrusts am ah am she screams a echoing scream as he pounds the air from her lungs and shoves his cock in deep up her vagina he grabs her by the upper thighs then slams his cock into her pussy staining his whole cock deep up her tight vagina she keeps screaming then comes he pounds her with rapid hard and fast thrust then shoves his knob in her arse then she screams louder arghh he rams his erection deep into her tight arse hole then keeps shoving his whole pole deep up into her arse hole smashing her arse hole ring with his girth he thrashes her and pounds her with hard and fast upwards thrusts he keeps pounding her arse hole then as he shoves his girth into her arse hole during she screams argh then comes he keeps pumping her arse and she is screaming holding onto the back of the lounge me keeps sliding his cock up her arse and shoving his girth into her arse hole ring he keeps pumping her arse hole ring with his erection she is screaming ah ah ah he keeps pumping her and feels his cock sliding up I to her arse hole he slams his stiff cock up her arse then re braces her hips then slams his erect pole straight up her arse with hard and fast pumps he keeps ramming her and plugging her arse hole ring with his stiff cock as she screams argh then comes he keeps sliding his cock up her arse then thrusts upwards and slams his girth into her arse hole ring he pushes her arse forward and she slams over the back of the lounge he gets up then lunges into her with his erection slamming straight back up her arse argh she screams as she is bent over the back of the lounge he grabs the back of the lounge then slams her arse hole ring with his stiff erection pounding her arse hole into the back of the lounge he keeps using his arms to thrust forward and up into her arse hole as she screams argh then comes he is pounding her arse hole slamming her arse hole ring with his erect pole pounding her with hard and fast upwards thrusts that stimulate his knob as it slams up her arse me feels his shafts sliding rapidly back and forth along her tight arse hole ring then keeps sliding his shafts along her tight arse hole she scram argh then comes he uses his arms to keeps slamming his body forward his erection stabbing up her arse hole as his girth smashes into her arse hole ring and she keeps screaming he pounds her arse hole with hard and fast upwards thrusts and deep anal penetration he thrashes her arse hole and spits on her arse hole ring then slides his cock rapidly up her arse bending her over the back of the lounge and using his arms to slams his cock up her arse she is screaming argh argh argh with each upwards thrust her head bent over the back of the lounge as he slams her arse hole with hard and fast thrusts he keeps pounding her pussy then pulls her hair back and gets her in a headlock she makes a choking sound then he can smell her hair as he holds her in a headlock and thrashes her with hard and fast upwards thrusts he keeps pounding her arse hole and slamming his girth into her arse hole ring then as he is choking her and shoving his erection up her arse he slams his cock deep up into her arse hole and she comes he takes his arm away then she coughs and splatters he pushes her straight back over the lounge she screams then he grabs the back of the lounge then pounds her arse hole in with a heap of rapid hard and fast thrust using his arm to propel his body forward and his cock slams up her arse hole he slams his girth into her arse hole then slides his erection deep up into her arse hole she screams argh then comes he pumps her with hard and fast thrusts he heaves her up from over the back of the lounge then turns left and falls with her onto the lounge argh she screams as he lands on her and starts prone boning her he slides his cock rapidly back and forth along her arse hole she keeps screaming he pounds her with hard and fast upwards heaves shoving his cock deep up into her arse hole he grabs her hips then thrashes her shoving his cock deep up into her tight arse hole he keeps pumping her and then spits on her arse hole argh she screams as he keeps pumping her and pounding her arse into the lounge he keeps spitting on her arse hole then slides his cock deep up into her tight arse he feels his cock sliding rapidly back and forth along her tight arse hole then holds her by the hips then thrashes her arse hole ring she screams argh then comes he keeps pounding her arse hole then thrusts back and forth and his cock drills her arse hole he thrusts upwards then plugs her arse hole with his girth he feels his whole cock sliding deep up into her tight arse hole ring then pounds her arse hole into the lounge he does a heap of rough deep upwards thrusts then steps off the lounge as she sits up he shoves his cock in her mouth then comes she is gagging and splattering as he grabs the back of her head then shoves his cock deep down the back of her throat she keeps coughing as he shoots come into the back of her throat as he keeps filling her throat with come she makes a choking sound and keeps splattering then as he keeps shoving his cock deep into the back of her throat she swallows and gulps and stops splattering he looks down at her she looking up at him with his veiny thick cock in her lips he lifts her up then kisses her and rushed the hair back from her face then then holds the back of her neck and open mouth pashes her and shoves his tongue down her throat he slides his lips across to the other side of her mouth then open mouth pashes her one the other side

Ivan is with the queen in the bedroom when she goes and starts getting dressed to gi3 to breakfast he tells her one more time and she pretends to be wanting to gi3 to breakfast he slides over then grabs her wrist and pulls her onto the bed she is putting on her shoe and falls back onto the bed giggling he kisses her them lifts her up like a doll lifts her nightie up over her head then walks with her in the air kissing her as he goes to the end of the bed she opens her eyes from kissing him then sees herself in his arms at the end of the bed and she looks up and sees the knots then screams to put her down he outs her down and she runs off he laughs as he snatches her wrist as she runs off then lifts her up by it like a piece of washing then hangs her up with rope and ties her up instead of a peg takes her other hand then does the same and ties her up facing the bedhead her arms tied up to the top of the bedhead he takes the whips they cracks it above her shoulder and she screams then he does it across her other shoulder she clenches and screams louder screaming no Ivan look I already sore from last night he just whips her arse then watches as she screams and thrusts upwards clenching the restraints she screams argh then as he whips her again she screams stop he does faster and harder whips all across her arse cheek and upper thigh as she just keeps screaming argh then louder arghh he ties her legs out to the sides then whips her upper thighs and watches as she screams stop with whip marks all across her back he goes up to her then kisses her lips she flicks his head away then he belts her with his hand and she fly's up in the air from the impact then as she comes back down he puts his hand up to stop her then kisses her again he shoves his tongue down her throat then keeps kissing her she moans as he open mouth pashes her and keeps groping her he takes his lips away then walks back behind her then crack he lifts the whip up and crack the whip over her back and puts lines all down her back argh she screams arghh he keeps whipping her then she keeps screaming stop argh it hurts please stop it argh he keeps whipping her then whips her arse cheeks argh argh argh she keeps screaming as he whips her back and watches as she thrusts around screaming argh argh argh it hurts crack arghhh she keeps screaming as he just stands there swinging the whip up and over his head and whipping her arse cheeks putting long red lashes all across her back and arse cheeks as she keeps screaming he keeps whipping her argh stop stop stop argh she screams as he keeps whipping her arse and back then he runs up to her with his cock up and erect he shoves it up her arse then thrashes her argh she screams as he shoves his whole stiff cock straight up her arse then he talks dirty to her then as he goes to grabs her hips and thrashes her he pulls her hair then quickly grabs her by the hips and pounds her arse hole with hard deep stabs he feels his cock grate and thread her tight hot arse hole he feels his knob and shafts being penetrated by his erection he pumps her with hard and fast thrusts ramming her arse from behind he does hard and fast thrust and upwards heaves pumping her rapidly with his erection slamming into her arse hole he keeps plugging her tight arse with his cock then slides his cock hard and fast up her arse hole ramming her and hammering her she screams argh then comes he keeps pumping her and shoving his cock up her arse then lunges upwards and spears her arse hole with his erection going straight up her arse from behind he re braces her hips then thrashes her pounding her arse hole ring he slides his cock hands and fast up her arse then rams her arse hole and plugs her arse e hole ring with his girth she screams argh then comes he holds onto her arse cheeks and hips then smashes her pumping her arse hole he feels his cock sliding into her arse hole and his girth slamming into her arse hole ring he thrashes her arse hole with hard a and fast pounding upwards thrusts that Invigorate his cock then he feels his cock harden then slides his erection hard and fast up her arse with penetrative thrusts and hard upwards pumps he drills his penis up her arse then does diagonal thrusts and slams his girth up her arse hole and hammers his erection deep up her arse and shoves his girth into her arse hole ring and thrusts upwards smashing his cock up her arse thrashing her as she screams argh then comes he keeps pumping her and does hard and fast upwards thrusts pumping her with rapid deep anal penetration he pounds her arse hole ring with his erect pole sliding straight up her arse he keeps pounding her arse hole with his cock and she screams argh then comes he grabs her by the hips then thrashes s her ramming her arse hole ring he does hard and fast upwards thrusts that jam his cock deep up her arse he keeps pounding her arse hole with his cock then does a heap of hard up wards thrusts that keep her screaming and invigorate his cock then he re braces her hips and thrashes her pounding her arse with hard and fast upwards thrusts she screams argh then comes he keeps pounding her arse hole with hard and fast upwards thrusts and can feel his cock pounding her arse hole ring he keeps sliding his erection deep up her arse hole then rams his cock hard and fast up her arse he puts his arms hands around her throat then she makes a choking sound he keeps choking her with his hands then pumps her with hard and fast thrusts pounding her arse hole he thrashes her arse e hole ring with his stiff cock he keeps pounding her arse from behind then does a heap of hard and fast upwards thrusts she comes then he takes his hands from her throat and she gasps for air inhaling she screams argh as he keeps thrusting his erection up her arse e hole and does a heap of hard and fast upwards thrusts he thrashes her arse e hole then shoves his girth up her arse and comes he ejaculates and shoots come straight up her arse and pumps her with come she screams argh then comes he keeps ramming her with deep upwards anal penetration he groans then leans forward and unties her rest for breakfast she is huffing and puffing as he slides his cock out and unties the knots she falls onto the bed then teases him goes a pose where her arse is showing and her side breast looks sexy as she lays there she lays her arms down and slides across the bed as if she were diving into the water her whole body layed out across the end of the bed then she takes her left leg off the bed and leaves her right knee on it bending over looking sexy Ivan goes and spanks her and she screams argh then he belts her again this time harder arghh she keeps posing there shaking her bum for him to spank it harder than whack he puts his all right across her arse and smacks her onto the bed then turns her facing up the bed then leaps onto her and shoves his cock up her arse she screams then he keeps pumping her arse with hard and fast upwards thrusts she keeps screaming as he pumps bones her up the bed he grabs her hips then down wards thrusts and slams his cock I to her arse then keeps pumping her arse then gets up and squats and keeps pumping her arse as she screams he dies low hard and fast squats and shoves his cock into her arse hole she screams as he keeps doing hard and fast squats and sliding his cock in her arse hole she screams argh then comes he slams her arse hole ring with hard deep stabs and drills her arse hole squatting he keeps plugging her tight arse hole ring and holds her sides then slams his cock into her arse hole he keeps squatting and plugging her arse hole ring with his cock then lifts her up and throws her up the bed she lands on the wall arghh she screams as he re plugs her arse with his stiff erection then does hard and fast upwards thrusts that to straight up her arse his cock slamming her arse hole ring as she screams argh then comes he keeps pumping her then slides his cock deep up her arse whole pumping her he slides his erection deep up into her tight arse hole she screams as he slams her into the wall he slides his cock directly up her tight arse into her arse hole ring pounding her arse cheeks as his cock slides up her arse hole she screams argh then comes he keeps plugging her arse hole with his erect cock then shoves his bonor deep inside her tight arse hole she keeps screaming as he unleashes as heap of rough upwards thrusts and slams his cock deep up inside her tight arse hole he spits on her arse then slides his cock up her arse and keeps pumping her arse hole ring with his erection plugging her arse hole he feels sensations all along his knob and shafts he keeps spitting on her arse hole then slides his cock up her arse running her breasts he reaches around then fondles her breasts and nipples then uses both his hands to gently squeeze her breasts as he pounds her arse hole ring his cock he keeps doing hard and fast upwards thrusts then shoves his cock harder and faster up her tight arse hole he keeps sliding his cock up her arse then pumps her with hard and fast pumps she screams argh then comes he shoves his cock deeper and harder up her arse then as she screams he holds her throat and chokes her she makes a choking sound then it goes quiet only the sound of flesh hitting flesh as his erection goes deep up inside her arse hole he slides his rock hard erection deep and hard up her arse then pounds her arse hole ramming her with hard and fast upwards pumps he uses his erect cock to plug her arse hole he keeps slamming his cock up her arse she comes then he takes his hands off her throat she gasps for air as he keeps pumping her and shoving his cock deep up into her tight arse hole and she screams as he dies hard and fast upwards thrusts pumping her arse hole he keeps shoving his cock deep up into her tight arse he feels his cock slam into her arse hole ring then does a heap of hard and fast thrusts that stimulate his erection as his knob pounds her arse hole he keeps doing intense thrusts then uses his cock to slam up her arse he keeps pumping her arse hole and pumps his cock up her arse and grabs her hips anthem keeps sliding his cock up her arse then rams her he pounds her arse hole with his erection and lunges upwards then his erection slams into her arse hole he drill his cock up her and keeps pumping her tight arse hole then keep shoving his cock up her are arse he holds her hips then pumps his cock into her arse hole ring sliding his shaft back and forth along her tight arse hole then lunges upwards and shoves his cock deep up her tight arse hole ring then re braces her hips and thrusts up she is screaming he has her hips in his hands and is bracing her as he slides his shafts back and forth along her arse hole ring then leaps upwards and keeps shoving his erection up her arse pounding her arse hole ring into the wall she screams as he gets her by the hips then bangs his cock hard and fast into her arse then keeps lunging upwards and spearing her arse hole with his erect stiff cock she screams argh then comes as he lifts his arse back and forward and drills her arse hole ring he plugs her arse hole with his erect pole sliding up her arse hole he keeps pumping her arse hole then trips her leg and she falls on her stomach and he lands on top of her arghh she screams as he pumps her arse hole prone boning her he humps and pumps her arse hole from on top then heaves his cock up her arse hole she keeps screaming as he grabs her hips then pounds her arse hole ring with his stiff erection he grabs her up and under by the hips then drills his cock into her arse hole screaming he does a heap of hard and fast down wards thrusts that slam her arse hole into the bed then he thrusts upwards and spears her arse hole she screams argh then comes he keeps pounding her arse and shoving no erection deep up inside her tight arse lunging upwards he feels his cock slam up her tight arse hole he gets sensations all along his shafts as he spits on her arse hole then glides his erection along her tight arse hole ring he grabs her by the hips then keeps pounding her arse hole doing a heap of hard and fast upwards thrusts he feels his whole cock plug her tight arse hole then as she s reams and comes he rams her arse hole and slides his erection straight up her arse hole into her he stands s her as hard and fast as he can then she screams he comes then turn a her over then slides up her body then shoves his cock in her mouth and holds the back of her head then shoots come in her throat she gags and coughs as he keeps shoving his cock down the back of her throat she splatters then gulps as he keeps shooting come into the back of her throat she gags then coughs he keeps holding her head down then she swallows then keeps splattering before she gulps he slides back down her body then kisses her navel then her inner thighs then kisses her groin then slides her legs open with his arms then spreads her pussy lips and spreads her vagina lips with his fingers then slowly licks her clit with his tongue he licks all up and down her clit then slides his tongue up and down her clit till she moans she lets out a passionate sexy accented moan as he licks her clit with the tip of his tongue she keeps moaning as he re parts her pussy lips then locks her clit up and down sliding his tongue along her clit her feels her clit on the bottom and top of his tongue then keeps sliding his tongue up and down her clit as she moans then moves left and right he keeps re parting her pussy lips and spreading her vagina lips right back popping out her clit that he licks with his tongue up and down up and down sliding the tip of his tongue over her clit she screams then exhales rapidly he keeps licking her clit then with the tip of his tongue he slides it up and down her clit then keeps licking her clit with his tip of his tongue she screams again then he puts his tongue more firmly onto her enflamed clit then licks up and down she moans then screams then screams loudly as she comes he watches her throat and move around moaning he keeps his tongue on her clit licking it till she snaps her legs shut then lays on her side he goes up and spoons her on her side then lifts his body up and slides his cock up her arse and keeps spooning her and slides his erection straight back up her arse and pumps her she is screaming as he slides his cock up her arse hole then keeps lunging upwards and slamming his cock into her arse hole ring she screams as he holds her hips then pumps her with his cock ramming her arse hole he drills her arse hole ring with his cock and plugs her arse hole with his erection lunging upwards he spears her tight arse hole ring with hard and fast upwards thrusts then re braces her by the hips then keeps pumping her arse hole ring ramming and slamming her he shoves his cock hard and fast up her arse hole she screams as he lunges up her arse with his stiff pole slamming her tight arse hole he plugs his girth into her are e then drill his erection up her are e hole smashing his stiff cock up her arse she screams argh then comes he keeps pumping her arse hole then he reaches around and rubs her clit and plays with her clit rubbing her clit up and down with his fingers as he pounds her arse hole from be-hind she screams then he keeps lunging upwards and spearing her arse hole with his erect pole as he runs her clit with his fin-gers she keeps screaming then he runs her clit up and down firmly using his fingertips then she's screams argh then comes he turns her over then prone bones her she is screaming as he slides his erection up her arse hole and keeps pumping her and sliding his cock up her arse hole she screams as he keeps pumping his erection up her arse hole he slides and shoves his cock up her arse hole then thrusts upwards and slams his erection up her arse he keeps plugging her tight arse hole with his erect cock then gets off the bed then shoves his cock in her mouth as he is standing up she is laying on the bed with her cheek to the mattress he has his cock in her mouth at the same time he stands there rubbing her clit and pleasuring her clit with his fingers he slides his fingers up and down her pussy and keeps sliding his fingers along her clit as he starts to come he keeps fucking her face he uses his hips to thrusts and to shove his cock back and forth along her lips then feels her warm mouth as she sucks and licks his knob he keeps rubbing her clit then she screams and thrusts he keeps rubbing her clit then she snaps her legs shut then gets up on her knees on the bed and faces him then he spreads his legs then steps closer to her sliding his cock closer into her mouth then she goes up and down and sucks his cock he watches as she parts her hair back behind her ears then keep going up and down on the side of the bed on her knees with her hands sliding up his balls and her other hand on his girth as he sucks his knob he keeps standing there and listens and watches as she makes swallowing sucking sounds and slurps as she keeps kneeling and going up and down sucking his cock he can feel her sliding her hand from the bottom of his balls to the top as if she were bringing the come or blood up it feels amazing her hands rubbing up his balls and her lips sucking his cock he flexes his pc muscle then help her out the concentrates then shoots come out of his cock surprising her she makes a oh you came in my mouth noise as he grabs her back of her head then keeps it down on his cock then she swallows he takes his hand away then she sits up on her knees with a happy smile on her face as she wipes her mouth then slides over on her knees to kiss him he lays her down then lays on top of her on the bed and kisses her his knees and elbows in beside her he tilts his head then open mouth tongue kisses her and shoves his tongue down her throat as soon as he feels her suck his kiss and he is naked on top of her and she purposely brushes her nipples on his chest he feels his cock to hard or starts to goes hard again then as he keeps leaning down forward and over her on his hands and knees the blood flows into his knob and shaft as he kisses her and she darts her tongue into his mouth and sucks his kiss he can feel it gone hard again he can't put it in her pussy if it's just been in her arse he grabs her by the back of her knees then lifts her legs right back over her head then slides his cock into her arse hole ring his knob feel her tight arsehole then the rest of his cock feels her arse hole as he pushes his cock back up inside her arse she screams as his cock slides all the way up her arse hole basic standards arse hole ..

Ivan and the queen get back from breakfast they are at the end of their bed kissing Ivan has his head tilted and his kissing her lips and slides his tongue down her throat and then open mouth pashes her as he lifts off her shoulder strap and her nightie falls down he scoops her body into his arms then holds her breasts close to his chest then feels her warm perky breasts on his chest as he keeps groping her then he kisses her at the same time un- buttons his pants then his pants come down and his cock ex- tends he leans forward to put it under her vagina no hands then pushes it up into her vagina then licks his pants off then lunges upwards and shoves his whole cock up her vagina at once argh she screams as he tackles her into the bed then thrusts up and down and shoves his erection straight up her pussy then keeps shoving his cock up her vagina then uses his arms and hands up above her to grab the mattress s then launch his stiff cock up hard into her pussy he fully grabs the mattress and heaves his whole stiff body as well as his throbbing cock up hard deep into her tight pussy watching her scream and make orgasm faces as he keeps grabbing the mattress and heaving his whole body up into her his erect stiff pole scrapes and grind and threads her wet tight vagina as he keeps pulling himself up into her body his top shaft pleasuring her g spot he keeps pumping her as she screams argh them comes he sees how hard and fast he can to she is screaming handling it well as he throws his whole body into hers and his pole slides vertically up her vagina parallel to the bed he keeps using the mattress to launch his body upwards and ram his stiff erection into her pussy each time he lunges upwards he uses his arms holding onto the mattress to propel his body upwards and purposely shove the whole lot of his throbbing cock up her she is screaming under him the whole time going wild herself he is looking at the bedhead and concentrating on pumping blood into his erection each thrust he feels her vagina leak then it becomes a pleasure for his cock instead of being in a world of pain from her tight pussy it becomes hotter and tender he doesn't feel the sting of her tight vagina ring he keeps grabbing the top of the mattress then goes like a sky diver over her legs and arms up his cock maxes out he shoves it as far as it can go up her with every thrust it can't to any further that's how far he throwing it up her he can feel it hitting the end as his girth gets shoved up her vagina ring she screams argh then comes he keeps grabbing the mattress then heaves his hips onto her ground making a loud slap sound followed by argh each time slap arghh slap arghh as his body slams Into hers he keeps using his arms and hand on the mattress to launch his stuff hard erection into her tight wet vagina he kisses her and open mouth pashes her then bear hugs her then spins her on top of him then pumps his hips and his cock drills up vertically into her vagina as she lay on top of him he keeps squeezing her against him and hammering his erection up and around up into her vagina hooking his pole up and around up into her vagina she is screaming into his face and he keeps pumping his erection up her pussy he can feel his cock going deep inside her vagina doing rapid fires where he pumps her with fast energetic humps and pumps she is going argh argh argh into his face as he keeps bear hugging her and drilling his erection up her vagina and hammering her pussy his cock getting pumped up her vagina as he thrusts his hips she screams oh then comes he keeps pumping her then rolls her back over again getting back on top then chokes her into the mattress she makes a choking sound as he leans on top of her with his upper body husbands around her throat applying pressure to her windpipe he keeps pumping her and looking into her sexy brain eyes as she says fuck me harder or that's what he think she is saying to him he does it he pumps her pussy and keeps pumping her sliding his cock up her vagina he keeps pumping her and she is making a sexy eyes rolling back face she comes then he lets go of her throat she gasps for air then keeps screaming he keeps pumping her and sliding his erection into her vagina he feels his cock sliding up her pussy and keeps pumping his erect penis into her tight vagina he keeps sliding his bonor up her vagina she screams and he feels his cock slide deep into her tight wet pussy he keeps pumping her and then slides his cock up into her vagina she keeps screaming then he pumps his stiff cock into her vagina and slides his erection up her vagina then he slides his cock up her arse she screams arghh he keeps sliding his cock up her arse then pumps his cock up her arse hole ring he slides his erection up her arse hole then pumps her arse hole with his cock she screams then he just thrashes her he shoves his erection deep and hard up her arse and stiffens his cock then slams it up her arse hole he keeps pumping blood into his cock then threads her arse and grates her arse hole ring smashing his cock up her arse she screams argh then comes he keeps pounding her arse hole with hard and fast thrusts ramming her he keeps up then slides his hand around her neck and chokes her she makes a choking sound then he pounds her arse into the bed and smashes his erection up her arse he stiffens his cock then lunges upwards and slams his cock up her arse hole he leans forward and keeps choking her into the mattress then upwards thrusts his erect pole up her arse he goes hard and fast than plugs her arse hole with his bonor ramming her and ploughing her arse hole he plunges his erection up her arse doing diagonal strokes he slides his cock into her arse hole he takes his hand away she gasps for air then screams as he pumps her arse with his erection he slides his cock up her arse then keeps pumping his bonor up her arse hole he slides his erection deep and hard up her arse hole then comes he pumps her and shoots come up her arse hole she is screaming and comes as well he pumps her arse e hole with upwards thrusts as he keeps shooting come up her tight arse he groan then pounds her arse hole and then plugs her arse with his girth then takes his cock out then walks up her body with his knees then shoves his cock in her mouth then puts his palms on the bed then fucks her mouth he pumps his hips and his cock slides back and forth in her mouth he keeps pumping her then comes again he shoots come in her mouth then keeps pumping and groaning as the second time his cock feel a like it's made of metal and iron he feels his intense erection unload another load into her throat he looks down and can see her choking on his cock as he is deepthroating her he lifts his leg up and she gasps for air choking and splattering she smacks him on the bum and says you come in my mouth

Ivan goes out to the balcony and can see the queen wearing a see thru nightie the summer nights breeze lifts it up slightly as she looks ago in he pushes up and in behind her then kisses her neck he tilts his head then shoves his tongue in her mouth at the same time he hold a her by the hips then slides his cock up her vagina she screams then keeps kissing her at the same time slides his cock up her vagina and can feel his girth slam into her pussy as he starts to push harder his cock up in her vagina he stiffens his erection then with each upwards thrust he feel his cock going deep up inside her vagina and threading grating and scraping her tight vagina ring as his oversized cock squeezes up her tight vagina ring she keeps screaming then comes he feels her vagina leak and her pussy becomes slippery inside and hotter he is sliding his girth into her pussy then hears flesh hitting flesh as his body slams into hers and he keeps sliding his erection up her arse and into her tight vagina she screams argh then comes he keeps pumping her he feels his knob hitting her cervix he holds her by the hips the thrashes her and drills her pussy with hard and fast thrusts smashing her pussy from behind he rams his girth into her vagina then pounds her into the railing and grabs onto her hips then shoves his cock deep up inside her vagina he keeps lunging upwards she is screaming the whole time he heaves his cock up her arse and drills it into her vagina then hammers his erection up her tight pussy she screams argh then comes he keeps pumping her then his cock turns to metal and he shreds and grates her vagina ring and threads her pussy as his girth pounds into her p I say lips and he shoves his erection up deep up into her tight wet pussy she keeps screaming as he drills her pussy from behind pounding her vagina ring with his girth he slides his cock up her vagina then grabs the railing and lunges upwards and hurls his body into hers his cock slides straight up her pussy and he keeps shoving his cock deep into her vagina as she screams argh then comes he moves in close to her then kisses her neck and keeps shoving his tongue down her throat she moans then he grabs the railing and thrashes her pussy banging her into the railing he slams his cock up her vagina using his arms to propel his body towards her and spear her pussy with his erection he rams his body into hers and his stiff cock pounds into her vagina ring she screams argh then comes she goes up on her tippy toes stuck between him and the railing as he uses all his upper body strength to heave his body into her backside and shove his bonor up deep up into her vagina he feels he rotates from his hands on her hips and pumping her vagina to his arms and hands on the railing and smashing his sword up her vagina and pounding her vagina ring as he kisses the side of her neck and tilts his head and shoves his tongue down her throat she screams argh argh argh as he bends her over the railing and pumps her pussy with upwards thrusts as he is pumping his erection up her vagina from behind she screams argh then comes he keeps heaving his whole body into hers and launching his knob up her cervix as he pumps her from behind using his hand he slides them over her breasts and nipples them keeps rubbing her and fondling her breasts he can feel her erect plump nipples on his palms as he uses his right hand to feel all across her sex y breasts his left hand guides his cock up her vagina as he rests it on her left hip he keeps pumping her with rapid hard and fast upwards thrusts he re grabbing both her hips he thrashes her over the railing and hears her screaming ah ah ah as he thrusts forward with his erection and gets it up and under her arse and deep into her vagina he keeps sliding his erection up her vagina from behind as he pumps her over the railing he does a heap of hard and fast upwards thrusts that keep her screaming he places his massive hands around her tiny throat then chokes her at the same time he is thrusting his erection up her arse and deep up inside her vagina he hears her makes a choking noise as he just groans and huffs and puffs hot air into her ear as he is choking her from behind the keeps shoving his stiffened cock straight up her vagina with hard and fast thrusts pumping her as he chokes her throat in his hands he keeps pounding her with upwards thrusts and hard and fast pumps drilling his erection up deep up I to her tight vagina he feels his cock grate scrape and thread her tight vagina ring as he heaves his erection up her from behind her and pumps her vagina with hard and fast thrusts that stimulate his cock and thread her vagina he keeps sliding his erection up her vagina then keeps kissing her at the same time pumping his cock in her wet tight pussy he keeps sliding his erection up her vagina then shoves his girth straight into her vagina ring then keeps pumping her he shoves his cock in her arse then she screams and he pumps her arse hole ring with his cock he keeps pumping her tight arse hole with vertical upwards thrusts he keeps pumping her then places his hands on her hips then slides his cock further and harder up her arse hole she screams argh then comes he keeps pumping her with rapid hard and fast as he shoves his cock up and down her arse hole pounding her arse hole with his erection he does upwards thrusts as he is stiffening his cock threading her arse hole as he keeps grating and scraping her arse hole ring with his erection she screams argh then comes he keeps sliding his cock up her arse in then grabs the railing then braces his arms and legs then drills her arse hole with hard and fast upwards thrust that keep her screaming ah ah ah as he pumps his erection straight up her arse and keeps pumping her arse hole he spits on her arse then keeps spitting and shoving his whole cock deep up inside her tight arse hole ring he slides his erection up her arse and she screams argh then comes he keeps sliding his pole up her tight arse hole then plugs his stiff erection up her arse then pumps her arse hole ring with hard and fast thrusts ramming his erection deep up her arse as she screams he holds her throat choking her with both his hands around her throat then keeps pumping her arse hole standing in close to her from behind he vertically slides his cock up her arse then keeps pumping her arse hole with his cock sliding up her arse as he keeps choking her he feels her whole body tighten as she comes he lets gi3 of her throat and she gasps for air inhaling as she breathes in and pants he keeps pumping her and then turns her face around and shoves his tongue down her throat at the same time he sliding his cock up into her arse hole he keeps kissing her and sliding his cock up h3r arse hole then grabs her hips and smashes her he thrusts his cock up her arse then slams his hips back and forth and his erection stabs into her tight arse hole ring and she screams he keeps pounding her and grabbing her hips throwing his body into her he slams her arse hole with hard and fast thrust lunging upwards he shoves his cock hard up her arse then re braces her by the hips and thrashes her arse hole ring slamming his girth into her arse hole ring and shoving his who is cock deep up her arse then spits on her arse hole then goes deeper and harder thrashing her arse hole ring as he keeps spitting she is screaming he pounds her arse hole ring with his girth and shoves his cock deep up inside her arse then thrusts upwards and shoves his stiff erection straight up her tight arse hole she screams argh then comes he keeps thrashing her arse hole and leaping upwards grabbing the railing he goes into ramming speed and keeps thrashing her arse hole ring by heaving his arms fo4ward and slamming his cock deep up her arse hole shoving his girth into her arse hole ring he lunges upwards his erect pole sliding straight up her arse from behind as she screams argh then comes he keeps spitting on her arse and grabbing her hips and thrashing her pumping his erection straight up her arse she is screaming as he keeps holding her hips and pumping her tight arse hole ring with his stiff cock hammering up her arse hole ring she screams argh then comes he keeps plugging her tight arse with his stuff erection shoving his vertical pole up her tight arse hole ring then sliding his cock up further up deep up inside her tight arse hole here braces her baby the hips then pumps her hard and fast up the arse with a heap of rough deep upwards thrusts he makes her scream argh argh argh then he holds the railing and thrashes her arse hole wo the hard up wards stroke argh she screams as he get in deep and hard up into her tight arse hole ring he plugs his erection up her tight arse then slides his pole straight up her tight arse hole drilling her arse hole ring with his erection hammering into her arse hole as he plunges his pole up her arse then keeps sliding it further and harder up her arse hole she screams argh then comes he is pumping her hard and fast using the railing he lunges his erection up her arse and she leans over the railing screaming he belts her arse cheek ouch she screams ad he re braces her by the hips then thrashes she's arse hole that hard and fast that he comes up her arse she slides his cock up her arse and then groans as he ejaculated he slaps her on the arse to get off then pops his cock out from her arse she dances around in a sexy runs into his arms he leans her back with his arm behind her back then leans forward and kisses her leaving his hand on her lower back to support her as he leans over her and shoves his tongue down her throat tilting his head he keeps open mouth pashing her lips as he keeps leaning her right back over his other hand on the back of her neck

Ivan is walking thru the castle halls when the queen us at the end of the hall posing she is looking out the window for him at the same time he is coming in from behind her she is on her tippy toes bent over looking out with her arms on the window sills looking for him he walks up from behind her then she turns around he outs his lips straight to hers and slides his tongue down her throat tilting his head and passionately kisses her while pushing her back into the window argh she lets out a pant as he pins her up against the window then lifts off her dress in a hurry then straight back kisses her again at the same time he is tearing down his pants then lifts her legs up then holds her up by her sides then lunges upwards with his erection it hits her pussy lips then slides up into her tight vagina as she screams he feels his cock to all the way up her vagina he keeps sliding his erection up and down her vagina ring he can feel his erect thick shafts sliding along her vagina walls as he keeps pumping his cock up her vagina and she screams argh then comes he keeps pumping her and sliding his cock up her vagina then turns and slams her up against the wall shoving his cock hard and fast up her vagina he feels his top shaft scraping the upper roof if her vagina as he heaves his whole body upwards and his stuff cock slides straight up into her wet tight vagina ring he keeps feeling his girth stretching her vagina ring as he bounces her up and down off his erect stiff cock he lunges upwards and slams her back into the wall and keeps stuffing his cock up her vagina as she screams argh then comes he keeps pumping her with his erection sliding up her vagina then puts her down turns her around then lunges upwards and re inserts his pole up her tight vagina as she screams he watches as her palms to up on the wall and she clenches her arse cheeks as he pounds upwards into her vagina with his stiff cock she leaks and his cock slides rapidly up and down along her tight vagina ring as she keeps screaming she is looking around on her tippy toes her palms up against the wall as she braces from his upwards thrusts that slam her vagina ring with his girth as he keeps plugging her vagina with his erection she screams argh then comes he keeps using the wall to do upwards heaves and shove his stiff pole straight up her arse and I to her vagina she keeps screaming as he pins her between him and the wall and thrashes her vagina with his cock sliding his whole erection straight up into her tight vagina his girth scrapes her vagina ring as he keeps shoving his cock up her he holds her hips then keeps pumping upwards she is screaming hotting the wall with her palms as he keeps ramming his knob up her cervix and he lunges upwards with penetrating upwards thrusts he slides his cock straight up into her vagina and keeps plugging her tight pussy with his cock sliding up into her pussy he feels his erection throbbing then as it turns and triples in hard ness it grates her vagina ring and scrapes her vagina as she screams argh then comes his cock sliding rapidly in and out of her tight vagina ring as he thrusts upwards and plugs her vagina ring with his girth he keeps pumping her and can feels his erection pumping with blood that he uses to grate scream and thread her tight hot vagina then shoves his stiffened erection deep up into her tight vagina as she screams argh then comes he uses his veiny top shaft to scraped her vagina ring and keep her screaming argh argh argh as he pumps her with rapid upwards heaves lunging up into her tight vagina with his stiff hard erect cock she screams argh then comes he can feel her vagina leaking and her pussy becomes slippery then he slides his erection up her arse into her tight pussy then wraps his hands around her throat then listens as she makes a choking sound as he keeps choking her and sliding his erection up her vagina he feels his knob tapping her cervix as he keeps shoving his erection straight up her vagina from behind then gets his stiff cock to gi3 up deep up into her vagina he can feel his shafts throbbing and as his cock stiffens he slides it up her vagina and scrapes her vagina ring she comes then he lets gi3 of her throat she gasps for air then screams as he lunges upwards with his bonor and keeps sliding his whole cock deep up her tight wet vagina she keeps screaming as she puts her palms up and braces looking back at him as he holds her hips and pumps her arse cheeks his cock is sliding straight up her vagina she screams argh then comes he keeps holding her hips with his palms and hands then shoves his knob up her vagina tapping her cervix as he keeps lunging upwards she keeps screaming as he rubs her breasts and feels her nipples with his palm as he rubs his hand across her breasts and keeps sliding his erection straight up her vagina she screams argh then comes he keeps pumping her then upwards thrusts onto his ties and gets his cock right up and in deep up into her tight pussy as she screams he keeps pounding her pussy up wards and slides his whole cock up her vagina ring she screams a argh then comes he slides his erection up and down her vagina then keeps upwards and thrusts his cock slides deep up her vagina ring as she keeps screaming he belts her arse cheek spanking her ouch she screams out as he places his palms and hands on her sides then upwards heaves his erection straight up her wet pussy oh my god she screams as he lunges upwards and slides his cock up her vagina them stiffens his erection then scrapes and threads her vagina ring with a heap of ramming upwards heaves that slide his cock straight hard up into her tight pussy she screams argh then comes he keeps pumping her then plugs her arse hole with his cock then she screams loudly as he holds her hips and pumps her arse hole ring back and forth he lunges upwards and shoves his erection hard and fast up her tight arse she is screaming ah ah ah as she holds onto the wall with her palms going yes yes oh yes he spits him her arse then keeps spitting then slides his cock straight up her arse hole feeling his erection slides up her lubricated arse hole ring up into her tight arse he lunges upwards then slides his erection straight up her tight arse hole ring then pumps her arse hole holding her hips he shoves his erection upwards pumping her arse hole ring with a heap of energetic upwards heaves he is stiffening his erection and it threads and scrapes her arse hole ring as she screams argh then comes he keeps plugging his cock up her arse then slides his erection straight up her arse hole ring and spits on her arse hole then keeps sliding his erect stiff cock up her arse hole as she screams argh then comes he keeps lunging upwards and shoving his cock up her arse hole then pumps her arse hole with rapid upwards thrust slamming her tight arse hole ring with his whole erection sliding up into her tight arse hole she screams argh then comes as he keeps sliding his erection into her arse hole he spits then shoves his cock straight up into her arse hole ring he sees his girth stretching her arse hole ring as he keeps sliding his whole cock up onto her arse hole she is screaming as he keeps threading her arse hole ring and sliding his cock up her tight arse hole he spits then holds her hips then shoves and slams his erection hard and fast up her tight arse hole argh she screams and comes as he pumps her arse hole ring with his stiff cock sliding straight up her tight arse hole he throws her to the other side of the hall then runs in and lifts her up and kisses her then slams his erection straight back up between her legs into her arse hole she screams oh my god as he bounces her up and down and shoves his whole cock straight up her arse then slams her back into the wall then re braces her then heaves his erection up her arse hole ring and slams his whole cock up her tight arse hole he keeps pounding her arse and plugging her arse hole ring with his thick girth sliding his cock up into her arse she keeps screaming ah ah ah as he is lifting her up his cock sliding straight up her arse he can feels her tight arse hole ring around his shaft as he keeps plugging her arse hole with upwards heaves that slam her back against the wall as he drills his erection up her arse hole he gets his cock to obliterating her arse hole ring she screams argh then comes as his whole body thrusts upwards and his cock drills up onto her arse hole he slams his girth into her arse hole ring then shoves his whole erection straight up her arse hole with hard and fast upwards thrusts that make a loud clapping sound as his body hits her groins and he pumps her upwards with hard and fast rapid thrusts slamming his stiff pole vertically up her tight arse as she screams argh then comes he keeps plugging her tight arse hole with his erection then puts her down that grows her towards the window sill she lands on it putting her hands on the windowsill and looking back as he runs in and shoves his pole straight up her arse hole then holds her hips and slides his erection up her arse hole ring she keeps screaming as she is bending over up against the windowsill looking back of her shoulder as he pumps her from behind stabbing up he uses his palms and hand stop rest on her arse cheeks and hips then slides his erection up into her arse hole plugging her arse hole ring with his cock as she screams ah ah am as he pumps her and rams her arse hole he keeps spitting on her arse hole ring them slides his erection up her arse hole she screams argh then comes as he rams and pounds her are e hole ring in with his cock he shoves his girth into her arse hole ring them slides his erection deep up her tight arse hole he gets sensations all along his shafts and knob as it slams up into her tight arse hole he keeps pumping her and heaves his erection up her arse his girth stretching her are whole ring as she screams argh them comes he keeps spitting and sliding his cock up her arse hole then spanks her arse cheek ouch she screams as a loud clapping sound fills his eras and she keeps screaming and looking back over her shoulder as he spits on her arse hole ring then slides his erection up into her tight arse hole he must his left palm on the window then wraps her throat up in a headlock pulling her body into his he keeps choking her then slides his erection up her arse hole while he is choking her in a headlock with his forearm wrapped around her neck he pumps her arse cheeks with his body as his cock slide up into her arse hole he h3aves his cock up her and she tenses then as he does a heap of rough upwards intense deep strokes he shoves his girth up her arse hole ring then lunges upwards and spears her arse hole with his erection he does hard and fast cock thrusts shoving his erection deep up into her arse hole she comes then he takes his forearm from her throat and she gasps for air and then screams as he holds her hips and pumps her age e hole standing up she is screaming ah aha ha as she stands there he slides his erection up her arse hole then keeps pumping her she keeps screaming then as he reaches around and runs her breasts and brushes his hands across her nipples and breasts she screams argh then comes he keeps sliding his cock up her arse then does hard and fast upwards pumps that lift her up and down she is screaming as he keeps shoving his cock that hard up her arse that she keeps going up on her tippy toes as he holds her hips and thrashes her arse hole to come as well he keeps sliding his cock up her arse then quickly pumps her with his shaft sliding up her arse hole he keeps plugging her arse then turns her around he hears her knees make a thud on the floor then he grabs the back of her head and shoves her head into his cock as he comes it goes silent only the sound of her choking on his cock as he keep pulling the back of her head into his cock as he shoves his girth into her lips and shoves his erection down the back of her mouth and shoots come in her throat he keeps orgasming and feels his cock throbbing and pumping come into the back if her throat she coughs and gags then splatter as he keeps coming she swallows then coughs and gulps he has his hands on the back of her head forcing her mouth then he pulls her up then turns and kisses her into the wall and tilts his head and pashes her up against the wall tilting his head and shoving his tongue down her throat he outs his lips on hers then changed sides and kisses her mouth and lips the other way and keeps sliding his tongue down her throat she darts her tongue into his mouth and sucks his kiss then he feels his cock stay hard he feels her hand slide up his groin then up his balls as he feels her hand slide up his groin and balls his cock stiffen he quickly turns her around then feels his knob slide into her arse hole then his shafts slide up into her arse hole ring he plugs her arse hole with his erection then pumps her rapidly with upwards heaves he slides his erection straight back up into her arse hole and she screams he keeps pumping his erection up her arse hole as she keeps screaming then slams her hands onto the wall screaming and bracing herself as he holds her hips and slides his stiff cock up her arse hole and pumps her arse hole with his stiff cock thrashing her arse hole ring with hard and fast upwards thrusts that have her screaming and slamming the wall with her palms he keeps sliding his erection up her are whole then spits and keeps spitting on her arse hole ring them plugging her arse hole with his erect stiff cock she screams argh then comes he feels his erection sliding up into her arse hole ring then keeps pumping her she keeps screaming as he pumps her arse hole ring with his cock he feels his knob and shafts being pleasured by her tight arse hole ring as he slides his cock up into her are hole she keeps screaming and turning her head back around as he lunges forward and slams her into the wall it makes a loud thud as she screams he keeps pumping her arse hole then shoves his cock up her arse hole ring and slams her up onto the wall she keeps screaming he keeps pumping his erection up into her arse hole ring he turns her around the chokes her up into the wall lifting her up off her feet he get a his erection up and under her then slides it vertically up her arse hole and threads grates or scrapes her arse hole ring with upwards thrusts his erection plugs her tight arse hole and he keeps vertically sliding his erect cock up her tight arse hole ring she makes a sexy orgasm face then as he body tenses and her eyes roll back she comes he keeps sliding his erection up her arse then puts her down as she gasps for air he lifts her up by the back of the knees then slams her up against the wall then heaves his erection up her arse hole she screams oh my god as he keeps pounding her arse hole ring up the wall sliding his cock up into her arse hole ring as she screams argh then comes he keeps pumping her arse hole ring with upwards heaves that have his cock sliding rapidly vertically up her arse hole as he pulls her breasts onto his chest and feels her warm breasts and nipples on his body he keeps using his hips to vertically slide his stiff cock up into her arse hole he starts to come then keeps pumping her as she is screaming he slides his cock straight up into her arse hole then kisses her and slams her back into the wall then heaves his erection up her tight arse she screams argh then comes he is slamming her into the wall plugging her tight arse with his erection as he comes he groans then goes into ramming speed pumping her arse hole rapidly he feels his cock slide deep up into her arse hole ring then explode and shoot comes at tight up her tight arse hole he keeps groaning as the feeling of orgasming with his cock article up her tight arse the come shooting up feels amazing he keeps pumping her arse hole then feels his cock spasming as he slides it up her arse he outs her down then he cock slides out from between her legs as he pins her back up wrist the wall and tilts his head and pashes her and shoves his tongue down her throat

The have a shower together then as Ivan is washing her back she poses and puts her palms up on the tiles and pokes her arse out then shakes it for him to come closer he runs up into her from behind with his erection and plugs her vagina w8th it she screams as he does a hard up wards thrust that makes his cock t he was grate and scrape along her vagina ring as she screams argh then he keeps pumping her with wild upwards thrusts holding her by the hips he pumps her arse cheeks with his stiff erection sliding straight up her vagina keeps thrashing her with energetic pumps and upward lunges that has his erection spearing her tight vagina from behind pounding her vagina with his girth he slams his cock deep up into her vagina with smashing upwards heaves he launches his erection deep up into her tight vagina from behind she keeps screaming as he plugs her arse hole then slides his erection up her arse then keeps pumping her arse hole ring with his cock slamming up into her arse hole he slides his erection straight up into her arse hole and she screams the he keeps sliding he's erection up into her arse hole she is screaming bent over in the shower her palms on the tiles he is pumping her arse hole with his erection sliding his cock up into her are whole he can see her breasts bouncing underneath her the cups her breasts and slides his palms across her breasts and nipples as she screams argh them comes he keeps sliding his hands across her breasts and nipples then slams his cock up her arse and grabs her hips and thrashes her pounding her arse e hole he does hard and fast upwards strokes pounding her arse hole ring with his cock he feels his cock stiffen then uses it to grate scrape and thread her arse hole ring as he stands there holding her hips and pounding her arse hole with his erection going hard and fast up into her tight arse hole ring he can hear her screaming ah ah ah as he pumps her arse hole with his stiff cock sliding straight up into her arse hole as he keeps pumping his erection up into her arse she screams s argh then comes he uses his palms to hold onto sides then slides his stiff cock up into her tight arse hole ring she keeps screaming as his erect cock slides up akin to her arse hole ring he keeps pumping her arse hole then feels his knob and shafts being pleasured by her tight arse hole ring as he lunges upwards and spears her arse hole with his stiff pole he shreds her arse hole ring as he shoves his knob up her tight arse hole and his girth slams into her arse hole ring he keeps pounding her arse hole ring and ramming her with deep and hard upwards thrusts her hear a her arse hole ring and pumps blood into his erection then shoves it deep up into her arse hole ring she keeps screaming as he unleashes a heap of rough deep upwards strikes pounding her arse hole he drills his erection into her arse cheeks and hammers her arse hole with his erection sliding his cock up her arse with powerful energetic upward pumps his cock slides harder and deeper up her arse hole ring she screams argh then comes he keeps pounding her arse hole with hard and fast upwards thrusts that grate tear and scrape her tight arse hole ring as home slams his girth up her arse hole she screams as he keeps hammering his erection deep up her arse hole and pounding her arse hole ring with his shafts sliding up her tight arse hole he keeps pumping her and pounding her arse hole ring shoving his erection deep up her arse hole he slides his whole pole up I do her arse he keep pumping and plugging his cock up her arse and she screams argh then comes he thrashes her and pounds her arse hole with his ere t cock sliding straight up her he keeps sliding his pole up her tight arse hole she keeps screaming as he thrashes her with hard and fast upwards thrusts he feels his cock slide up into her arse hole then he keeps pumping her then starts to come he hold a her hips then pumps her with hard and fast upwards thrusts he feels his cock sliding up her arse cheeks and I to her arse hole he rams her and pounds her arse hole as he is coming then slides his erection up into her arse hole and keeps pumping her arse hole with his erection sliding straight up her arse she screams argh then comes he keeps pumping her arse hole then she screams argh then comes he is pumping her arse hole with his erect cock sliding his cock up her arse and ramming her arse hole as he comes he slams his gi3 the into her arse hole ring then shoves his whole cock deep up her arse hole and pounds her arse hole ring with hard and fast rapid upwards thrusts he plugs his erection deep up her arse as he shoots come up her arse hole he groans then keeps pumping her arse hole ring with his shafts he feels his cock explode then keeps pumping her arse hole with rapid deep upwards heaves as he slides his cock deeper and harder into her arse hole he turns her around then pasha shed and then slams her into the wall and kisses her mouth and tilts his head and keeps open mouth tongue kissing her and then slides his tongue down her throat and keeps groping her

.

Ivan keeps slapping the queens arse as she runs at the stairs he gets her and she screams argh he keeps spanking her then whack he belts her arse cheek as she screams argh she gets to the top then he lifts her up by her arms then carry's her onto the room kicking and screaming he pulls her dress off then goes her arm up to the top of the bed she keeps screaming as he gets her other arm then ties her up to the bed frame she is hanging and swaying back and forward as he whips her arse argh she screams then argh argh as he whips her he lifts the whip up and over his head then crack he whips it across her arse cheek arghh she screams as he keeps whipping her she thrusts up and down screaming stop it it hurts he lines her up then crack argh crack argh her whips her upper thighs and arse cheeks then can see how red they are from the lashes of the whip then keeps whipping her the whip hits her hard and she screams argh it hurts and ouch he keeps whipping her anyway and can hear the crack of the whip as it hits her skin and the lashes tear across her arse her arse cheeks leaving a series of red whips marks and lines that are protruding as he walks up to her telling her sshh he slides his palms over her arse cheeks and can feel her a raised skin as he keeps sliding his hand across her arse cheeks she screams argh you fucken bastard whack he spanks her arse and belts her with his hand then watches as she goes swaying up thru the air then as she comes back down he thrashes her with the whip argh she screams as he lays into her with a heap of hard whips and pashes that tear thru her a skin and leave massive red gashes across her red arse cheeks he then puts his left foot forward and puts his body into the whips and crack argh he hots her on the arse cheek then crack arghh she screams as he hits her again he keeps whipping her argh stop she pleads arghh a lot hurts he keeps whipping her and watches as she thrusts around screaming her whole body shaking as she keeps screaming at the top of her lungs argh argh argh he keeps whipping her and she thrusts her body tensing he puts his hand on her body and stops her from thrusting she calms down then crack he whips her back and she screams he rips into her with a heap of rough whips that tear her back and leave massive lines across all of her back as he decorates her with numerous whip marks and slashes then slides his hand along her back as she keeps screaming he runs his palm across the wounds to feel the braised skin on his palms as she screams argh the whole time he kisses her side then her breasts and tilts his head around then sucks her nipple then walks around the other side then unties the top her feet touch the ground as if she were abseiling then he takes her from behind he shoves his cock up her arse she screams argh then he pumps her again argh she screams as his cock slides straight up her tight arse hole he pumps her and his cock goes up her arse hole ring then keeps pumping her arse hole with his erection sliding straight up and up into her tight arse hole as she keeps screaming his cock stiffens and he slides it up her arse hole ring then uses his whole body to lunge upwards and launch his erect stiff pole straight up her tight arse hole lunging upwards he spears her arse hole ring with a heap of hard and fast thrusts pounding her and thinking her arse hole ring with his cock he slides his cock directly up her tight arse hole then keeps pounding her arse hole ring with hard and fast upwards thrusts drilling her arse hole with heap of upwards thrusts and hard and fast heaves pumping her with rapid intense up wards thrusts that have his stiff pole ramming up her arse hole as she screams argh then comes he keeps pumping her then places his hands on her hips and slides his erection hard and deep up her tight arse as she screams he feels his cock grating threading and tearing her arse hole ring as he vertical thrashes his erection into her arse hole pounding and thinking her arse hole ring with his girth as it slides up her arse hole ring he keeps pumping her with hard and fast upwards heaves as he launches his stiff cock up her arse then keeps pumping her and watching as she screams ah am ah with each upwards thrust he keeps sliding his erect at hi cock up her arse hole as she screams argh then comes he keeps pumping her then with his left hand on her hip and his right hand over her shoulder be pounds his cock up her arse and holds onto her and smashes his erection up her arse hole and deep into her arse hole ring as she just screams the whole time he keeps bracing her there and sliding his erection vertically up her tight arse hole ring he feels his girth pounding her arse hole as she screams argh then comes he is standing behind her holding her and pumping his stiff erection up her tight vagina hole thrusting forward at the same stone stiffening his erection it slides harder and deeper up her tight arse hole he keeps pounding helix stiff erection up her arse then unties her and throws her onto the bed she falls face chest the he holds her by the hips spits on her arse hole then slides his erection rapidly into her arse hole with hard and fast thrusts she just smashes up into her arse hole with his erection he is standing at the end of the bed she is bent over it as he is holding her up by the hips and shoving his cock up and right up and into her tight arse hole with vertically upwards thrusts he jams his girth into her arse hole then slides his whole erect cock up hard into her tight arse hole he keeps pumping her as she screams argh then comes he keeps pumping his erect ad in cock up hard into her arse hole then reaches his hand around her and runs her breasts she is screaming as he feels all over her breasts and erect nipples with his fingers and hand than uses his forearm to run and holds them as he slides his cock straight up and into her tight arse hole with a heap if hard and fast upwards thrusts pumping her and sliding his whole cock up deep into her tight arse hole she screams argh then comes he keeps pumping her and then slides his cock deep and hard up her arse hole and stretches her arse hole ring with his girth as it slams up into her he keeps feeling her breasts and pumping her arse hole as she screams then he p have a her into the mattress and she falls face first he straddles her back legs as they hand off the back of the mattress then he shoves his erection up her arse hole and he slams her with hard and fast upwards thrusts that have his cock pounding her arse hole ring as she screams he just keeps plugging her arse hole and feels his erection slide straight up and into her tight arse hole he keeps pounding her then thrashes his cock up her arse she screams argh them comes he is there pounding her with up-wards thrusts that keep her screaming argh argh argh with each upwards thrusts then slides his erect at hi cock up deep up her are whole and threads her arse hole ring with his stiff cock he keeps pumping her with rapid a hard and fast upwards thrusts that slam her arse hole ring she screams argh then comes as he keeps lunging his whole body upwards and he feels his cock pounding her arse hole ring as she keeps screaming he just keeps launching directly up wards and heaving his vertical stiff pole straight up her tight arse hole ring slamming his girth up her arse as she screams oh my god he thrashes his erection straight up her tight arse hole ring and plugs her tight arse hole with his throbbing cock he shoves his erection up into her arse with a heap of rough upwards thrusts that has his erect stiff pole shoves up her tight arse as he slides it in and out she screams argh then comes he keeps belting his erection up deep into her tight arse hole throwing his stiff pole straight up her arse hole ring as he keeps sliding upwards and doing vertical thrusts upwards his cock pounds up Into her pussy as he plugs her tight arse hole with his cock he holds her throat then pumps his erection up her arse from behind as she makes a choking sound he keeps pumping his pole straight up into her tight arse hole ring then slides his cock up her arse hole she keeps screaming then he just keep pounding her arse hole she comes then he takes his hands off her throat then she screams was he rams his erection up her arse hole then stands there pumping her and shoving his erection up into her are whole she screams argh then comes as he keeps sliding his whole pole straight up her tight arse hole she keeps screaming he slides his girth back me forth along her arse hole ring then spears her arse hole ring with his girth shoving his erection up deep up into her arse hole ring as she screams argh then comes he keeps sliding his erect stiff cock up her arse then turns her around then lifts her up into his arms then shoves his erect cock into her pussy then take his hand away as she screams he slides his erection up her arse hole and keeps pumping his cock up her arse she keeps screaming he keeps pounding her up and down off his erection as he slides his cock hard and fast up her arse hole with rapid deep upwards thrust he slides his cock deep up her arse hole she screams argh then comes he keeps pumping her standing up at the end of the bed with his erection sliding up her arse hole then he slams her o to the bed the chokes her and leans up over her then spears her arse hole with his cock and thrusts upwards and keeps shoving his erection deep up her arse hole with a heap of hard and fast upwards thrusts heh slides his cock in her arse then pumps her arse e hole with rapid thrusts pumping his erection in and up deep I to her tight arse hole as she makes a choking face he keeps leaning over her with his arms down straight choking her into the bed lifts his arse up and down he slams his erection straight up and around up into her tight arse hole pounding her arse hole ring into the bed with his erect stiff cock down wards thrusting and ramming his pole up her tight arse hole then fest his knob far and deep up her arse hole ring as his girth pounds her arse hole ring her eyes are rolling back as she comes then he takes his hands off her throat and she gasps for air and inhales then screams as he keeps pumping his cock in her arse he re braces her by the hips then slides his e section up deep up into her arse hole then pounds her arse hole into the edge of the mattress then spots on her arse hole ring then keeps pumping his erection up her arse hole with a heap of upwards thrust that split tear and grate her arse hole ring as she screams argh then comes he uses his hand to hold the back of her knees then pins her down into the bed and slides his erection straight up into her arse hole and does his bonor up her arse hole ring he keeps thrusting upwards and launching his erect pole straight up her tight arse hole ring then keeps pumping her arse hole ring with upwards thrusts and hard and fast upwards pumps she keeps screaming argh argh argh as he pins her down to the edge of the mattress and slides his erect stiff cock up her arse hole and keeps ramming his cock up her arse hole ahe scre ma argh then comes he keeps pumping her and shoving his cock up her arse then hold her throat and pins his erection up her arse hole he keeps sliding his cock up her arse then keeps pumping her and shoving his cock up her arse she comes then he lets gi3 of her throat and she gasps for air then starts screaming as he is pounding her arse hole into the mattress and sliding his cock up her arse hole he keeps pumping her and shoving his cock up her arse then slams her arse hole with upwards thrusts of his erect penis she is screaming he flips her over using her sides and she goes up o to all fours he goes up on his toes to shoves his erection up her arse then holds her hips and pumps his cock up her arse as she screams he keeps pumping her arse hole with his erection and slides his cock straight up her arse hole then keeps pumping her arse hole ring with his cock she screams argh then comes he keeps pounding his erection up her tight arse hole she screams as he holds her by the hips and thrusts his bonor up her arse hole ring he keeps pumping her arse hole ring with hard and fast upwards thrusts sliding his erection up deep up into her arse hole as she keeps screaming he feels a tight sensation around his knob and shafts as his slides his cock up her arse hole then holds her arms up then braces her and thrashes his erect pole up into her tight arse hole ring pounding his cock up her arse hole as she screams a echoing scream ah ah ah as he keeps holding onto her arse and pumping his stiff cock up her tight arse hole pounding her arse hole ring shoving his cock up deep up into her tight arse hole he can see his erection goes in up deep up into her arse hole ring as she screams argh then comes he pumps her arse hole with upwards thrusts of his erect stiff cock pumping his erection up her tight arse hole as she keeps screaming he lets gi3 of her arms the throws her up onto the bed then leaps on and prone bones her shoving his knob on her arse hole with his hand around his shafts Ponting it down he slams it into her tight arse hole and she screams as he pounds her arse hole into the mattress then holds her hips to the mattress and down wards pounds his cock up her arse hole she screams as he keeps ramming her arse hole into the mattress and sliding his erection up deep up into her tight arse hole with rapid upwards thrust he rams his erection straight up her arse hole she screams argh then comes he keeps pounding her arse hole with his stiff cock then slides his erection straight up her tight arse hole ring then reaches around and slides his hand under her side breasts and rubs her breasts with his hand and palm she screams as he keeps sliding his erection up her arse hole then rains her beast and nipple with his palm then both her breasts and nipples with his palms pounding his erection into her arse hole ring as she screams argh then comes he keeps slamming her arse hole with upwards thrusts from his stiff erection then slide his bonor up into her arse hole he keeps sliding his cock up her arse then she keeps screaming as he pounds her arse hole ring he holds her hips then thrashes his erect cock up deep up into her tight arse hole ring shoving his erect cock up her tight arse hole as she screams argh then comes he keeps shoving his bonor up her arse then holds her throat with his hand and chokes her she makes a choking sound as he slides his erection up her arse hole he slides his cock deep up into her arse hole with hard and fast upwards thrusts he shoves his erection deep up her tight arse hole threading scraping and tearing her arse hole ring he lunges upwards then shoves his erection up her arse hole she comes then he takes his hands off her throat and she gasps for air then starts screaming as he pumps his cock up into her arse hole spitting on her arse hole ring he slides his cock up her arse hole then keeps spitting on her arse as his erection slides up into her tight arse hole she screams as he threads tears and grates with his erect cock her tight arse hole she screams ah ah ah arghh then comes as he pounds his erection up into her arse hole pumping and pounding his erection up her arse he slides his cock straight up her arse hole with upwards heaves he plugs her arse hole and keeps sliding his erect stiff cock up her arse hole she screams argh then comes he keeps pumping his erection up her arse then throws her up the bed he chases her then lifts her up and slams her into the wall making a loud thud and scream as he slides his cock back up her arse hole then plugs her arse hole with his erection and keeps shoving his cock up her arse hole she screams as he lunges upwards and heaves her into the the wall his cock pounding up her arse hole as he slides his erection up deep up into her arse hole ring plugging her arse hole ring with his erection he keeps pumping her with hard and fast upwards thrusts then braces her by the hips then spears her arse hole with his erection spitting on her arse hole ring he slides his cock up into her arse hole she screams argh as he pins her hips to the wall then slides his erection straight up her arse from behind she keeps screaming as he slides his cock up into her arse hole belting her arse cheek he spanks her arse cheek with his palm then re braces her hips and slides his erection up her arse hole she screams he keeps sliding his cock up into her arse then spanks her again then keeps sliding his erect stiff cock up into her tight arse hole he keeps pumping his cock up her arse then whacks her arse cheek re braces her hips shoving his cock up her arse hole and thrashing his cock up into her arse hole ring as he holds her hips his cock slides straight up vertically up into her tight arse hole she screams argh then comes he keeps pumping her and shoving his cock up her arse pounding his erection up into her arse hole holding her throat she makes a choking sound as he wraps his hands around her throat he lunges upwards sliding his erect cock up her arse he keeps heaving his cock up into her arse hole and pumping her he keeps grasping her throat and stands there behind her sliding his stiff cock up into her arse hole he lunges upwards heaving his cock up into her arse hole as she comes he takes his hands off her throat gasps for air then inhales he then slides his erection up into her arse hole she screams then he holds her hips then slides his cock hard up her arse hole then explodes he feels his knob and shafts tighten as he shoots comes up her arse then keeps sliding his whole cock up into her arse hole scraping and thread-ing her arse hole she screams argh them comes he slides his cock up into her arse then keeps coming he feels his cock pumping come up her arse as his erection spasms inside her tight arse he keeps sliding his cock up into her arse hole after he has come then holds her shoulder turns her around then tilts his head and pashes her into the wall and slides his tongue down her throat as she is panting he can feel the hot air from her lips as he changes sides then keeps open mouth pashing her and sliding his tongue down her throat

Ivan wakes up and is spooning the queen then lifts up her night is and is looking at her arse when she wakes up and laughs then turns over he leaps on top if her then tilts his head and kisses her into the bed then pulls his shorts down then his cock erects up and he points it down then hooks it up and into her vagina he feels his knob push against her pussy lips then as he lunges up he feels his top veiny shafts grate her vagina ring he keeps launch-ing himself upwards and his cock goes up deep into her vagina his knob pounds into her cervix as she screams and goes wild underneath him she holds his side's and wraps her legs around his body as he keeps upwards and spears her vagina with his stiff erection he thrusts and pumps stroke and thrashes upwards worse them a wild animal as she screams he keeps heaving and lunging upwards up the bed his erection drills up into her pussy deep as he uses his whole body to launch upwards his pole stabs her vagina and he grates tears scrapes and threads her tight vagina ring as she screams argh then comes he keeps launching his whole body upwards his cock pounds into her vagina ring he feels his girth threading her pussy ring she screams argh then comes as he keeps pumping her pussy with his cock and sliding his cock deep up her vagina he launches up grabs the bed head then heaves his cock hard up into her vagina smashing his cock into her pussy making loud clapping sounds as Hume slams into her groins and his cock slides deeper and further up into her tight wet vagina his girth maxes out on her vagina ring he keeps stroking her and going faster and deeper with harder upwards thrusts using the bedhead to launch his stiff cock straight up her tight vagina she screams arghh the whole time then as he stiffens his cock then strokes her with that she screams oh my god as he pounds his cock deep up into her vagina she comes he pumps her with his cock sliding it up and into her vagina slamming his erection deep up her tight vagina he feels his girth stretch her vagina ring with each upwards lunge as he keeps using the bedhead to slam and ram his cock up deep up into her vagina she leaks then he feels his cock threading scraping and grating her wet vagina walls as his ribbed erection goes hard up into her pussy he lunges upwards then slams his knob into her cervix he thrashes his pole up into her pussy and keeps pumping his cock deep up into her wet tight vagina he launches upwards grabbing the bedhead he throws his whole body up the bed his stiff cock threads her vagina with fast rapid upwards thrusts he slams his girth up her vagina ring and she screams argh then comes he slides his erection up deep up into her vagina then keeps pumping her with his cock by grabbing the bedhead and heaving his body upwards and smashing his pole into her pussy his balls slap into her arse cheeks then he stiffens his cock then vertically spears her tight vagina with his erect pole using straight up her vagina as she screams arghh in a echoing tone as she comes he is pounding her whole body as he uses his arms to heave his cock up deep up into her vagina as he is sliding his cock up her vagina she leaks and wettens the he does powerful upwards thrusts that shove his pole deep up into her vagina he puts his hands around her throat then leans forward it goes silent only the sound of her making a choking noise and his cock as it slides up her vagina his knob tapping her cervix as he does downwards thrusts and pounds his erection deep up into her vagina he keeps scooping his cock up and around up and in deep up into her vagina with his knob and tops shafts pleasuring her g spot he keeps sliding his cock up her vagina then she comes he lets gi3 of her throat she gasps for air then screams as he re grabs the bedhead and heaves his whole body upwards and slides his stiff cock straight up and onto her vagina he shakes the whole bed and slams his cock hard up her tight wet pussy threading scraping and tearing her vagina ring with his stiff cock he keeps grabbing the bedhead and lunges his whole body up hard and fast and his cock slides deeper and further up into her pussy as she screams argh then comes he is shovelling his cock up and up deep into her vagina he re braces the bedhead then heaves his body upwards and stiffens his cock at the same time he scrapes grates and threads her vagina with his throbbing shafts sliding up along her vagina wall as he keeps grabbing the bedhead and humping her pumping and pounding her vagina up the bed she places her palms on the bedhead flat to stop herself and is screaming as he is grabbing the bedhead and heaving his whole body up into her as his cock slides deeper and further up into her pussy he grates her vagina with massive upwards thrusts the bedhead making loud squeaking and banging sounds as he grabs o to it and throws his whole body upwards his erect cock sliding up into her pussy she is screaming as the sound of his body slapping into her groins keeps his cock stiff and grating her tight vagina ring as he keeps grabbing the bedhead and launching upwards she screams arghh then comes he is pumping her with his cock sliding up into her vagina as his is using his whole body and grabbing the bed head to heave his cock up her vagina she takes his cock and slips it into her arse as he is heaving his cock up into her he feels it to into her arse then feels a tight sensation around his knob and shaft as well as her scream louder he groans then keeps grabbing the bedhead and launching his body into hers as his cock slides up into her arse hole she keeps screaming he is doing wild upwards heaves using the bed head to launch his cock up her arse hole he launches up the bed and uses his arms to heave his cock deeper and further up into her arse hole she is screaming as he thrashes his cock up her arse and thrusts upwards using the bedhead to launch faster and harder up into her arse hole with powerful upwards heaves he stiffens his cock as it slides up her arse and she screams argh then comes as he feels his cock grate her arse hole with rapid upwards thrusts he feels his body slamming and pounding into hers as his cock slides up into her arse hole as he launches up the bed using his arms to heave himself up into her arse hole he stiffens his erection then slides his stiff erect cock deep up her are whole then re braces the bedhead and plugs her arse hole with his cock sliding up into her are she is screaming oh my god as he keeps launching upwards and heaving his cock up her arse hole ring he grabs the bedhead then launches directly upwards with a stiffened cock that slides up her are hole she screams argh then comes he keeps pumping her and shoving his cock up her arse then with both arms tight on the bedhead holding on he thrusts his cock and slides it deep up into her vagina she is screaming then he holds her throat and leans forward and applys pressure to her windpipe choking her then slides his cock up her arse as he keeps choking her he feels his cock slide up into her arse hole he keeps pumping his cock up her arse then watches as she opens her mouth he kisses her and then keeps sliding his cock up her arse with upwards heaves and massive upwards launches he slides his cock up her arse hole pumping her he feels his erection throb and the sides of his shaft grate her arse hole ring as he keeps sliding his stiff cock up her arse he is choking her his arms out straight and leaning up over her looking into her eyes and sliding his cock up deep up I to her arse hole her eyes roll back and she comes he lets gi3 if her throat and she gasps for air he wraps his right arm around her upper body then braces her there then slides his cock straight up her arse he feels his girth stretching her arse hole as he gets up deep up into her arse hole ring with his whole cock up inside her arse hole he slides his stiff cock up her arse then she bites his neck and he thrashes her he holds her hips and slides his cock straight up her arse as she screams he keeps sliding his cock up her arse and feel his cock slide deeper and further up inside her arse hole then throws her over and she slams o to the bed he keeps on top of her then grabs the bedhead with one hand his cock in the other and slides his knob up her arse then grabs the bedhead and launches upwards and his cock slides up her arse hole into her arse hole ring she screams as he pounds her arse cheeks into the bed and his cock slides fast up her arse hole he keeps using the bedhead to absolutely tear her arse hole with rapid deep upwards thrusts he uses the bedhead to launch his cock up her arse hole she is screaming he gave and cheeks om the mattress holding the wall and bedhead with her palms as he slides his cock up her arse hole he keeps plugging her tight arse hole with his whole cock pumping her arse hole ring he keeps pounding and pumping her arse hole with his stiff cock she is screaming as he keeps upwards and thrusts his cock slides straight up her tight arse his cock parallel to the bed up her arse hole he keeps sliding his cock up her arse hole tearing grating and scraping her arse hole ring as his cock gets launched up into her tight arse as his whole body thrusts upwards and his cock slides up her arse hole she screams argh them comes he keeps pumping her arse hole with his cock sliding up her arse as she keeps screaming he lifts up her neck and chokes her with his hands around her throat then keeps prone boning her sliding his cock rapidly up her arse hole ring he keeps shoving his cock up her arse and choking her with his hands then as he stiffens his cock and threads grates and scrapes her arse hole ring with his throbbing shafts he keeps sliding his cock up her arse hole he feels his body slamming and pounding into hers as his cock slides up her arse hole ring she comes then he lets go of her throat she gasps for air inhaling as she breathes deeply she slams

the side of her face and cheek back onto the mattress screaming
as he slides his cock up her arse she keeps screaming as he re
grabs the bedhead and foes fast upwards pumps his cock sliding
deeper and harder up into her tight arse hole ring she screams
argh as he keeps grabbing the bedhead and sliding his cock up
her arse hole he spanks her are ouch she screams then he keeps
pumping her arse hole ring he feels his shafts sliding along her
arse hole as he keeps using the bedhead to launch upwards and
slides his cock deeper and harder up into her arse hole ring he
does a heap of hard and fast thrusts then slides his cock straight
dire fly up her tight arse hole she screams argh then comes he becomes a machine with hard and fast upwards thrusts he heaves
his cock up her arse she is screaming as he thrashes her with hard
and fast upwards thrusts he keeps pounding her arse hole ring
with his girth then keeps pumping her and shoving his cock up
her arse hole with his erection sliding straight up her arse hole
she keeps screaming her arm sup holding the bedhead and her
palms straight as she braces herself he slides his cock up her arse
hole he keeps grabbing the bedhead and his whole body up the
bed his cock sliding up into her arse hole she screams argh then
comes then he stands up and lifts her up onto the wall then argh
she screams as he slides his cock up her arse then stands there
behind her sliding his cock up her arse hole as she screams and
puts her palms onto the wall he holds her hips and slides his
cock up into her arse then belts her arse cheek spanking her
ouch she screams as he keeps sliding his erection up her arse
hole then she screams argh them comes he keeps pumping her
arse hole ring with his erection sliding his cock up her arse from
behind holding her hips he keeps sliding his cock up her arse as
she screams he grabs the bedhead then stands there pumping his
cock up her arse he keeps using the bedhead to slide his cock up
her arse further and deeper pounding her thrashing her and
drilling her plugging her arse hole ring with his whole cock she
screams argh then comes he keeps sliding his cock up her arse
and pumping her then re braces the bedhead and launches his
cock up her arse hole as she screams he keeps heaving his cock

up her arse hole and slam stiffening his cock as it slides up her arse hole grating tearing and scraping along her arse hole ring as he purposely uses the bedhead to launch himself harder and deeper up into her arse hole and slams her arse hole ring with his girth she screams argh then comes he finds himself launching upwards and grabbing onto the bedhead to heave his cock up her arse and keep her screaming his cock sliding up into her arse hole ring he keeps launching upwards and heaving himself up her arse hole with vertical upwards strokes his cock slides straight up her arse hole ring and she screams argh then comes he keeps pounding her arse hole into the wall and sliding his cock up her arse hole she is screaming he keeps pumping her with hard and fast upwards thrusts he keeps pounding her arse hole then re braces the bedhead and slides his cock vertically up into her arse hole she screams argh then comes he keeps pumping her and slides his cock up her arse hole he can feels his body slamming into hers as he slams her into the wall she makes a loud thud and he re braces the bedhead pulling himself closer to her and pinning her between him and the wall then slides his cock up her arse she screams as he re grabs the bedhead and thrashes her he thrust upwards and shoves his whole cock up her arse hole and grates thread and scrapes her arse hole ring with a heap of hard and fast upwards thrusts that slide his cock deep up into her are hole he keeps plugging her tight arse with his throbbing erection sliding up her are hole he grabs the bedhead then spears her and impales her arse hole with his bonor getting shoves deep up inside her tight arse hole he slams his girth into her arse hole ring then shoves his cock vertically up into her arse lifting her up onto her tippy toes screaming as he slides his cock up her arse hole he keeps standing there she is up against the wall her elbow and forearms up as he grabs the bedhead and slides his cock up her arse hole thrusting upwards and heaving his erection up her arse hole he drills and hammers his cock up her arse holding her throat he chokes her she makes a choking sound as he slides his erection up her arse hole with rapid upwards heaves and hard and fast vertical thrusts he slides his cock up her arse hole and keeps plugging her arse hole with his girth stretching her arse hole ring as he slides his cock up her arse hole he keeps pumping her arse hole then slides his cock up her arse hole she comes then he takes his hands off her throat then she inhales and gasps for air he does a rough vertical thrust that spears his cock up her arse hole she screams then he re grabs the bedhead and heaves his cock up her arse he keeps sliding his cock up her arse then she screams as he pumps his cock deep up into her arse hole he keeps pumping her sliding his cock up her arse then pumps his cock harder and further up her arse hole whack ouch she screams he belts her arse cheek then he keeps sliding his cock up her arse hole she is screaming as she comes he keeps heaving his cock up her arse hole and shoves his cock deeper and harder pounding her arse hole he thrusts upwards and slides his cock up her arse then drills and tears her arse hole grating her arse hole with his cock he keeps sliding his cock up her arse then keeps pumping her he turns and falls with her onto the bed then as she screams he holds her throat and chokes her he keeps sliding his cock up her prone boning her then slides his cock up her arse hole he keeps pumping her and drilling her arse hole thrashing her with hard and fast thrusts pounding her arse hole he rams her from behind he keeps choking her and sliding his cock up her arse hole she comes then he takes his hands off her throat and she gasps for air he puts both palms flat on the mattress then digs his knees in then uses his body as a battering ram to slide his cock up her arse she is screaming as he does a heap of hard and fast powerful thrusts that have his cock sliding up into her arse hole as she screams he keeps sliding his cock up her arse she screams argh then comes he keeps pumping her and plugging her arse as he thump her arse hole ring with his girth and hammers her arse hole up the bed with hard and fast drilling strokes pounding her a se hole up the bed she screams argh then comes he keeps sliding his cock up her arse hole then turn her onto her back flipping her over he positions his cock under her arse then slide his cock up her arse hole then holds the back of her knees then slides his cock up her arse as he pins her down into the mattress using the back of her knees argh argh argh she screams as he pumps her into the mattress slamming his cock into her he keeps sliding his cock up her arse then pounds her arse hole sliding his girth into her arse hole ring and pumping her with his cock sliding up her arse she screams argh then comes he keeps pumping her and sliding his cock up her arse then get her legs on his shoulders then puts his palms on the bed beside her body then in a push up position he slams his cock in her arse she screams as he slides his cock up her arse pumping her arse hole ring he feels his cock sliding up her arse as he groans he keeps pumping her and sliding his cock straight up her arse hole then feels his girth slam into her arse hole ring as he pounds her arse hole into the mattress he hops onto her throat with his hands then pins her to the mattress and chokes her she makes a choking sound as he keeps pounding her arse hole into the mattress sliding his cock deep into her arse hole he keeps sliding his cock up her arse hole and lunges upwards his cock slides up her arse her eyes roll back as she comes he takes his hands off her throat she gasps for air then he keeps sliding his cock up her arse she keeps screaming he goes and put his hand under her left shoulder then flips her onto her back then slides his cock up her arse she screams as he keeps sliding his cock up her arse hole he feels his shafts slide up her arse hole ring and his girth slam into her arse hole then grabs her hips and thrashes her pounding her tight arse hole with his cock she is screaming as he stiffens his erection then spears it up into her arse hole and thrusts forwards and lunges upwards his cock slides up her arse she is screaming he keeps pumping her then fish hooks her mouth and she screams he keeps sliding his cock up her then gets off the bed and sits on the edge of the mattress as she comes around then sits on his cock then he slides his cock up her arse she screams as he keeps sliding his cock up into her arse hole and pumps her arse hole with rapid pumps and slides his cock up her tight arse hole she is screaming argh argh argh as he pumps her arse hole he stands up then throws her o to the bed then comes up behind her she is kneeling over the mattress he slides his cock up her arse hole then thrashes her he rams his cock hard and fast up her arse hole and slams his cock up her arse pounding her arse hole ring she screams he keeps pumping her arse hole with hard and fast upwards thrusts she screams argh then comes he keeps sliding his cock up her arse then places his hands around her throat choking her then hears a choking sound he keeps sliding his cock up her arse hole pumping her with hard and fast thrusts he keeps pounding her arse hole and drills her arse hole pounding and ramming her he heaves his cock up her arse slamming and plunging his erection up her arse hole he keeps choking her and sliding his cock up her arse hole she comes then he lets gi3 of her throat she gasps for air coughing he keeps pumping her arse hole and sliding his cock up her arse hole ring as she is screaming he turns her around then slumps her down on the floor up against the mattress then shoves his cock in her mouth and comes he slides his cock down the back of her throat then shoots come out from his cock and pumps her throat with come she coughs and splatters as he shoves his cock deep down the back of her throat and keeps coming she has and coughs then swallows as he keeps holding the back if her head and forcing his cock down the back of her throat as she gulps the gasps for air he slides his cock out then lifts her up then lays on the bed with her he puts his cock between her legs then as he is kissing her he slowly slides his cock back into her vagina then as he slowly slides it back and forward and he is kissing her he feels it stiffen as it slides along her vagina walls he keeps kissing her then as it swells up and goes erect he feels his shafts starts to grate her vagina ring and thread her tight pussy he sits up on his knees then keeps up the bed and his cock spears her vagina and he starts humping and pumping her she is screaming as he heaves his cock up her vagina and launches upwards stiffening his cock it goes harder the second time as the blood pumps throughout his body his erection is ribbed and has veins stick-ing out from it that thread her vagina ring making a grating feel-ing around his girth she screams argh then comes as he is sliding his cock up her vagina her breasts and nipples are hard as he keeps launching upwards and heaving his cock up her vagina pounding her and pumping her he hammers and drills his cock up her vagina he feels it already warm and wet then it goes hot and tight her vagina leaks and he launches upwards and feels his knob tapping her cervix she screams argh then comes he uses his veiny top shaft to stimulate her g spot as he slides his cock up her vagina she screams argh then comes he keeps sliding his stiff cock up her vagina and pumps her pussy with hard and fast upwards thrusts ramming her vagina in he thrashes her pussy with his cock he slides his cock up her vagina then keeps pumping her pussy his hands fall around her throat and chokes her and she goes silent only the sound of his cock smacking into her pussy he keeps sliding his cock up her vagina then launches upwards and stiffens his cock then shoves it up her vagina he looks at her face as she is coming then thrashes her vagina sliding his cock hard up her vagina her eyes roll back and she comes he takes his hand off her throat she gasps then screams as he launches his cock up her vagina and heaves his erection deep up into her pussy she keeps screaming as he launches his cock up her vagina with hard and fast upwards thrusts that keep her screaming as he launches upwards he stiffens his cock then threads her vagina ring he keeps pumping her pussy and threading her vagina ring slamming his girth deep up into her pussy lips as she screams argh then comes he keeps pumping her and sliding his cock deep up her vagina then launches upwards and slides his cock up her vagina she keeps screaming as he goes on his knees then lifts her up by the hips then drills her vagina with his cock hammering into her tight wet pussy as he grabs her by the hips slightly elevates her and thrashes his cock up her vagina she keeps screaming as he keeps rocking his veiny top shaft back and forth along her vagina and pleasuring her g spot he does vertical thrusts that spear his cock up her vagina she screams argh as she comes he keeps sliding his erection up her vagina then lifts her up and slams her up into the wall and humps her and pumps her sliding his cock up her arse he slams her back into the wall making loud thuds as well as her screaming he keeps shoving his cock up her vagina and feels his girth slamming her vagina ring as he keeps pumping her vagina into the wall and heaving his erection up her vagina with vertical thrusts he slides his cock straight up into her vagina with deep hard upwards thrusts bracing her by the legs and sides he keeps sliding his cock up her vagina she screams argh then comes he lunges upwards and keeps sliding his cock up her vagina then shoves his knob into her arse hole she screams as he keeps sliding his cock up her arse heaving his cock up her arse hole he slides his erect stiff cock up into her arse as she screams yes yes yes he is sliding his cock up into her arse hole pumping his erection up her arse she screams argh then her whole body tenses as she comes he keeps launching upwards and sliding his cock deep up into her arse with hard and fast upwards thrusts he stiffens his cock then grates and threads her arse sliding his cock vertically up her arse as she screams argh then comes he keeps sliding his cock up her arse and shoving her back into the wall and sliding his cock up her arse hole she screams then he re braces her then slams her arse hole up the wall and keeps sliding his erection up her arse then keeps pumping her and sliding his cock up her arse he outs her down then turns her around quickly then slides his cock up into her arse hole then grabs the bedhead and drills her arse hole with his cock pumping her and slamming his cock up her arse hole she is screaming as he grabs the bedhead then slams her arse hole ring with his cock he drills hammers and pounds her arse hole she keeps screaming as he plugs her arse hole ring with his erection pumping her with hard and fast upwards heaves he keeps grabbing the bedhead and shoving his cock up her arse hole pumping her with hard and fast upwards heaves he slides his cock straight up her tight arse hole she screams argh then comes he uses his arms to heave his whole body forward and slam his cock up her arse hole he feels his knob and shafts tighten then he keeps pumping and sliding his cock up her arse then holds her neck and chokes her he wraps his hands around her throat then keeps sliding his cock up her arse hole he keeps pumping her and shoving his cock up her arse hole then does a heap of upwards pumps that slides his cock up her arse hole ring she orgasms then he takes his hands off her throat and she gasps then he keeps sliding his cock up her arse hole and lunging upwards she keeps screaming as he holds her by the hips and pounds her arse hole ring and slides his cock up her arse hole he keeps sliding his cock up deep up into her arse hole then grabs her hips and heaves his cock up her arse and shoves and pounds her arse hole ring ramming her and plugging her tight arse with his cock spanking her arse cheek she screams ouch he keeps pumping her and sliding his cock up her arse then comes he groans and slides his cock up her arse with hard and fast thrusts he thrashes her arse hole she screams argh then comes he keeps pumping her arse hole and shoots come up her arse then feels his cock spasm and tighten as he keeps pumping come up her bum then slides his cock up her arse after he has come he turns her around then tilts his head and open mouth pashes her and slides his tongue down her throat holding the back of her neck he pulls her lips onto his as his tongue slides down her throat and he open mouth tongue kisses her

Ivan takes the queen up to the bedroom after dinner then she is in his arms he is kissing her and walking up the stairs open mouth pashing her at the same time she is undoing his buttons he keeps kissing her then lays on the bed with her then takes off his shirt then lifts her dress up over her head then keeps kissing her into the bed open mouth tongue kissing her as he feels her breasts with his hands she keeps panting then he grabs her wrist and lifts her up off the bed and ties her arm and wrist up she hits him with her left hand and he sucks then she keeps slapping him he turns his head and she just keeps hitting the back if his head as he finishes tying the first knot off then as he goes across her body and ties her other hand up she keeps trying to get free and thrusts around screaming he gives her mouth and it goes silent then he has to take his hand off to tie the knot she screams in his ear then tries to get her arm free he re braces it then gets it re- strained she screams then he watches and smiles as she thrusts around screaming and kicking him he moves his body and she air swings and kicks the air he gets the whip then cracks it around her side's it hits the back of her arse cheeks and she screams argh then goes up on her tippy toes he gets a better angle then crack argh she screams as he whips her arse and she keeps screaming he does a heap of whips in a row that all hit perfect on her arse cheeks she stands there thrusting and screaming her whole body tenses as she tries to break the restraints then keeps thrashing around and screaming crack argh he whips her arse cheek again then he keeps whipping her she screams constantly argh argh argh with each whip he can hear her scream and thrust around with a deafening scream he just stands there humming to himself and whipping her arse cheeks he walks up to her then kisses her she flicks her lips away then spits at him he touches her breasts with his fingers and feels her breasts she screams in his face as he keeps admiring her breasts and neck then slides his hands up her neck then chokes her lifting her off her feet she panics and thrusts around he puts her down then as she kicks him he blocks it lift up his knees and he keeps feeling her breasts then goes backwards and lines up her breasts and then crack argh she screams argh argh argh it hurts as she leaks over screaming he can see the mark it has left from a distance crack argh he whips the other side of her breasts she screams then he just keeps whipping her front he whips her breasts again then her up thighs then as he whips her pussy she screams loudest a war piercing shriek that goes up t throughout the castle he steps closer then can feel her screaming her veins in her neck are showing and her whole body is red like a lobster with whip marks across it her eyes are wide and she is just screaming argh arghh arghh he sees how much she can take then keeps whipping her then when her legs give and she can't stand anymore he walks over to her then tells her to stop screaming and stand up then heaves her back o to her feet he props her back up then slap her on the arse like that's better she swings her leg and kicks him he blocks it with his hand then tightens the restraints and she goes up higher then as she is on her tippy toes he whips her and can see lines in a pattern across her front he stand s back then tells her to turn around she is screaming then he whips her arse argh she screams as she turns her arse and shows him her side crack he whips her a proper hard whip that keeps her screaming then he whips her breasts she screams he whips her other breasts she screams louder then as he whips her vagina she screams arghh arghh ouch he keeps whipping her vagina and can hear the cracking if the whip as it hits her flesh and leaves lash marks like stripes all across her front she is screaming as he just keeps whipping her front she screams stop argh he whips her again then she tells him stop it hurts he goes harder and she screams argh he stands closer then crack he whips her breasts and she screams stop please stop argh he whips her again then he 2atches as she thrusts around screaming and trying to untie her restraints he whips her arse cheeks then she keeps up in the air screaming he likes to see her jump like that and keeps whipping her arse cheeks as she thrusts up in the air clenching her arse and screaming he tells her to keeps moving argh she screams as he keeps whipping her she screams stop then he whips her harder and then goes a heap of whips that all hits her arse cheeks and she jumps up and down screaming her head off at him he tells her to relax then crack arghh she screams louder and then he tells her to please stop moving around so much she tells him to fuck off then he whips her arse cheeks and watches as she keeps moving around and screaming the sight inspires him to do a heap more whips cracking the whip around her he watches as she screams and thrusts around on pain he goes around on a better angle then tells her to stop fucken moving then he whips her arse cheek and she screams arghh it hurts then thrusts her body around trying to snap her restraints he goes o her to her then blindfolds her then tells her that he won't whip her anymore she starts to calm down then crack he whips her vagina and she leans forward screaming argh then thrusts back and forth having a tantrum he whips it out of her whipping her arse he keeps whipping her arse cheeks argh argh argh she screams then she lifts her body up and goes on her tippy toes he whips her again and again she screams and exhales breathing rapidly in between screams he can hear her huffing and puffing then screaming as the whip hits her arse cheek argh he whips her again then she screams argh he walks up to her then pulls her nipple then the other one she screams then he steps back and whips them arghhh she screams he thrashes she whipping her entire front he whips her breasts and her front her belly and her vagina her upper thighs then her breasts again she keeps screaming arghh then he lays into her he goes a heap of powerful hard whips that land perfectly on her the whip cracking and hitting her flesh she screams arghh her whole body covered in a fine layer of sweat that makes the whip sound crisp as it hits her skin then he goes up to her and keeps whipping her and watches as she jumps up and down screaming he is standing close to her and can hear her deep breathes he tells her to suck it up and she hear a that he is close and kicks him he moves back then whips her away lifting the whip quickly up and I we his head he whips her breasts and she screams and stops kicking instead thrusting around and jumping up and down screaming in pain he asks her which hurts more the breasts and he whips her breasts and she screams arghh then he says or the vagina then crack he lifts the whip up and whips her vagina argh he09 keeps whipping her breasts then tells her I can't hear you then crack he whips her breasts again arghh he lays into her with a heap of rough hard and fast whips that whip her front and he can see her breasts have limes across them and massive whip marks that he is proud of that he looks at and hums to himself as he lifts the whip up then with his whole body throw a the whip then crack he whips her vagina and she screams he walks up to her then kisses her and tries to open mouth pash her she kicks him and keeps kicking him he stands back then crack he whips her in the middle of her breasts and she screams then he goes on his side and tilts his head then aims perfectly for her pussy crack arghhh stop it argh it hurts me tells her to stay still she making it more difficult for him arghh arghh arghh he keeps whipping her then watches as she goes wild thrusting around she screams and thrusts up and down left and right trying to snap or break the restraints he whips her arms then she stops trying to pull them off he then aims around her back and gets her back argh she screams he walks around then crack argh he whips her back and she screams argh he keeps whipping her back then she screams and thrusts forward her shoulders back and her hips in the air screaming as he keeps whipping her she screams argh then he gets the electrical cord he stands behind her on the bed then hiding the top of the bed frame with his left hand he lifts his eight hand up towards the bedhead then whack he belts her arse cheek with the electrical cable then watches as she arches her whole body from the impact and screams arghh In an ear piercing shriek he tells her stay still stop moving then uses his hand to brace himself then with his whole body swings the electrical cable then whacks her arse cheek with it she screams first then her whole body tenses after and she thrusts upwards screaming arghh as she keeps screaming and tensing her body up and down in the air he lifts his arm up then like he were pegging a cricket ball for a run out he smashes the electrical cord onto her arse cheek and she keeps up on her tippy toes screaming arghh he can see the impact as her whole body goes forward and then she keeps screaming then as he lunges forward and goes it again he takes her legs out from under her and she dangles in the air screaming arghh he jumps down off the bed then lifts her back into her feet and props her up using his arm around her back he gets her back to her feet she is screaming then tries to kick and head butt him he tells her to relax then she screams and goes agro and tries kicking him and swinging her leg up in the air he glimpses her pussy lips then he starts to get horny she keeps kicking and his attention is drawn to her pussy lips and her arse cheek that's when he gets her feet and ties her leg up to the top of the beam he ti2s her right ankle up to the beam with her hand then her other 13g and watches as she sways screaming her head off he stands back then tells her that this will hurt then belt her arse cheeks with the electrical cord she screams then her whole body thrusts around as she tries to get herself free she panics and thrusts around and tries to get herself unrestrained wriggling and thrusting she keeps screaming then tries to get her wrist free or her legs then as she is doing that Ivan lifts his arm right back over his head with the electrical cable then whack he belts her hitting her arse cheeks she scr3ams then her whole body shudders from the impact she keeps screaming then he does it again as she swings back he tines it then whack he belts her a beauty right across the arse cheeks she screams arghh stop it then twists and turns screaming and thrusting in pain he re braces the electrical cord gets a good grip then re aligns himself sliding his feet and lining her up she sways back towards him then whack he belts her arse cheek and she screams then he can see her thrusting and screaming saying argh he lifts his arm back then throws the cable onto her arse cheek making a loud smack sound as it connects she screams arghh then jumps around screaming and thrusting left and right in agony he quickly places his hand on her to stop swinging then whack he belts her again argh she screams and thrusts up and down screaming her lungs out he waits for her to swing back then whack he hits her again and she screams argh then he unties her then slams her onto the bed then keeps her blindfold

He keeps her blindfold on then runs on his knees forward then dives up the bed his cock spears her vagina and she screams he thrusts upwards and shoves his cock hard up her vagina then keeps humping and pumping her and pounding her vagina he keeps launching his body upwards then stiffens his cock as he does his erect pole slides straight up into her vagina and he keeps pumping her pussy with hard and fast upwards thrusts he can feel his cock grating and threading her vagina as he lunges upwards and heaves his cock up her vagina she keeps screaming then he just keeps pounding her vagina into the bed drilling her pussy with hard and fast thrusts of his cock he lunges upwards stiffening his erection he feels his cock slide deep up inside her vagina ring he keeps launching upwards and shoves his cock up her vagina she is screaming then he heaves his cock up her vagina then slides his cock deep up into her tight pussy he can feel his knob hitting her cervix then as he goes hard and fast with deep upwards vaginal penetration he thrashes her pussy with his cock and she screams argh then comes he keeps pumping her vagina and drilling his cock into her right pussy she keeps screaming as he keeps upwards and thrusts his erection up deep up inside her vagina as he is lunging upwards and stiffening his cock and sliding it up her tight vagina he feels his shafts threading her vagina ring as she screams he keeps upwards then drills his erection deep up inside her pussy the keeps lunging upwards and sliding his cock up into her vagina as he keeps up the bed he feels his shafts scraping and threading her vagina he keeps launching upwards and shoves his girth into her vagina ring and pounds her pussy up the bed she screams argh then comes he keeps pumping her and heaving his stiff hard cock up her tender wet pussy he keeps pumping her pussy with his cock and dies a heap of upwards thrusts that keep her screaming argh argh argh with each upwards thrust he slams his stiff cock up her vagina then grabs her hips and thrashes her vagina with upwards thrusts and hard and fast thrusts he feels his cock grating her vagina ring as he slams his erection deep up inside her vagina he keeps thrusting upwards and spearing her tight pussy with his thick cock then heaves his erection deep up into her vagina she screams argh then comes he shoves his cock deep into her vagina pounding her pussy with hard and fast upwards thrust that's keep her screaming grabbing her hips he thrashes her pussy with energetic upwards heaves pounding her vagina into the bed he keeps pumping her and sliding his cock deep up into her pussy as she screams he feels his top shaft scraping along her vagina ring as he keeps upwards and tears her pussy with his thick girth he slams his erection deep up into her vagina and she screams he thrashes her with his cock pounding her pussy he feels her vagina leak and then slides his cock further and deeper up I side her vagina his knob slams her cervix as he keeps pumping her with hard and fast upwards thrusts then launches upwards stiffening his cock it grates and threads her tight vagina ring she keeps screaming then he holds her down by the throat and chokes her she makes a choking sound then he slides his cock up her vagina and keeps stiffening his erection then shoving it up her pussy he feels his girth stretching her vagina ring with each upwards thrust he keeps sliding his cock up into her pussy as he keeps pumping her he can hear his body slamming into hers making a loud clapping sound as he keeps sliding his cock up into her vagina her eyes roll back in her head as she comes he takes his hands of her throat then she gasps for air then screams as he holds her by the hips then slides his cock up her vagina he keeps lunging upwards then feels his cock slides up into her vagina she screams he keeps sliding his cock up her vagina then slides his cock up her arse hole she screams as he keeps sliding his cock up into her arse hole he feels his knob and shafts tighten as he squeezes his cock into her tight arse hole ring and she screams argh then comes he slides his cock up into her arse hole she keeps screaming he feels a tight sensation then as he keeps sliding his cock up her arse hole he starts to come he thrashes her with hard and fast upwards thrusts he keeps pounding her arse hole ring with his girth she screams argh then comes he keeps pumping her and sliding his cock up her arse hole ring she keeps screaming then as he is lunging upwards and sliding his cock up her arse he starts to blow and thrashes her he goes wild ramming her and pounding her arse hole ring he plugs her arse hole with his erect cock he keeps lunging upwards then feels his cock deep up inside her tight arse hole he keeps coming she screams argh then comes he keeps sliding his cock up into her tight arse he feels his cock shooting and pumping come out as his cock spasms inside her tight arse hole he groans then keeps pumping and sliding his cock up into her arse hole he keeps sliding his cock up her arse after he has come and feels his cock harden then keeps sliding his cock up into her arse hole then kisses her and open mouth pashes her tilting his head he slides his tongue down her throat and keeps pashing her then his cock stays hard and he keeps pumping her and sliding his cock along her arse hole ring and up her arse he feels his cock stiffen as he is kissing her then starts to thrash her again lunch her arse hole he does hard and fast upwards slides that have his cock pumping up Into her arse hole he keeps thrashing her then pounds her arse hole with his girth she starts screaming as he launches upwards and slides his cock deep up I to her arse hole pounding her arse hole ring with his girth he slams his whole cock hard and fast up her arse then heaves his cock up her arse hole pounding her arse hole ring he does rapid upwards thrusts that slide his cock deep up into her arse hole she screams then as he keeps sliding his cock up her arse he starts to come as well and thrashes her pumping her with hard and fast upwards thrusts he plugs her arse hole with his girth then as he keeps ramming his erection up her tight arse hole ring he comes and thrashes her arse hole ramming and slamming his cock up her arse he re braces her hips and pounds her arse hole with upwards thrusts she screams argh then comes as he is sliding his cock up into her vagina he is holding her hips and coming as his cock slides up I to her arse hole he shoots come up her arse hole then keeps sliding his cock up her arse he feels his cock spasm then he keeps sliding his cock up her arse after he has come he like a the feeling of his ribbed cock threading and grating her arse hole ring he keeps kissing her and tilts his head and shoves his tongue down her throat and keeps kissing her passionately

Ivan is listening to the queen singing as he comes into the room she is dancing and singing she dances over to him as he is walking up to her then he dances with her before leaning her back and kissing his arm around her back and shoulder as he slides his tongue down her throat and keeps open mouth pashing her she giggles as he 2alks her back towards the bed then lays her down and kisses her inner thigh and up the inside of her leg he kisses her groin then lifts her dress up and off then kisses her other groin and her inner upper thigh before parting her pussy lips then sliding his tongue up her clit then back down it he re braces her vagina lips then keeps licking the top of her clit with the top of his tongue she moans then he licks directly up and down over her clit with his tongue sliding up and down her clit as he licks her and goes down on her she is moaning he re parts her pussy lips properly and spreads then her clit pops out then he dives his head between her legs and keeps using the top of his tongue to slide up and down the top of her clit she keeps moaning passionately he just uses the top of his tongue to keep licking up and down her clit he slides his tongue up along her clit then back down as she starts to pant as well she is moaning and panting breathing deeply he keeps sliding just the top of his tongue up and down her clit she is making sexy moaning sounds he can hear her as he looks up she is looking straight at him in a sit up as he looks up at her she throw a her head back and lets out a scream as he keeps licking her clit then as he slides his tongue up and down her clit she keeps moaning and then he re parts her pussy lips her enflamed clit popping out he keeps licking her clit with his tongue she screams then he keeps licking her clit with his tongue sliding up and down over her slippery clit he keeps licking her clit with his tongue going up and down up and down then she screams and thrusts lefts and ring he holds her thighs and keeps her down pinning her to the bed then re parts her pussy lips then keeps licking she screams and comes as he keeps licking her clit she keeps screaming then snaps her legs shut and goes into the foetal position and keeps moaning as he gets up onto her he pushes her onto her stomach then shoves his cock up her arse then grabs her hips and thrashes her pumping her arsehole ring with his girth he pounds her arse hole hard and fast as she screams argh then comes he keeps ramming her arse hole ring and heaving his whole body upwards and tears her arse hole ring with his erect stiff cock pounding into her arse hole and he keeps sliding his cock up and into her arse hole she screams he re braces her by the hips then lifts her up onto all fours and rams her from behind pounding and slamming her arse hole he starts to come then thrashes her he slides his cock deep and hard up her arse hole ring then feels his girth stretch and grate her arse hole as he thrashes her she is screaming and coming as he is tearing into her arse hole ring with his stiff cock pumping her with hard and fast upwards heaves he launches his bonor straight up her arse hole re grabbing her by the hips he pumps her harder and faster as she keeps screaming he can hear the pounding sound of flesh on flesh as he drills his cock up her arse hole and then slides his erection deep and hard straight up her tight arse hole ring then pulls her hair and comes he keeps grabbing her hips and slamming his cock up her arse and shooting come up her arse as she keeps screaming he just kneels there sliding his cock up her arse hole ring then as he is ejaculating he re grabs her hips and thrashes her and bangs his cock up her arse hole with rapid intense penetrative upwards thrusts she is screaming and comes then he pumps her with a heap of rough hard and fast pumps then slaps her arse off his cock ad she falls onto the bed on her back he leap on top of her and kisses her then tilts his head the other way changes sides then open mouth pashes her on the other side and slides his tongue deep down her throat

Ivan is laying bed the queen is in front of him on all fours facing down the bed he pushes her arse down with his hand then she sits up on her knees he points his bonor forward off his stomach then points it up as she goes to sit on it he watches as she does the splits onto his cock am with her knees he feels his cock to hot and wet as she dips her vagina down all over his erection he feels his side shafts slide along her vagina walls he thread grates and scrapes her vagina walls as she keeps twerking and grinding her pussy o to his cock as he just lays there with his hands be-hind his head she dances and moves her body around in a sexy heap of moves she slides dumps slams and pumps her pussy all into his erect pole he can see her pussy lips and her vagina as they gi3 up and down along his pole then she screams and he keeps watching as her a sexy body slides up and down he can feel her pussy slide along his shafts then she goes backs and for-ward and his cock screaming argh as she comes he can feel her vagina leak then she slides and glides up and down on his pole stimulating his shafts he can feel her vagina ring on his shaft scraping and grating threading his stiff pole as it sticks up her vagina she keeps screaming as she goes up and down on his cock then she slash his cock and goes back and forward on his girth grinding it into her pussy he keeps pumping blood into his cock then as it stiffens the veins thread her vagina ring and she screams she makes passionate moaning sounds and lets out a scream then keeps moaning as she reaches orgasm he lifts his arse up off the bed and pumps into her pussy and hammer and drills upwards pumping her with his erection going deep up into her pussy making loud clapping sounds as he keeps pumping his cock up her she is screaming and bracing herself on her forearm and elbows bent over on her knees as he keeps pumping his cock up into her and lifting his arse up and down drilling her pussy with his cock she screams argh then comes as he keeps humping and pumping upwards his cock drills and thrusts upwards be is pumping her pussy with rapid upwards thrusts that have his cock threading and grating her vagina ring as his girth slams into her vagina ring and his knob pounds her cervix he keeps doing hard up wards thrusts that pump his cock up her vagina he can feels his girth threading her vagina ring she screams argh then comes he keeps pumping upwards and drilling his cock up her vagina then sits up and pushes her into the bed then leaps onto her prone boning her he slams his cock into her arse hole then pumps her arse hole ring into the mattress she screams as he who we his cock up her arse and thrusts upwards and spears her arse hole ring with his girth impaling her she screams argh then comes he keeps jumping and pumping her pounding and slamming her arse hole with his cock ramming her into the mattress as she lay on her face and cheek screaming argh argh argh as he pins her arse hole with hard and fast downwards thrusts shoving his cock in then up her arse hole tearing her arse hole ring with his girth and shoving his whole cock deep up I to her arse hole ring she keeps screaming as he grabs her hips then elevates her up on all fours then kneels there pounding her arse hole ring with his cock and thrashing her from behind spanking her arse cheek she screams as he keeps holding her hips and sliding his cock up her arse and spitting in her arse hole then shoving his girth into her tight arse hole ring with rapid upwards heaves he plugs her arse hole ring with his girth and she screams argh then comes he keeps kneeling there holding her hips and sliding his cock deep up into her arse hole then thrusts rapidly and hammers her arse hole ring with his girth and pounds her arse hole with his cock slamming deep up into her arse hole ring he re braces her by the hips and pumps his erection up her arse hole she keeps screaming as he pulls her hair ouch she screams then he re braces her hips and pounds her arse hole with his girth smashing her arse hole ring as she screams argh then comes he keeps pumping her and pounding her arse hole with his whole cock sliding up her arse hole then he thrashes her to come as well he holds her hips then kneels there pounding her arse hole ring with his shafts sliding back and forth along her tight arse hole ring she screams argh then starts to orgasm as he goes into ramming speed thrashing her arse hole ring he shoves his cock deep up into her tight arse then turns her over and runs on his knees up to her mouth and shoves his cock down her throat and comes he groans as he feels his cock shoot come onto the back of her mouth and she coughs and gags splattering on his cock as he keeps it shoved down the back of her throat he feels his cock spasming in her mouth as he deep throats her and keeps coming she is gagging and splattering as he forces his cock deep down her throat and holds the back if her head as he fills her throat full of come she keeps coughing then goes silent as she swallows then gulps then starts coughing again he takes his hand soft the back of her head then she lets back on the mattress and wipes her mouth as he lets on top of her then tilts his head and pashes her then keeps passionately kissing her and sliding his tongue down her throat then tilts his head and open mouth pashes her and keeps sliding his tongue down he throat as he lifts his hand around the back of her neck then pulls her lips onto his and keeps sliding his tongue down her throat

The queen runs and a leaps off the bed as he whispers to her in her ear he going to tie her up he watches as she gets up and goes to leap off the bed he catches her by the ankle then she falls back on the bed face first he gets off the bed with her ankle in his hand then drags her up the bed she is kicking and screaming then he does her ankle up to the top of the bed frame no she screams and thrusts kicking and screaming he has to avoid her outbursts and she punches and thrusts he dodges her arms then gets her other leg and ankle tied up then she sways back and forth upside down facing away from the bed with her hair all hanging down he walks up to her then ties her hair up then puts it from her face then goes back and back pedal all excited then gets the whip she is screaming no oh no no oh no he can't help but smile then as he runs in and whips her breasts and she screams he hears her scream the castle down argh she screams as he lands s the whip straight across her breasts the six lines running across her breasts as she keeps screaming he goes up to them and feel a them with his hand and palms then kisses them she punches him away then he walls back and crack he whips her breasts again and she screams louder arghh then does a powerful heap of hard and fast whips that tear skin off her breasts and she screams louder arghh he steps closer to her then crack argh crack argh he keeps whipping her breasts and she keeps screaming then he whips her vagina argh she screams loudest as he keeps whipping her pussy he watches as she thrusts up and down doing sit ups and screaming argh it hurts stop it Ivan please stop it it hurts he tells her stop complaining then crack he whips her breasts and she screams arghh then he walks up to her then crack he whips her vagina and she screams ouch argh that hurts he keeps whipping her anyway then listens as she screams arghh loudly and thrusts up and down he ties her hands up to the bedhead then has her back and arse in his face he walks to her back then slides his hands along her skin then slides his hands all over her arse then steps back she is already screaming no Ivan please stop then he whips her back and she thrusts up and down screaming he keeps whipping her back then as she screams and thrusts he whips her arse cheeks argh she screams as he keeps whipping her then watches as she bounces up and down screaming and thrusting screaming stop it argh he crack the whip again on her back then watches as she screams he keeps whipping her back and then turn around and jump on the bed then shoves his cock up her arse then starts pumping his cock up her arse hole as she sways back and forward screaming he uses the ropes as a sex swing then keeps pumping her she screams yes oh yes as he thrashes her and pounds her arse hole with his cock ramming straight up her arse he keeps pumping her then slides his cock deeper up her arse hole then he slides his cock straight up her arse hole and keeps sliding his cock up her arse hole ring as she screams argh then comes he spits on her arse hole ring then slides his cock up her arse hole and keeps pumping his cock up her arse hole ring and pumping her sliding his cock up her arse as she screams argh then comes he stands there using the ropes he holds the top of the beam then thrusts his hips and his cock drills and pounds her arse hole ring he keeps pumping her with rapid hard and fast thrusts as she keeps screaming he slides his cock deeper and further up into her tight arse hole then with both hands on the beam he uses it to balance on and slides his cock up into her arse hole with hard and fast thrusts he keeps pumping her arsehole ring with his girth and then rams and plugs her arse hole with his girth she scream argh then comes he keeps pumping her arse hole ring with his cock and she screams argh then comes he keeps pounding her arse hole then leans over and chokes her and keeps his hands around her throat at the same time he sliding his cock up her arse hole he feels his cock stiffen then keeps sliding his cock deep up into her arse hole ring as he thread grates and scrapes her are whole ring with his girth he feels his shafts sliding along her arse hole ring as he keeps choking her her eyes roll back and she comes he takes his hand soft her throat then she gasps for air and inhales he keeps sliding his cock up her arse hole then pumps his cock deep and hard up into her arse hole ring thrashing her and pounding her arse hole he feels her breasts and slides his hands over her breasts and fondles her nipples and keeps using his palms to slide across her nipples as his cock stiffens he feels it thread and stretch her arse hole ring as she screams argh then comes he keeps pumping her and can feel his cock swelling his shafts scrape her arse hole ring and he keeps sliding his erection her arse hole and she screams as he spanks her with a uppercut slap underneath her it makes a loud crisp clap sound as she screams ouch he keeps sliding his erection up her arse hole and can feels his shafts sliding along her arse hole ring she keeps screaming then he thrashes he ran sounds her arse hole ramming his cock up her arse he feels his cock throbbing as he grates and threads her arse hole ring by slamming his cock in and out if her arse hole she keeps screaming then he thrusts upwards and keeps pumping her and while she screams argh then comes as he thrashes her with hard and fast upwards thrusts he feels his shafts sliding along her tight arse hole ring then he pumps her with hard and fast upwards thrusts that keep her screaming and invigorate his cock as he spits on her arse hole than keeps pumping her as he stands there pounding her arse hole ring standing on the bed she is tied up and he keeps pounding and slamming her arse hole as she sways back and forth hanging by the restraints he keeps spitting on her arse then glides and slides his cock up into her arse hole he thrashes her then pull his cock out and comes on her face and neck then unties her restraints and she drops on the bed

Ivan uses his axe to block a barbarian as he is running up a path towards their fortress he lifts his axe up then blocks his sword then lifts the plasma canon up them blasts him point blank then keeps running up the path a barbarian with a sword points it at him and runs at him Ivan smashes the sword away then hits the axe into his head dropping him Ivan runs along the wall then straight thru the entry way two barbarians see him then come from both way at him he turns to his right first and leaps up and slams the axe onto the top of his head then turns and has to quickly block the other one as he lifts baseball bat swings a sword into him clunk metals collide as his axe blocks his sword Ivan front kicks him back then lifts the plasma canon then blasts him Ivan looks up they have a mythological creature double the size of a dragon that lunges at Ivan whack the axe across its head as it goes to bite him then

back hands it the other way and smashes it again Ivan then lunges forward and gits it in the head and smashes it backwards the gets the
plasma canon and turns it around and boom he shoots it up and under
its neck blasting it then watches as the mythological creature starts to
choke and die Ivan looks to his side then clunk he lifts his axe up just in
time as a barbarian chops him with a sword Ivan pushes forward heaving him back and then swings the plasma canon into his ribs and side
then lifts his axe back over his head then cracks his skull with to as he
falls back on the ground another barbarian leaps over him and attacks
Ivan with a club hitting his Ivan kicks him back then leaps over the
body then left hooks the axe into his jaw dropping him Ivan runs
around the mythological creature into the fortress as he walks inside
he can see stairs across the room he runs towards them from under the
stairs comes a wolf it runs at Ivan and leaps up onto his body Ivan hits
it away with his axe and it slides across the floor then turns and runs
back at Ivan boom he blasts it across the floor then runs up the stairs as
he is running up the stairs a barbarian is running down the stairs at
him with a club at the same time another wolf runs from behind him
Ivan steps to his back against the wall then the wolf attacks barbarian
Ivan boots them both off the stairs then keeps running up he gets to
another room then looks around on the far side of the room he can see
a barbarian coming from the shadows with a shiny metal blade his
sword drawn then Ivan blasts him with the plasma then looks up from
above on the next level a barbarian drops down onto his with a club it
hits Ivan and they both fall on the ground Ivan gets up first them
uppercuts the axe into his head as he is getting up then takes his axe out
and quickly pegs it at a barbarian with a bow and arrow about to shoot
at him the axe spins thru the air then hits him in the mouth whoosh
the arrows fly's past Ivan misfiring and hitting a barbarian behind him
Ivan runs and takes his axe from the archers mouth just as he is dropping then climbs a ladder to the next level he can see a barbarian as he is
climbing up he runs to Ivan's ladder then goes to kick it off the level Ivan
pegs his axe at him first then as he drops Ivan reaches the level and
climbs off the ladder then takes his axe and runs along a balcony he
climbs up into the roof then runs across the roof and then can see into
the compound he can see a dozen barbarian with a dragon the dragon
spots him and the barbarian all look then as the pilot gets on the dragon
and goes to take off and fly Ivan runs and kicks the pilot off in mid-air
then grabs onto the saddle of the dragon in flight Ivan digs his heels
into the drain then heaves the reighns and the dragon lifts up and flaps
it's wings Ivan turns the dragon around and keeps hovering then

whoosh he burns the barbarians below then lands as they are running around on fire around him Ivan can see the maps on the far side of the room he runs the dragons across to them then tears then off the wall at the same time he has to lift his plasma and blasts a barbarian am as he runs and tries to chop the dragons neck off boom the plasma blast sends him across the compound floor as Ivan goes to leave and turns around he is face to face with another dragon and pilot boom Ivan's blasts it with his plasma it hits the pilot then the dragon starts attacking Ivan's dragon Ivan digs his heels in and it breathes fire at it then as Ivan can smell the burnt dragon on fire he blasts it with his plasma comp and it gets blasted into pieces across the room Ivan gets the dragon then ascends and takes off out if the courtyard and fly's out of the fortress when whoosh whoosh his dragon is attacked by rockets that fly up from a cart below as the dragon swerves to avoid the rocket blasts Ivan has to quickly maintain control over the dragon and fly it out if the way of the exploding rockets kaboom kaboom the rocket explode and Ivan's dragon crashes onto the roof and slides along the tiles then as it is sliding off the roof Ivan digs his boot into the tiles then stops it from sliding off then Ivan gallops the dragon back up the roof just as two barbarians with bow and arrows pop up from the it he side of the roof and shoot arrows at Ivan Ivan lifts the dragons wing up and the arrows hit it's wing them Ivan blasts his plasma at them boom they gi3 flying off the roof Ivan goes to where they were coming from he rides the dragon up and over the ridge if the roof then looks below whoosh they fire a rocket from their cart Ivan heaves the dragons reighns back and it misses it's head and neck then kaboom it explodes in the air Ivan quickly runs the dragon up and over the top of the roof then leaps down onto the cart Ivan smacks his plasma canon over one barbarian head then as another one goes to slice Ivan with his sword Ivan blocks it with his axe then boom he blasts his plasma canon it lifts the barbarian back off the cart and he fly's thru the air Ivan looks up and they sky is blackened as barbarians on dragons swarm above him like wasps Ivan gets off the dragon then whoosh he fires rocket up at one kaboom it hits one on the wing and it crashes below then he gets the rocket then aims directly up at another one then whoosh kaboom it hits then as they all comes in and attack Ivan breathing fire Ivan takes the dragon leash and head of off and under the cart with him Ivan reaches around with his plasma canon then shoots upwards boom he hits a dragon and it crashes on the cart above them then i vs steps out of cover then boom boom he blasts his plasma canon up at another dragon blasting it the dragon crashes onto the wall then slams into the cart Ivan heaves the dragon out from sleeping under the cart then tells it come on he has to heave it one more time and it comes out from under the cart then to ascend and to wrong take-off he fly's out from the compound on his way up the dragon flapping it's wings to take off a barbarian runs and leaps thru the air then slides Ivan with his sword Ivan stands up on the dragon then with his axe leans out and hits him first and he falls thru the air to the cart below then as Ivan looks around a archer is about to shoot a flaming arrow into the dragon boom Ivan shoots him first boom the argh a gets vaporizes Ivan keeps ascending then another barbarian with a club leaps onto the dragon and tries to bring he back down he hangs onto the front of the dragon and the dragon starts to spin around and lose control Ivan reaches up then whack he hits him off with his axe and he falls onto the cart below Ivan lands the dragon on the roof then can see the fortress wall in the distance he hovers and glides across to it on the way whoosh whoosh they shoot rockets up at him from the fortress wall Ivan has to quickly turn the dragon then fires off the side of his dragon at them shooting the rockets from the wall boom boom boom Ivan shoots the store they can reload the other rockets then Ivan is attacked from below a mythological creature reaches up and grabs Ivan's dragon in its hand Ivan quickly lifts his plasma canon then as the beast goes to eat Ivan and bite his head off Ivan lifts the plasma canon forts them boom he shoots it in the head the beasts growls and hisses then drops Ivan's dragon and him to the ground below Ivan is grabbed from a barbarian from behind and teared off the dragon the barbarian grabbing Ivan with both arms and hands then he takes out his sword from his holster then goes to impale Ivan Ivan licks him in the body from laying down then knocks him backwards Ivan spins around at the same time gets up then as the barbarian runs at him and slices him Ivan lifts up his axe then blocks them then jabs the plasma barrel into his jaw knocking him back Ivan runs then kicks him straight into a wall then pegs his axe at his face then collects his axe and hurls it at a barbarian getting on his dragon it hits him in the back of his head as he was going to take off Ivan takes out his axe then goes to throw him when from the sky a dragon breathes fire at Ivan whoosh Ivan lifts the human shield up then at the same time digs his heels into the dragon and it ascends Ivan keeps using the human shields as the dragon takes off then Ivan throws the human shield blasts the dragon with the plasma canon them fly's up out from the courtyard as the dragon crashes onto the walls then falls down below Ivan flaps the dragons wings and it takes off then Ivan can see below they have carts everywhere they aim their rockets at Ivan whoosh

whoosh whoosh the sky is full of rockets Ivan blasts his plasma canon and shoots them kaboom kaboom they explode underneath him the dragon soars upwards from the hot air under its wings as Ivan flies upwards he can see more carts on the other side whoosh whoosh they fire their rockets Ivan has to manoeuvres thru the exploding rockets then boom he shoots the rockets boom boom he keeps firing at the rockets and hitting them before they hot him whoosh whoosh more rockets come from all angle a Ivan keeps rising his plasma then shoots them then aims at the carts below boom Ivan's plasma bursts hit the carts below and they explode whoosh another cart is still firing at him he looks around then can see on the roof a barbarian with rockets whoosh he aims at Ivan's dragon Ivan blasts his plasma boom he hits the barbarian on the roof except his rocket hits Ivan's dragon on the wing Ivan looks then crashes into the fortress roof and goes thru the roof and crashes straight into a mythological creatures den Ivan is thrown off the dragon into the straw then can smell it a creature he looks around then the beasts bites Ivan Ivan shoots his plasma first at it's head and the beasts head catches alight Ivan heaves his dragon out from under it then jumps onto the dragon then lifts up springing up in the air Ivan's dragon starts to fly up when the beast on fire swings it's arms around in a tantrum then smashes Ivan's dragon and Ivan's dragon spins around in the air then crashes back down boom boom Ivan shoots the beasts then it walks backwards it's whole body on fire Ivan digs his heel into the dragon then whoosh it breathes fire at the beast Ivan goes to take off when a barbarian stabs a spear into Ivan's dragon then controls of forcing it back down Ivan swings his plasma canon it hits the spear then brakes it in two then he lunges across and whack he hits the barbarian across the head ad drops him Ivan's dragon takes off and goes to ascend when the beast on fire goes to fall on them it falls on its knees then is pushing Ivan and his dragon down with it Ivan heaves the reigns and digs his heels into the dragon it shoots up on the air and breathes fire then hits the beasts Ivan fly's up out up to the roof when whoosh rockets fly up from the wall and the barbarian gather in carts near the wall shooting rocket up at Ivan Ivan shoots his plasma long range at them boom boom the plasma blasts hit and the carts catch alight a barbarian runs and leaps up and pulls the dragons leg onto the roof them another barbarian runs and holds onto the dragon and brings it down onto the roof Ivan feels the dragon descending them looks around and over the dragon the barbarian are holding onto its legs Ivan leans over the side of the dragon with his axe he reaches down then chops the barbarian arm off then the dragon lifts back up Ivan heaves the dragon up in the air and it flaps it wing hard enough to take off with the other barbarian hanging on Ivan keeps whipping the reins then he fly's close to the wall the barbarian gets clothes lined from the wall and drops off the dragon Ivan spears out towards the forest then looks back whoosh whoosh barbarian in carts are galloping after him shooting rockets up at him Ivan has to quickly swerve left and right the rockets barely missing his dragon then looks down and boom he shoots then keeps firing he lean back and over the back of the dragon fires his plasma canon directly down at the barbarian aiming at their moving carts he shoots plasma after plasma blast boom boom hits the barbarian carts and they explode he keeps during at then then boom he hits another one whoosh a rocket fly's straight past him then he has to cover his eyes kaboom the rocket explodes in front of him and his dragon is hit from the impact and the dragon fly's towards the trees and goes to crash Ivan heaves the dragons reigns and lifts it up just before it hits the trees and it scrapes along the trees and then lifts up at the same time they keep shooting rockets at him boom boom Ivan shoots back and hits another cart it explodes at the same time a rocket hits the trees in front of him he can't see then covers his eyes and goes thru the flames then lifts the dragon up and whoosh another rocket fly's up boom he hits the cart thru the trees with his plasma canon blasting directly down he watches as the cart explodes he looks up the crashes thru branches then lifts the dragon up out from the tree line then gets airborne he can see on the oath below barbarian on a cart the are aiming a rocket at him to shoot then whoosh they fire Ivan quickly swerves and the rocket goes around him then he aims and fires at the cart boom he fires at then then they swerve and the plasma blasts hit the oath Ivan swoops in close to them right on their tail then whoosh he digs his heel in his dragon breathes a fireball that fly's thru the air then hits their cart and the cart loses control then crashes into a tree and catches alight Ivan keeps shooting it with plasma bursts and it explodes Ivan looks up and there is a cart waiting aiming and shooting its rockets at him whoosh whoosh they fire two rockets Ivan spins the dragon between the two rockets and does a barrel roll and holds on then as he comes out if the barrel roll he aims his plasma canon then boom as he is flying towards it he shoots his plasma canon directly at it then it explodes as Ivan looks back there are more carts chasing him and they fire rockets whoosh whoosh he turns around and blasts them back boom boom he hits one then as the other one comes towards him he quickly dodges it and it goes past him kaboom it explodes I front of him Ivan's dragon flies straight thru the blast then Ivan aims at the art then boom he hits it with his plasma bursts as it explodes a dragon swoops Ivan and crashes into him and forces Ivan to crash into the trees Ivan quickly shoots the dragon boom with the plasma canon then blasts it off Ivan's dragon Ivan lands the dragon and it lands between the trees then runs along the forest floor when up ahead is a cart that has barbarians on it Ivan shoots his plasma canon boom boom then takes off the dragon lifts up and Ivan flips up over the cart when whoosh they fire a rocket boom Ivan fires back and hits the richer with his plasma canon burst kaboom a massive explosion lifts Ivan's dragon up thru the air and Ivan holds on then heaves the reigns up and the dragon lifts up they the trees and soars thru the air Ivan can see barbarian gathered on the hill they fire bows and arrows at him and throw spears thru the air at him boom Ivan shoots his plasma canon then whoosh he digs his heel I to the dragon the plasma bursts and fire from the dragon burn the arrow and blasts the spears Ivan can see a cart on the hill that fires rockets up at him whoosh whoosh Ivan swerves and misses them then aims at the cart busts before they can shoot any more rockets boom Ivan aims his plasma canon and lasts the cart whoosh they blast a rocket whoosh it hits the sky o from of Ivan kaboom it explodes Ivan swerves around it and comes out from the flames then lifts the dragon up and soars across the hill then as he is going up and over the hill a mythological creature hits Ivan's dragon from the sky and Ivan crashes into the field he is flung off the dragon then crashes into the grass he loses his plasma canon then gets up the beast is massive Ivan runs towards it then with his axe he runs and with both hands chops into its legs with his axe argh the beast roars at Ivan the swings it's claws at him whack Ivan chops it arm off with the axe and it goes wild it uses its other arm and hand to scoop oban up then as it goes to eat him Ivan gets his axe then whacks its face and head with the axe slamming it into its head and mouth the beast drops Ivan from his hand then he runs and hacks into it's leg again and watches as it starts to lose balance Ivan keeps hacking and chopping it's leg then its swings it's claws at Ivan clunk Ivan uses his axe to block it's hit then runs up and whacks its legs and cuts thru it the beasts groans and falls onto the ground Ivan gets the plasma canon then boom he shoots it in the head then blasts its head off it kicks and twitches them stops moving Ivan's dragon is getting attacked by barbarians Ivan leaps over the beast then runs and smashes one over the head from behind with the plasma canon dropping him as they all the and attach Ivan boom he blasts one then the other ones keeps coming at Ivan boom Ivan aims with both hands and shoots another one when his plasma canon is knocks downward the barbarian goes to swing at

Ivan again like a baseball bat Ivan lifts his plasma canon up and blocks the club then sweeps his legs out kicking him he falls on his back as goes to get up Ivan leaps at him with his axe out and cuts his head off then watched as he drops to the ground Ivan is tackled from behind by a barbarian Ivan is slammed into the ground face first then gets up and turns around then whack he left hooks him in the head then runs and upper cuts him in the ribs then grabs the back of his head then knees him in the face dropping him Ivan sees a barbarian with a sword running at him Ivan grabs the sword by the handle then throws the barbarian thru the air then runs after him and stomps on him and keeps stomping on him then as a cart of barbarians comes then leap off and attack him with weapons he has to quickly take the plasma and lift it up to block a barbarian with a sword Ivan side kicks him back then lifts up his axe and blocks another one then jabs him with the plasma then left hooks the axe into his head Ivan can see a barbarian on the cart with a bow and arrow about to fire at him he grabs a barbarian then holds him in front of him the arrow hits him in the back Ivan reaches over his shoulder then fire the plasma canon and boom it hits the arches and he flies off the back of the cart arghh a barbarian runs at Ivan with an axe over his head Ivan turns and holds the barbarian up with a arrow on his back holds him up then the axe splatters onto his back then Ivan heaves the barbarian forward and throws him into the other barbarian they crash to the ground then Ivan lifts the plasma canon up and boom he blasts them boom vaporizes them Ivan can hear a barbarian running up behind him he turns then heaves the plasma forward then lifts him up in the air then turns and directs him thru the air into the side of the cart he lands and crashes into the cart Ivan runs up and as he is getting up uses the edge of the cart to hold onto then stomp him into the ground with his boot then has to leap onto the cart then fire rockets as dragon seem above him and fly around and come to fire fireballs at him whoosh whoosh Ivan fire a two rockets up that hit the dragons they explode into pieces a dragon swoops down and tries land on Ivan whoosh he fires a rockets then kaboom it hits the dragon as more dragons and carts arrive Ivan uses his plasma cannon to shoot the carts and fires rockets it hits the dragons then can see barbarians in a cart about to attack Ivan's dragon whoosh he fires a rocket at the cart and it explodes Ivan aims the rocket up at a dragon the dragon breathes fire at Ivan's cart whoosh Ivan's rocket hits it and it explodes a cart stops next to Ivan's and barbarian runs off it Ivan stand sip then lifts his plasma canon up with both hands and blocks the barbarian with a sword then front kicks him he falls back and goes between the two carts and falls down between the carts as another barbarian leaps across then comes a Ivan with a sword Ivan smashes it out of his hands with the plasma canon then lifts the plasma canon up over his head then whacks him in the head then kicks him down between the two carts and he falls down then aim their rocket straight at Ivan from the other cart Ivan runs then leaps onto their cart then kicks the rocket whoosh it explodes the other way Ivan reaches and grabs the barbarian then slam his face o to the rocket then does it again harder than lifts his body up onto the rocket then whoosh he fires it the barbarian spears into the air then kaboom he explodes Ivan can hear footsteps on the cart then turns around swinging whack he left hooks a barbarian with a club then lunges towards him then gets the plasma canon with both hands then uppercuts it up onto his chin and he does a backflip Ivan aims the plasma canon as another barbarian runs up to the cart boom Ivan shoots and blasts him it hits him and he catches alight a cart arrives with a mythological creature in a cage the barbarian opens the cage then stands on top of it in safety up high it goes out from it cage then gallops at Ivan boom Ivan shoots it with both hands aiming at it he hits it the giant beast keeps running Ivan quickly aims the rocket at it then whoosh he fires it straight at it then kaboom it explodes the barbarian on top of the cart releases the next one Ivan aims at the beast then shoots his plans a canon boom he hits it then he goes to fire the rocket the beast leaps onto the cart then Ivan quickly shoots the rocket whoosh the beasts is lifted up thru the air by the rocket then kaboom it explodes over the cart the barbarian curse at Ivan then turns the cart around and goes to take off he trots away Ivan goes to get the dragon then heaves its reins and the dragon flaps it wings and fly's after the escaping cart then Ivan lands s the dragon on the cages the barbarian turns around and sees Ivan on his cart with a dragon then gets his cross bow then aims it at Ivan whole he is steering whoosh Ivan digs his heel into the dragon and a fireball burns the barbarian Ivan looks up and the cart is head off the cliff then it crashes over the edge as in the cart goes thru the air Ivan springs the dragon up and it flaps it's wings and takes off thru the sky then goes out over the oath in the forest where all the burning carts are and over the burning fortress Ivan fly's towards the kingdom

Ivan looks out from the castle and can see a whole army of barbarians then Scots them the chokes after that only him and the queen and servants are their the queens army are fighting another war Ivan's tells the queen he will be back soon she can't see the rows of tanks and carts and mythological creatures he throws her in the panic room then kisses her and closes the door then goes outs use and runs to get the dragon then fly's to the castle wall he starts firing rockets whoosh he aims for the closest barbarians first then watched as the rocket hits the barbarians on horses and cart and explodes then keeps firing rockets whoosh kaboom he hits more if the barbarians they spread out and firm a line then as Ivan keeps firing rockets the first if the arrow starts to rain in the castle wall Ivan keeps firing the rockets and grabs a shield the arrows hit the shield at the same time he fires rockets whoosh he aims at the arches whoosh whoosh he fires multiple rocket that all hit the archers and they explode then as the barbarians are eliminated the Scots come from behind them with canon and rockets on their carts in a heavy line up of artillery they fire at the castle walls the ground vibrates around Ivan as the cannonball hit the walls Ivan keeps firing rocket after rocket whoosh whoosh Ivan aims at the carts then kaboom kaboom they starts to explode then as they get closer the walls starts to shake as the cannonball hit close range Ivan keeps firing rockets whoosh whoosh then watches as they hit the carts and explode all around cannonball hit the wall and Ivan keeps firing rockets towards the scots carts whoosh he hits another cart as it explodes Ivan keeps firing rockets after rockets and watches as they hit their targets the carts go up in flames cannonballs hit the castle walls from close contact carts Ivan watches as the carts come around from the sides then fire Ivan quickly aims the rockets at moving targets whoosh whoosh kaboom the carts explode then as more come and take positions closer to the castle walls Ivan has to quickly fire rockets a whole line of enemy carts can be seen Ivan shoots rockets at the carts whoosh he fires at one close range it hits kaboom it catches alight then as he shoots more rockets they keep coming he fires multiple rockets then watches as the carts explodes he aims the rockets at the closest carts then kaboom they get hit then as Ivan keeps firing rockets he starts to eliminate the Scots he watches as two carts come in close he follows them aiming the rockets he fires whoosh whoosh the rocket fly's towards the cart and explodes the carts go up in flames and Ivan keeps firing rockets as another cart comes flying towards the castle walls Ivan re aims the rocket then fires at it kaboom it explodes Ivan can see a cart has come directly in from of the castle walls he aims the rocket at it then fires at it the cart explodes and as another one comes from the flames behind that Ivan turns the rocket then shoots it the rocket fly's thru the air then kaboom from the Scots the Chinese come in vast numbers spread out across the whole of the from wall from one side to the next Ivan takes the dragon then fly's towards them and shoots his plasma canon at the same time fire fireballs he soars up close to them then fires boom boom whoosh whoosh the fireballs and plasma canon blasts hit the first of the Chinese soldiers and they explode Ivan quickly flies alongside the rest of them then boom boom he fires his plasma at their carts when all of a sudden whoosh whoosh they have high powered rockets that shoot thru the air Ivan dodges one then quickly dodges the other then keeps firing his plasma canon and digs his heel in to shoot fireballs from the dragon whoosh whoosh he burns a cart and blasts another one flying close to their enemy line he aims his plasma canon over the side then boom boom he watches as the plasma bursts hit their soldiers when all of a sudden he starts taking machine gun fire and multiple rockets as they launch their assault he fires the plasma canon while waiting towards then then keeps firing plasma bursts towards their carts and soldier a whoosh he digs his heel into the dragon then shoots fireballs boom boom the plasma bursts hit a cart and it explodes just as they let of several rockets boom boom Ivan shoots back then keeps firing plasma bursts towards the carts then watches as his plasma bursts rain down on them and cause massive explosions that blow up their carts he fly's ring above them then boom boom he fires several plasma bursts that all hit their targets and their carts keep exploding they have a cart that is at the walls with ladder up and are climbing up over the wall Ivan turns around and flies towards then then soars in close boom boom he hits their cart then fly's the wing along the top of the wall and pushes the ladders away with the soldiers flying the thru the air Ivan keeps turning back around to see them in carts all aiming rockets at the wall and are about to fire Ivan fly's towards them blasting he flicks the plasma canon trigger and quickly fire boom boom he shoots the cart and watches as they explode and burn that's when Ivan can see the Chinese making a device a bomb to blow a hole in the wall they are gathered around in a group near the wall and constructing it Ivan swoops down and like a crane he pierces them then lifts them back up and fly's off with them then drops them back towards their carts then boom the device goes off and they explode at the same time Ivan drips them onto their carts Ivan shoots and keeps blasting his plasma canon he aims at their carts that are coming towards the castle walls kaboom boom the carts explode then as Ivan gets close to then whoosh whoosh they fire rockets at him boom boom he shoots back and hits them boom boom kaboom another cart explodes as the Chinese start to retreat Ivan keeps blasting his plasma canon then watches as his plasma firsts hit their carts whoo whoosh they fire up at him boom boom he shoots and hits their rocket then hits them with his plasma blasts he fly's towards a cart that is about to ram into the castle gates whoosh he fires ad fireball digging his heels in at the same time he fires plasma canon kaboom a massive direct hit sends the cart up in flames as soldiers retreat from it Ivan aims at them individually as they run from the burning cart boom boom he keeps killing their soldiers then can see they have made a whole in the wall with cannonballs Ivan swoops down then lifts up a cart then drops it in front of the hole blocking them from getting in then turns the dragon and whoosh from on top of the cart he shoots fireballs from the dragon and shoots plasma canon blasts towards their oncoming vehicles kaboom the first one explodes then as another two carts come from behind them Ivan has to shoots fireballs to the left's at the same time shoot plasma canon blasts to the right shooting both carts at the same time as they go up in flames behind them are the tanks Ivan quickly flies towards then then with his plasma comp aims directly at one and hits it with plasma bursts and fireballs he keeps shooting plasma bursts and fireballs at the front of the tank then kaboom the plasma blasts and fireballs direct hit the first tank then as another tank comes from behind that one of fires into the wall and then rams thru it Ivan fly's down towards it then boom boom as it is fitting thru the hole that it made the tank explodes as Ivan hits it with plasma blasts and shoots fireballs at it Ivan can see the hatch open and the soldiers try to leap from the burning tank he uses both hands to hold the plasma and aim at them kaboom the tank is hit and the soldiers catch alight then as the other tanks start to fire at the wall Ivan fly's above then then boom boom he hits them with the plasma canon that's when he hits one and it explodes the other ones still are firing tank cannons at the wall boom boom Ivan fly's in close to one and he makes it explode as the plasma blasts hit the tanks and they catch along the chokes keep coming then Ivan fly's at them and shoots boom boom he keeps firing his plasma anon at them then they explode Ivan can sees an enemy dragon circling the roof of the castle he fires at it long range boom boom he aims directly at it then boom he watches as it crashes in flames Ivan sees more dragons that have firmed a v formation and are flying from the Chinese soldiers side if the battle Ivan keeps blasting carts below with his plasma canon then aims up towards the dragons boom boom he fires his plasma canon towards them then he can hear machine gun fire as they shoot at him he keeps shooting at them then kaboom the firsts of their dragons explodes and crashes into a cart below catching it on fire as well Ivan re aims the plasma canon then boom boom he shoots the other two dragons as they explode from the sky Ivan can see them aiming their rockets at the castle wall then boom boom he aims at them slow that kaboom carts explode in flames they have more ladders and ropes and are abseiling the castle wall Ivan fly's the dragon then it breathes fire at the top of their ropes then whoosh the fire burns straight thru their ropes ask they crash to the bottom of the wall Ivan fly's then whoosh he shoots fireballs at them then boom boom fires his plasma canon they explode Ivan keeps firing his plasma canon then can see a dragon on the watch tower the pilot is opening the gates Ivan fly's at him then boom boom he fires his plasma canon at him the pilot runs out if the watch tower it's too late Ivan's plasma burst s hit the watchtower and the pilot is thrown thru the air as his dragon is exploded Ivan lands on the wall then looks out the Chinese soldiers have re grouped and formed an attacking line Ivan gets on the canon then whoosh he fires rockets at them kaboom he hits a cart then kaboom he hits another he keeps firing the rockets at the carts and they fly thru the air and hit the soldiers carts and they explode then as he re aims the rocket and fires it the rocket flies towards the carts then kaboom they explode they start to move their carts and are mobile Ivan has to aim at them then fires whoosh whoosh he hits a moving cart kaboom and it flips in the air in a massive explosion as Ivan can see a cart headed towards the castle walls whoosh the rocket hits the cart and it explodes Ivan quickly takes the dragon then soars thru the air he aims his plasma canon then boom boom he shoots plasma whoosh whoosh he shoots fire the two meet up and expose and hit a cart kaboom the cart goes flying to pieces in an epic explosion Ivan keeps firing plasma and shoots fireballs at a cart the cart explodes at the same time it shoots a rocket at Ivan boom Ivan disintegrate it before it can reach him or the castle walls Ivan fires s Ivan can see they have gone around the other side of the castle wall and are using nets to throw over the walls and climb up he can sees them climbing up the nets he fly's towards then the digs his heels into the dragon and the fireball hits the net and it catches alight at the same time he fires his plasma bursts the net and soldiers go up in flames boom boom Ivan shoots the cart they came in on then watches as it explodes and all the soldiers are eliminated Ivan quickly turns then goes after the Chinese soldiers that are at the gates and walls he fly's towards them he can see them about to ram the cart thru the gates he fly's closer down lower then boom he fires his plasma to get the aim of it then boom

boom boom he fires multiple shots in a row that all hits the soldiers and they catch alight and burn whoosh Ivan is attacked and shot at with rockets from a soldier a cart he turns and swerves them the rockets juts missing him he aims his plasma at the cart shooting them then boom boom he aims and fires at the cart kaboom it explodes then Ivan keeps flying towards another one they have stopped the cart then are getting on the roof then climbing over the wall whoosh Ivan's dragon breathes fire at them whoosh they catch alight then as Ivan fly's over them he shoots hits plasma kaboom the cart explodes Ivan can see the soldiers lifting the cart from the hole and are are about to penetrate the castle Ivan swoops towards them then lifts the cart up and re plugs the wall then turns around and whoosh the dragon breathes fire at then at the same time Ivan shoots plasma blasts driving them back then boom the plasma blasts hit and the cart explodes Ivan can see in the distance they are sending thru the second wave of re enforcements Ivan springs the dragon off the cart then soars towards them he shoots plasma blasts and digs his heel into the dragon then the dragon breathes fire kaboom the plasma bursts hit the soldiers carts and they explode then the fire balls hit the other carts boom boom Ivan keeps firing the plasma the plasma hits as well blasting all the carts Ivan can see behind the carts are more soldiers on foot shooting machine guns at him he fires is plasma canon and shoots fireballs at them boom boom the plasma blasts hit the soldiers and they catch alight then as the fireballs reach them whoosh whoosh they catch on fire Ivan keeps shooting plasma bursts and they run back to their carts and as they are running back Ivan fly's in close at the same time shoots plasma bursts and fireballs kaboom he hits the carts and the soldiers explode as well as the carts Ivan can see that back at the walls soldiers have run from the forest and are entering with ladders and ropes Ivan fly's back towards them then as they see Ivan they open fire with machine guns burst Ivan shoots his plasma boom boom then watches as they explode and fly up on the air Ivan swoops the dragon up and lands on the wall

Then turns the dragon then whoosh he fires fireballs and shoots plasma canon blasts at the oncoming Chinese soldiers carts kaboom kaboom he hits them and they explode he keeps firing plasma bursts then as more soldiers run from the forest shooting machine guns up at him he aims his plasma and blasts them boom boom then keeps shooting at them boom boom he forces them back into the forest and they stop coming Ivan looks up and as the Chinese carts tear towards the castle Ivan has to quickly shoot at them and blasts them with plasma blasts kaboom kaboom the hit and the carts erupt in flames and explode Ivan soars the dragon off the wall then fly's towards them and shoots plasma canon blasts at their carts then kaboom they explode Ivan can see a dragon and pilot on the roof the pilot is climbing down using the reigns to abseil in Ivan fly's towards the dragon then lands next to it then lifts the pilot back up with the reigns then hits him on the head with the axe then cuts the reighns off the dragon and kicks the dragon away it flies off then Ivan gets the reigns ang wraps them around the pilots throat then snaps his neck and throw him off the veranda he can see more soldiers coming thru he takes the dragon and soars across the lawn then fires his plasma canon and shoots fireballs boom whoosh the plasma bursts hit the soldiers the fireballs as well Ivan shoots plasma bursts into the ground and gives up the hole with soil then soars up onto the wall and looks out to a sea of Chinese soldiers he starts blasting into them firing his plasma canon he shoots burst of plasma into them kaboom the plasma bursts hit Ivan keeps firing plasma bursts and flying towards then then whoosh he fires fireballs as well they all hit their targets and kill the soldiers whoosh whoosh they fire back with rockets Ivan has to dodge them and them keeps shooting plasma bursts whoosh whoosh he fires fireballs the explosion are huge and force soldiers into the air in pieces as shrapnel tears their limbs he keeps shooting his plasma canon then gets in close whoosh whoosh they shoot rockets to keep him back he dodges them then keeps firing plasma bursts and fireballs into their army and watches as they explode on impact kaboom it lifts up their carts and burns their soldiers he keeps firing plasma bursts then whips the reins and fires fireballs while hovering above the battle field kaboom more of his plasma bursts erupt blowing them up into the sky he keeps he kills the last of then with plasma bursts and fireballs then suddenly he looks back to see them coming from the forest into the castle walls they have blown a hole in the wall and are swarming the castle Ivan shoots the last of the soldiers then soars back towards the wall only to find they are already inside the castle Ivan keeps blasting his plasma canon then takes off towards the castle the stops the dragon on the roof he keeps down to get the queen then goes inside a soldier goes hiya then karate kicks him as he goes thru the veranda door then Ivan slaps hi lick away then grabs him by the throat he kicks Ivan Ivan twists his hand and snaps his throat then throws him out of the way to the hallway to the panic room to see if the queens alright he gets out the door then has to quickly take cover as machine guns bullets hit all around him he aims the plasma canon out and around without looking then shoots boom he follows after it shooting and blasting the soldiers at the end of the hall then as the smoke clears he can see how many he killed hiya one side kicks him into the wall Ivan grabs him by the back of the head then slams his head thru the wall then looks up the hall to the other rooms where the queen should be he hits the soldiers with his head thru the wall comes alive and kicks his foot up and hits Ivan in the head then shoves his head back thru the wall then round house kicks Ivan Ivan left hooks him and punches him down the stairs them goes to run up the hall then soldier hops out then starts firing a machine gun on the hallway Ivan takes cover then steps out of cover and boom he blasts him Ivan quickly rushes towards the panic room in a hurry he sprints down the corridors of the castle then a soldier steps into the hallway and elbows him and drops him on the ground Ivan sweep his legs out from under him them gets up then knees him into the wall them headbutts him just as another soldier pops out into the hallway and shoots his machine gun Ivan grabs the soldier and uses him as a human shield then runs up the hall with him then boom he blasts his plasma canon at him and watches as he fly's down the hallway on fire he goes to drop the human shield when from the end of the hall he just came from he hears a soldier pops out into the hallway and shoots at him he turns with the human shield bullets hit him as he slams around and shoots his plasma canon up the hall boom it hits the soldier Ivan drops the human shield then runs down the hall and turns right then can see where the room is he sprints towards it with his weapon drawn then kicks down one door then hit a soldier kick a him with a flying side kick Ivan dodges it then left hooks the soldier he ducks it then uppercuts Ivan in the ribs Ivan doesn't feel it then sticks his fingers in his eyes then slams his face and head into the wall then before he opens the panic room door he makes sure there is no one follow him in he looks onside then taps on the window and calls out her name she pops her head up them he smiles and tells her he'll be back he closes the doors then goes out into the hall in a rage then struts up the hall then goes into the roof then starts firing his plasma canon off the roof at the soldiers below boom boom he does accurate two handed head shots all across the lawn leaving there bodies looking like red paintballs as there blood sprays across the lawn he keeps firing at then then looks over and can see one climbing up Ivan shoots him in the top of the head then re aims towards the lawn as more run across the lawn Ivan shoots boom boom his plasma canon blasts them then from the roof above him from the other side a soldier pops up and holds a his machine gun up and shoots Ivan Ivan steps off the roof onto the veranda ducking the bullets then he reaches up with his plasma canon then boom he shoots his plasma then watches as the flaming body on fire rolls down off the roof and crashes into the veranda Ivan leans over the railing and starts shooting down at the soldiers as they get her below and starts shooting up at him he takes cover as bullets hit all around him then with one hand reaches out and over then shoots down and blasts them boom boom he looks over and can see them on fire Ivan can see they have gone in thru a down stairs window have smashes it and are running thru the castle this was not what I planned the queen was not meant to have been in the panic room I write that she was there just to make you happy I will go with this alternate ending this is if the queen was in the panic room he runs back down stairs then keeps off the stairs a flight at a time plasma canon in hand them goes to the lounge-room and has to duck and slide in front if a lounge as they open fire on him from the other side of the room he curses as all around him machine gun fire hits then he pops up and shoots his plasma canon at them boom he hits two of them with one plasma blast them can see the window they coming thru the looks around the rest of the room they are in between bookshelf and beside lounges there is one shooting at him from the window Ivan quickly fires three quick blasts accurately blasting each one of them boom boom boom then it goes quiet hiya one of them leaps off the lounge thru the air and kicks him in the head sneaky bastard Ivan gets up the wrong way and the soldier kicks him in the back Ivan spins around and grabs his leg then blocks his kick then as he goes to karate chop Ivan Ivan blocks it with his left arm then punches him in the head he is dazed then still manages to a jumping roundhouse kick that hits Ivan in the side of the head and he falls sidewards into a lounge Ivan quickly moves as he goes to karate kick him Ivan catches his leg then kicks and breaks his knee with a powerful right kick using his shin then punches him in the jaw and knocks him out then has to quickly duck as another one karate kicks him over the head Ivan turns to him then then grabs his shoulders and knees him in the guts uppercuts him backwards then lines him up and punches him out Ivan can hear glass or footsteps on glass then turns to the window as a soldier dives thru and takes cover behind a lounge then aims up and over the lounge at Ivan Ivan can see the barrel of his machine gun pointed at him Ivan shoots his plasma at the top of his head killing him then from the top of the stairs Ivan can see a soldier running down Ivan waits at the bottom then coat hangers him on the way down dropping him the as Ivan looks up and other one is there he quickly shoots upwards and blasts him just as he goes to lift up his machine gun Ivan runs up the stairs they must have gone into the panic room he gets to the panic room then looks in the queen is still there hiya a soldier punches Ivan into the door Ivan's head is squashed against the glass as the queens screaming he has to quickly elbow him in the guts then reach over grab his head and body then flip him over onto his back breaks his arm then stomps on his neck and breaks that too then looks out into the hallway he closes the panic room door to make it unnoticeable then keeps spitting up the hall he looks out the window to see how many there are as he is looking out the window he hears a hiya then quickly turns around and lifts up both his arms and blocks a karate kick to his face then jabs him as he stumbles back Ivan grabs him and throws him out the window then from behind him another one comes and lifts his machine gun up and goes to shoot Ivan Ivan slaps the machine gun out from his hands then punches him in the head then throws him off the stairs as another one is running up he sees Ivan Ivan see him then he lifts his machine gun Ivan wrestles it into the wall then smashes it against the wall dropping it out from his hands then headbutts him while keeping hold of him then takes the sidearm from his holster then holds it to the side of his head and shoots him then has to quickly aim it at a soldier running across the lounge room bang bang bang he shoots him in the head the back and the head again as he slides across the floor Ivan looks at the window as a soldier pops up shooting Ivan shoots him in the head as well then leans over the stairs and there is a soldier running under them he shoots him in the top of the head then throws the empty weapon just as another soldier runs across the loungeroom floor from cover to cover Ivan aims his plasma then boom he blasts him and the lounge across the room from the top of the stairs behind Ivan a soldier pops up then goes to shoot Ivan boom he shoots directly up and blasts him then runs up to see where they coming from their is a rope ladder on the veranda they are climbing up with Ivan looks behind him and one jumps from the roof Ivan catches him them throws him off the veranda then as another one climbs up the rope ladder Ivan takes out his axe then cuts the rope ladder and he falls Ivan check both side s to see if there are any climbing up then from the top a Chinese on a dragon on the roof bites Ivan and keeps hissing and snapping at him Ivan swings his axe around and chips it's head off then aims the plasma up with the other hand and blasts the pilot off as well rockets hit the veranda as Ivan leaps into cover whoosh kaboom whoosh kaboom the hit the outside balcony and veranda the walls vibrating and shaking around him then he goes out into the veranda then fires his plasma canon

He aims at the carts that have stopped their then quickly fires plasma bursts down at them boom boom the cart erupts in flames and explodes as a dragon swoops in Ivan has to swing his plasma canon around and smashes it off him as it bites him then as it goes to breath fire Ivan holds I'm the plasma canon up to its head then blows it off the dragons body slumps on the veranda as the pilot goes hiya then karate chops Ivan Ivan left and right punches him in the ribs then upper cuts him then knees him then takes out his axe then smashes him over the head with it dropping him he holsters his axe then aims the plasma canon both hands as an enemy cart comes towards the castle he blasts plasma bursts at it boom boom the cart swerves then kaboom it hits it Ivan hears a hiya and turns around a soldiers has both hands on the top of the door Frame and kicks Ivan with both feet Ivan falls back nearly over the veranda Ivan put a both hands on the railing then kicks him back into the room then runs in after him then punches him in the throat from the door way another soldier runs towards him Ivan runs at him Ivan punches him and hits him in the head then as he stumbles back he goes hiya then does a karate chop and a karate kick Ivan blocks one then the other then sweeps his legs out from him then stomps on his head then kicks him down the stairs as he is rolling down the stairs Ivan can see a soldier coming thru the window Ivan aims his plasma canon then boom he blasts him back thru the window then from across the lounge room two soldiers come with machine guns Ivan aims at the one on his left boom he blasts him with the plasma canon then as the other one opens fire Ivan leaps off the stairs and takes cover behind a lounge bang bang the machine gun bullets hit all around him and are closing in Ivan slides across the floor then pops up and shoots him from a different angle then he was expecting Ivan's plasma burst lifts him across the room into a fireplace then Ivan has to cover to entry points the window and the stairs he goes over to the window then heaves a lounge across it and cover their entry point then keeps his eyes on the stairs as they rush in from the roof and veranda Ivan can see them then keeps blasting his plasma canon as they falls down the stairs in fire he keeps blasting them as they come in then hears a smash glass of a different window and looks over to see glass on the floor and a soldier pop in thru the window boom Ivan shoots him in the back as he enters then looks up the stairs a soldier is coming down shooting his machine gun Ivan takes cover behind the stairs then as the soldier comes to the side of the stairs to shoot down at Ivan Ivan aims upwards and blasts him first boom he rolls down the stairs in fire then Ivan hears the glass a soldier runs thru and Ivan has blast him with his plasma canon then looks out the window as rockets hit the window and carts stop outside and fire rockets towards him whoosh whoosh he keeps into cover kaboom just as the whole of the down stairs section vibrates as glass windows smash and a heap of soldiers run thru at him boom boom Ivan shoots quickly boom boom hitting them as they enter Ivan points his plasma outside then aims at a cart just as they go to fire a rocket in at him he aims and blasts the plasma canon at them first then as a cart rams thru the castle windows and soldiers leap off and runs thru the windows shooting Ivan aims and shoots then keeps firing his plasma canon at them boom he hits one soldier as he enters then has to uses the butt of the plasma canon to close range elbow it over the head of the soldier as he runs in dropping him Ivan looks up as more soldiers leaps off the cart into the loungeroom he quickly fires at them boom he shoots one then swings his aim across to another one boom he blasts him back into the cart then as Ivan shoots all the soldiers he can see one about to fire a rocket inside of the back if the cart he runs then leaps up onto a lounge the pegs his axe at him the axe hurls thru the air then hits him in the head Ivan leaps up onto the cart then takes his axe out then a soldier lands on the cart from am above balcony Ivan runs at him then whack he hits him with the axe then as one grabs his leg from under the cart Ivan quickly chops his arm off with the axe then grabs him by the hair then chops his head off then Ivan looks across the lawn as another cart comes tearing towards him he quickly aims the rocket on the back then whoosh he lets it rip and it fly's thru the air then as the cart tries to swerve it kaboom it explodes across the castle lawn Ivan looks up and as soldier a abseil in around him onto the cart shooting their machine guns Ivan has to quickly shoot up at them boom boom he shoots then as they slide down the rope on fire one lands and then goes to point his machine gun at Ivan Ivan slaps it out if the way with his plasma then back hands the plasma canon across his head knocking him off the cart Ivan has another one climbs up the cart then he aims his machine gun at Ivan and shoots Ivan takes cover behind the castle wall then bang bang bullets hit around him he points the plasma canon around the wall then shoots it it hits the soldier and he catches alight screaming as he runs around towards Ivan Ivan elbow him off the cart onto the ground more soldiers co me up the end of the cart and into the loungeroom shooting Ivan aims his plasma canon then boom he keeps shooting as they come thru the window boom boom he blasts two of them then as the other one comes running in shooting Ivan slashes his gun out if his hands then headbutts him as he falls back Ivan lifts up his plasma canon then blasts him back out the window Ivan has a soldier abseil in and kick him back onto the cart as Ivan is sliding back he shoots off the ground the rope and soldier go flying backwards and the soldier gets blasted across the grass a cart comes onto the castle lawn then they fire a rocket at Ivan whoosh Ivan leaps back into cover in the loungeroom kaboom just as the rocket explodes around him he runs out if the flames blasting at them with the plasma canon boom boom he hits the cart and it explodes then as more carts come tearing up the lawn Ivan stands up on the cart and aims at them boom boom he fires his plasma canon directly at them then watches as the plasma bursts hit their targets and explode the cart me go up in flames Ivan can hear the sound of abseiling rope then turns around just as a soldier lands on him Ivan smashes him with the plasma then gets the rope and strangles it around his neck snapping it then another one abseil in and is shooting Ivan Ivan uses the other one as a human shield then the bullets hit him as abseils in shooting his machine gun Ivan keeps using him as a human shield then keeps him in a headlock while blasting his plasma canon at the other one a dragon swoops on and Ivan uses the rope to wrap around its neck then keeps it away from biting him as he smashes his plasma canon over the pilots head he keeps heaving the rope in his left arm and stray king the dragon as he clubs the pilot to death and then doubles the rope around the dragons neck then heaves it again taking his axe out he chops it's neck off just as he sees another one land on the roof above the pilot taking out a machine gun and shooting down at him Ivan runs and uses the rope to swing out on then aim up and blast him plasma canon at the one on the roof boom he shoots it and it explodes as Ivan swings back in in the rope and lands back on the cart he thinks he hears scream

Then takes off and heads towards the panic room across the lounge room he can hear footsteps on the way he just goes straight to the panic room then can see she has left he looks for footmarks then can see a dragons then follows them then out on the veranda is the queen getting kidnapped by the Chinese on a dragon Ivan runs and then leaps outside jumping on the balcony then in the air off the balcony and grabbing into the pilot the dragon goes down and starts to descend from too much people on it then as the pilot goes to take out his side arm Ivan grabs it first then takes it from the holster and puts it to his head then bang he blows his head off then pushes his body off then takes control of the dragon then digs his heel in and it ascends then as Ivan is ascending a soldier comes out from the veranda shooting and Ivan breast her fire on him digging his heel in then as another one comes from the roof Ivan uses the hand gun to bang bang he shoots him first and he falls face first off the roof onto the veranda Ivan keeps taking fire from below then looks down as a cart comes and then shoots a rocket up at him Ivan fly's the dragon into cover on the roof as the rocket whooshes past them onto the air Ivan lands the dragon on the roof then takes the queen back to the panic room he keeps thru the hall then goes up the hallway then tells her not leave there he kisses her backwards into the panic room at the same time closes the door then runs back out and onto the veranda a soldier leaps onto it the aims his weapon at Ivan Ivan grabs the barrel then wrestle him bang bang it keeps going off in Ivan's face as he wrestles with him then he heaves him backwards into and thru the glass doors then as he smashes thru them he give up the weapon he crashes thru the glass then as a dragon swoops on behind Ivan he turns with the machine gun pressing the trigger bang bang bang he keeps pumping the dragon with machine gun bursts the dragon starts to descend as it is hit the loses altitude and crashes thru a down stairs window Ivan looks up and sees sh3 cart headed towards the castle with a rocket Ivan opens fire with the machine gun holding the trigger he aims at the cart then it explodes as he hits the rocket from the roof a soldier goes hiya then karate kicks Ivan off the balcony Ivan falls over and backflips off the grabs onto the railing I've handed then with the other hand shoots the machine gun at him Ivan climbs back up then hears a rocket whoosh he turns around and sees one coming from a chokes soldiers cart Ivan runs and leaps inside kaboom it explodes outside as Ivan runs out then aims at the cart bang bang bang he runs out if ammo then as a soldier is climbing up he slams the empty machine onto his head then grabs the plasma canon then aims at the cart boom boom the cart explodes and Ivan hears soldier a on the hall he runs back inside then runs across the room and into the hall bang bang they shoot at him from the other end of the hall he shoots down at them boom boom then listens as it goes quiet hiya a soldier comes from behind him and kicks him in the back Ivan falls forward face first the quickly turns over and shoots boom the soldier goes flying back as Ivan gets up then checks the hall for the queen he does a secret knock then she opens the door he tells her to come as well then goes out into the hall then tells her to stay behind him then goes down the stairs and heads to the barn to the other panic room he runs down the stairs then crosses the lounge-room and goes out the back door then goes back in as bullets hit the door he tells her to wait here then leaps out the door firing and blasts the soldiers then as one runs from behind him he turns swinging the plasma and knocks him out he goes back in-side then gets the queen she is not there he only left her for a mo-ment he looks around the then call out her name then yells out her name she is home he looks around thru the hall then curse he goes out into the cart that was smashes thru the living room then sees her vetting taken lifted up by soldiers and kidnapped he runs across the field and sprints after them then as they go around the side of the barn he goes around the other way then cuts them off he runs and smashes one over the head with the plasma then head butts the other one then catches her as they drop her then holds the plasma canon up in the other hand and shoots the last one then tells her where did she go as he runs across into the barn with her then puts her down as he puts her down from the side of the barn comes more soldiers they are surrounding them and coming from both ways he climbs with her up the ladder to the top roof of the barn then as they sur-round them at the bottom he shoots down at then and blast them all then tells her to come back down he slides down the ladder then catches her as she slides down after him then he runs with her across the field towards the stables gun fire breaks out and she dives on the ground her stands in between her and where the bullets are coming from then lifts her up to keep running they make it to the stables then he gets the dragon then tells her to leave that he will keep fighting them and she will make it to the forest she is screaming then as the gunfire closes in and the glass starts to break around them he tells her to go that way he kisses her then he goes to the front of the barn and starts firing then takes the other dragon the take a deep breath then starts shooting them he blast his plasma canon and they are held back as he keeps firing at them the take cover in the house and he keeps firing at them then he looks back and he can see her getting away on the dragon into the forest then he fly's towards the house and shoots the soldiers as one comes out from where the cart crashed onto the loungeroom he blasts him with the plasma canon then fly's up to the roof then looks out towards the wall he can see rows of them coming thru the gates that they have gotten thru the fire rockets towards the castle and Ivan shoots back he goes back onto the veranda then whoosh he shoots fireballs and blasts his plasma canon whoosh they fire rockets into the castle boom Ivan blasts his plasma canon at them boom boom they keeps firing rocket whoosh whoosh then Ivan is taking heavy fire on the balcony he shoots the plasma canon boom boom he hits a cart and it explodes then he re aims and aims directly at a cart approaching shooting rockets whoosh whoosh they fire two rockets that nearly hit Ivan dives onto cover as they hit around him he can feel the castle shake them gets up quickly then aims with both arms sitting the plasma canon boom boom he hits a cart and it explodes them he keeps firing his plasma canon boom boom he hits another cart and it explodes them as a dragon swoops overhead and bites at him he lifts the plasma canon up to its head then blasts it boom it hits it's head and it falls from the sky and crashes Ivan runs and leans over them shoots at a cart boom boom it explodes then he can see another cart coming he aims at it then boom the plasma canon hits at the same time it fires a rocket at Ivan boom Ivan hits the rocket in mid-air and it ex-

plodes he keeps firing as more carts come from the gate and up
the lawn he fires his plasma canon then boom boom he watches
as the plasma blasts hit the carts direct and they explode he re
aims to his right at the other ones then boom boom he hits them
as well then as two carts come firing rockets at him he quickly
runs forward them aims and shoots plasma canon at them then
boom boom the plasma bursts hit the carts and they explode
Ivan runs and dives just as the rockets hit him and explode he
gets up then runs back out then can see a cart has a ladder and
they climbing up it to get to him he leans over then boom her
blasts the cart and it explodes from the lawn comes more carts
whoosh whoosh they fire rockets at him boom boom Ivan fires
back and the plasma bursts hit the rockets then he quickly re
aims then fires plasma blasts at the cart boom boom kaboom it
explodes and goes up in flames from around the flames another
cart tears towards him whoosh whoosh they fire rockets up at
him boom boom Ivan hits their cart and it explodes a mythological creature in a cage gets brought on then Ivan starts shooting boom boom he hits it and they release it from the cage as
well as fire rockets at him whoosh whoosh Ivan fires at them
boom boom he disarms the rockets as the creatures runs and
leaps up the balcony then climbs up Ivan leans over and boom
he shoots it in the head it catches alight then keeps clinninh up
on fire whoosh whoosh they fire rockets Ivan aims at the rockets
letting the creature get closer boom boom as he hits the rockets
then creature grabs onto him and tears him off the balcony Ivan
shoots it in the temple with his plasma canon and it releases
him Ivan falls onto the lawn outside then as the creature crashes
to the ground Ivan has to run up on top of it then shoot the carts
boom boom he fires at the carts then whoosh whoosh they get
off two rockets kaboom Ivan explodes the cart then takes cover
behind the creature kaboom Ivan runs out from cover onto the
lawn then boom boom he shoots at the last of the carts kaboom
he hits them whoosh whoosh other carts fire at Ivan Ivan runs
and dives into cover kaboom they hit all around him then he re
aims at a cart coming towards him boom boom he shoots the

last one then whistles to the dragon he has to make it to the forest to get the queen the dragon swoops down then he takes off with it he fly's towards the forest then goes to where she would be he finds her near the bridge I could do a love sex scene her or she is being kidnapped again by Chinese he flies over the forest then can see her near the bridge her dragon is dead and he can't see her he swoops down then looks for tracks and calls her name then looks at the tracks they lead onto the forest they are her tracks maybe the dragon took machine gun fire on the way and she made it to the rendezvous he gallops behind her tracks then can see where they lead to the wood cabin he keeps following them then lifts the dragon up flying it thru the air in a haste to find her he gets to the wood cabin then gets off the dragon then goes inside he walks in then she keeps onto him from behind and he turns around then kisses her then pins her against the wall then keeps kissing her as he takes his pants down then shoves his cock up into her tight wet vagina she is panting them screams as he slides his cock up into her pussy he rams her into the wall and thrashes her pumping her with hard and fast upwards thrust shoving his gi3 the knob to her

He keeps pounding her into the wall and shoving his cock up her vagina thrusting upwards he does hard and fast thrusts that grate tear and thread her wet tight pussy and scream as he pumps his cock up her vagina he re braces her by the legs properly then slams her up into the wall sliding his cock straight up into her tight wet vaginaramming her pussy into the wall as he slams her back up against it with upwards heaves he shoves his erection deep up into her tight vagina she is screaming and bouncing up and down off his cock as he stuffs his knob into her cervix and threads her vagina with his shafts he drills her pussy into the wall she is screaming as he keeps holding her by the arse cheeks in his arms and heaving his stiff cock up her tight pussy she screams argh then comes as he launches forwards and upwards up deep up inside her tight pussy pumping his cock up into her tight vagina he feels his cock threading her vagina as he keeps bouncing her up and down he feels his cock stiffen then uses it to scrape her vagina ring as his girth smashes into it and she screams argh then comes he keeps pumping upwards and holding her by the arse cheeks and sliding his cock up her vagina she screams argh as he keeps sliding his cock up into her pussy and ramming her into the wall thrusting his hips his erection still up into her pussy she leak warm pussy juices and he feels his cock sliding further and deeper up into her tight wet pussy he makes loud thumping noises as his cock slides up her vagina and he feels his knob pounding her cervix as his stiff cock slides straight up her tight wet pussy and she screams argh then comes he keeps pumping her and shoving his cock deep into her vagina he feels his shafts grate her vagina ring she screams as he keeps sliding his cock in and out of her vagina ring and threading her tight pussy with his shaft sliding up her vagina scraping her vagina ring with his girth then as she keeps screaming argh argh argh in a echoing tone he keeps bouncing her off his cock he can feels his girth stretching her vagina ring as she lands on it making loud clapping sounds as his body hits her groins and makes loud slapping noises as well he keeps thrusting upwards and shoving his cock deep up inside her vagina then she screams argh then comes he slams her into the back of the door and heaves upwards and shoves his tongue down her throat and kisses her then at the same time he kissing her he slides his knob into her arse and she screams argh into his lips he keeps pumping her and sliding his cock deep up I to her arse hole then pumps his cock deep and hard up her arse hole drilling her arse hole ring he pounds his erection up her arse she screams argh then comes as he keeps sliding his cock up her arse then pumps her with hard and fast upwards heaves sliding his cock deep up into her arse hole pumping her with hard and fast upwards heaves and slides his cock straight up her tight arse hole she screams argh then comes he keeps pumping her and ramming his cock up her arse while ring then does hard and fast upwards thrust pumping her he slides s his cock hard he keeps pounding her arse hole ring with his girth his stiff cock sliding along her arse hole ring his he can feels his shafts sliding along her tight arse hole ring as he keeps pumping her with hard and fast upwards thrusts that smash his girth into her arse hole ring as she screams argh then comes he keeps pumping her

Then pumps his cock hard and fast I'm up her arse hole and feels his cock sliding deep up inside her arse hole ring he keeps sliding his cock up her arse hole then stiffens his cock and keeps pounding her arse hole into the wall as he slams her back up against it with powerful upwards thrust he feels his cock pounding into her arse hole ring he keeps stiffening his cock then feels his cock slide hard and fast up her arse hole then re braces her by the arse cheeks and sides then slides his cock up along her arse hole ring his shafts sliding back and forth along her tight arse hole ring he keeps launching upwards and slamming his cock into her arse hole ring then she screams argh then comes he re braces her around her arse cheeks and her sides then pounds his cock into her arsehole ring then hammers his erection up her arse hole and feels his girth stretch her arse hole ring as he keeps losing her up with his cock sliding along her arse hole ring she screams argh as she comes he keeps pumping her then re braces her by the hips and around the sides then slams her back into the door he kisses her then tilts his head and open mouth pashes her tilting his head he keeps sliding his tongue down her throat at the same time he shoves his girth in her arse hole ring and drills her arse hole up the door and slams her back into the door then keeps doing upwards thrusts that slide his shafts along her arse hole ring he stiffens his cock then he feels his girth slide back and forth along her arse hole ring he bra as her there then keeps her on that position and keeps his thick girth sliding back and forth along her tight arse hole ring as she screams argh then comes he uses his arms to heave her body then slides his erection along her arse hole ring back and forth he feels sensations all along his shaft as he keeps pumping her and sliding his cock

in and out of her arse hole ring as she screams argh then comes
he re braces her then pounds her arse hole ring into the door and
slams her up against it sliding his girth back and forth along her
arse hole ring she keeps screaming them he pins her to the door
and chokes her into the door then keeps thrusting his hips as his
cock drills up her tight arse hole ring then keeps shoving his
whole cock deep up into her tight arse hole then drills her arse
hole with hard and fast upwards thrusts then she comes he stops
choking her and he takes his hands away she gasps for air he
keeps doing vertical upwards thrusts with his erect pole that
keep her screaming his cock girth stretches her arse hole ring as
he purposely slams his girth into her arse hole ring to hear her
scream louder he pounds her arse hole with deep upwards
heaves he lunges up and down and thrusts his pole up her tight
arse hole he kisses her then as he feels his tongue sliding it down
her throat his cock triples in hardness then he uses it to tripe her
arse hole ring in size slamming his girth into her arse hole ring
he slams her slams her against the door to shove his erection
harder up her arse she screams argh then comes as he keeps
pounding her arse hole ring he thrusts upwards as hard as he can
while stiffening his erection this threading screaming and grating her tight arse hole ring as his whole cock slams into it she
screams a argh then comes he stiffens his cock and his veiny top
shaft threads her arse hole ring as he heaves his pole straight up
vertically into her tight arse hole he shoves his girth as far up
her arse hole as he can to stretch her arse hole ring she keeps
screaming then he opens the door then blasts the Chinese with
his plasma canon at the same time he keeps pumping her then
slams her into the wall then keeps ramming forward and sliding
his shafts along her arse hole ring he feels his erection sliding
along her arse hole he keeps holding her by the hips and slides
his cock up her arse while ring then kisses her the keeps open
mouth pashing her with his tongue sliding down her throat he
keeps sliding his cock up her arse then slams her up I to the wall
and slides his shafts along her arse e hole ring stimulating his
cock he keeps sliding his arse hole ring along her tight arse hole

then them re bra es her by the arse cheeks and her legs then slides his shaft up along her tight arse hole he keeps sliding his cock up her arse hole ring then pounds her arse hole

He keeps pounding her are whole into the wall and shoving his cock up her arse hole with hard and fast upwards thrusts that keep her screaming and keeps his cock hard as he slides his shafts along her arse hole ring she screams argh then comes as he keeps feels his veiny top shaft slide along her tight are whole he feels his girth grating her arse hole ring he pounds her arse hole ring with his girth she screams as he keeps sliding his shaft along her arse hole ring then feels his cock sliding up her arse he re braces her by the hips and legs them pounds her into the door then slides his cock up her arse hole ring then puts her down then turns her around then slides his cock up her arse hole his girth slides back and forth along her tight arse hole ring then he rams his cock up her and thrashes her lunging his girth into her arse hole ring he smashes her arse hole she is screaming then he does hard and fast upwards thrust and pumps her arse hole ring with his shaft then lunges upwards and slides his cock back and forth along her arse hole ring she is screaming as he keeps thrusting upwards and spearing his cock up her tight arse hole he rams her into the door and slashes his cock up her arse hole shoving his whole cock straight up her arse hole ring his girth slams into her arsehole and she scram argh then comes he keeps grabbing her by the hips and thrashing her then stuff his bonor up her arse hole sliding his shafts along her tight are whole ring then belts her arse cheek with his palm she screams as he re braces her by the hips then slides his cock up her arse hole ring then keeps pumping her and sliding his cock up her arse hole ring he chokes her with his hands then keeps sliding his cock along her arse e hole ring he pumps his shafts along her arse e hole then slides his cock up her arse hole with hard and fast thrusts he smashes her arse hole ring pounds her with drilling upwards thrusts ramming her arse hole hard and fast as he can he plugs her arse while with his girth she comes then he lets go of her throat she is screaming as he thrusts upwards and spears her arse hole with his cock slamming his girth up he rare hole he keeps pounding her with air fans fast upwards thrust she scram argh then comes he takes his cock out then he hears her knees drop on the floor as she slams onto the ground he shoves his cock in her mouth then comes she gags as he slides his cock down the back of her throat and deep throats her she keeps gagging then coughs and splatters as he shoves his cock down the back of her throat and he keeps pumping comes down her throat he grabs the back of her head then forced it into his cock she swallows then he hears her gulp then lifts her up then he pins her to the wall and kisses her and keeps open mouth tongue kissing her and shoving his tongue down her throat then tilts his head the other side and keeps kissing her and open mouth tongue kissing her with passionate open mouth tongue in throat gropes he goes to leave the cabin then is surrounded

Ivan goes outside and they are surrounded by nature and trees then he takes her back inside then Ivan sees the queen sitting on the lounge she has her arse out to the side in a short dress that shows all her leg he goes over to her then feels her leg up them lifts her dress and squeezes her arse cheek then she gets up on the lounge on all fours he lifts her dress up then snaps off her g string then slides his cock up her pussy he feels his knob touch her pussy lips then his shafts slide up along her vagina walls then feels his shaft keep threading her vagina as he slides his whole cock up her tight vagina and his knob taps her cervix she screams then he just thrashes her be grabs her hips and slams his cock as hard and fast as he can up her vagina he feels his girth slamming her vagina ring as he keeps sliding his whole cock vertically up and in her vagina he keeps pounding his erection up her vagina as she screams he keeps pumping her with rapid upwards thrusts that have his girth smashing her vagina ring as he shoves his cock deep up inside her vagina he keeps plugging to erection into her pussy as she screams argh then comes he feels her vagina leak and become slippery then feels his shafts sliding along her vagina ring as he thrashes his erection deep up inside her vagina he feels his shafts gliding along her vagina walls especially the upper shafts near his knob they thread and grate her vagina walls as his girth just slams her vagina ring his knob is pounding up her cervix as he grabs her hips and throws them back into he slams her vagina forwards this makes a loud clapping sound as she screams he goes wild do energetic upwards heaves that have his cock threading grating and scraping her tight vagina ring he can feel all his cock stretching her vagina ring as he slides it back and forward he keeps feeling his whole cock threading her vagina ring he keeps getting this feeling along his cock that it is stretching her vagina ring as his veiny top shaft scrapes her tight vagina ring she keeps screaming as he purposely stiffens his cock then feels it throb and go three times as hard and get larger he uses it to keeps scraping her tight vagina ring she screams argh then comes he keeps pumping his erection full of blood then keeps scraping her vagina ring she screams then grabs the top of the lounge and looks back watching him as he punishes her vagina ring with his erection she keeps screaming and looking back at him her whole body is shuddering with each heavy impact as he lunges into her and heaves his whole body upwards so his cock slides deeper up into her tight vagina he feels his knob tapping her cervix as she screams argh then comes she keeps screaming as his cock slides all along her vagina ring he keeps smashing upwards heaves that have his cock deep up into her pussy then slides his shafts along her vagina ring and feels them scraping her she keeps screaming and turning ago in looking at him whack he belts her arse cheek then keeps sliding his cock up her vagina ring his shafts sliding along her tight vagina ring make him groan then he keeps feeling his shafts slide up and down her vagina ring and his ribbed shafts being stimulated as his top shaft scrapes her vagina ring ouch she screams as he belts her arse cheek again then slides his shafts back and forth along her tight vagina ring she keeps screaming then makes a sexy orgasm sound as she reaches climax she sounds like a kettle boiling then screams as she comes he keeps sliding his shafts along her vagina ring then grabs her hips and thrashes her and pounds her vagina drilling his cock deep up inside her pussy he feels his girth smash her vagina ring and he plugs her vagina with his thick girth pounding her vagina ring whack he belts her arse cheek then re braces her and spears her cervix with his knob he keeps pounding her with hard and fast upwards thrusts jamming his girth into her vagina ring she screams argh then comes as his erection slides deeper and further up her vagina he rebraces her by the upper outer thighs his hands on her arse cheeks he pounds her pussy with upwards vertical thrusts and whole body upwards heaves pumping his cock up deep up into her vagina she keeps screaming as he thrashes her pounding her he plugs her vagina with his whole cock smashing up into her tight vagina he reaches around and runs her breasts with his hand and slides his palm across her nipples then reaches around fully and squeezes her breasts then pinches her nipples and keeps sliding his cock up her vagina then lunges upwards with a fast upwards drilling motion he hammers her vagina with his cock then re braces her body then feels his girth stretching her vagina ring his shafts sliding back and forth along her vagina he lunges upwards then slams her pussy lips with his girth she keeps screaming the he does rough deep upwards thrusts that tear her vagina ring as he slams his girth into it she screams argh then comes he stands there holding her body he feels her vagina leak then as it leaks he slides his cock deeper and further up into her tight vagina ring his shafts glide along her vagina walls aa he rams his shafts into her vagina he keeps pumping blood into his cock then uses his erection to thread grate and scrape along her vagina ring she screams argh then comes he keeps slamming her then wraps his hands around her throat and cheek her at the same time he pumps her vagina ring with his girth he slides his shafts along her vagina ring and he feels his knob pound into her cervix he keeps heaving his cock up her vagina and his shafts slide all along up and down her vagina ring stimulating his shafts he keeps doing deep upwards thrusts that slide his shafts into her vagina ring as he lifts his shafts back and forth inside her vagina ring he feels them scraping her vagina ring she screams argh then comes he feels his shafts expand then slide harder along her vagina ring then keeps his cock sliding all along her vagina ring as she screams argh then comes he does a heap of hard rough stabs that bang her vagina ring she keeps screaming he can resist but to hold her hips and ram and pound her tight vagina ring with his shaft she keeps screaming as he thrusts upwards hard and fast then feels his cock pounding and slamming her vagina ring she screams argh then comes he keeps pumping his shaft all along her vagina ring then spears her cervix with his knob and thrusts upwards with deep hard and rough strokes she screams argh the comes he launches his cock vertically up her vagina ring then feels his top shaft and knob sliding up her vagina wall then keeps stroking his cock up her vagina his veiny top shaft is threading her vagina his body slams her arse cheeks as his cock slides straight up into her pussy he uses his right arm and hand to belt her arse cheek forward she screams ouch making a loud crisp smack sound followed by the sound of her screaming in a sexy accent and skin hitting skin as he goes up on his toes to get omg is knob up deeper into her cervix she screams yes yes yes as he hits her special spot he keeps pumping her and sliding his shafts along her vagina ring then does a heap of hard and fast upwards thrusts she screams then comes as he stand there holding her hips hitting her pussy with his bonor sliding his cock shafts all along her tight vagina ring as she keeps screaming then he goes deep and hard he pounds her with hard and fast upwards heaves that slam his cock shafts along her vagina then slides his cock further and deeper right up into her vagina he belts her arse cheek with his palm then keeps sliding his shafts along her vagina ring shove his hand onto his shaft then pushes his knob onto her arse hole ring then pops it into her arse hole then grabs her hips and thrashes her arse smashing his cock deep and hard up her arse hole ring he shoves his cock hard and fast up her tight arse hole she keeps screaming loudly as he re grabs her hips then slams his body forward at the same time he pulls her hips back and smashes her arse hole ring with his cock spearing her arse hole he slams his girth into her arse hole ring then keeps pumping her he re grabs her by the hips then thrusts upwards and shoves his whole cock deep and hard up into her tight arse hole ring he keeps plugging her tight arse with his whole cock stiffening it with every upwards thrust he grates tears and slams her tight arse hole she screams argh then comes he keeps pounding her arse hole ring then grabs her throat and chokes her squeezing his hand around her throat he clenches her throat with his hands then keeps banging his cock into her arse hole and thrashing her with deep upwards thrusts that spear her arse hole with his erection slamming his girth into her arse hole ring he does hard and fast upwards thrusts she comes then he lets go if her throat then she gasps for air and screams as he does smashing upwards thrust that tear her arse hole then slams his cock deep and hard up her arse then grabs her arse cheeks and throws her onto the lounge then stands up and shoves his cock down the back of her throat and comes he forced her mouth onto his cock as she gash and coughs he keeps shoving his cock down the back of her throat then shoots come in her mouth she keeps gagging as he slams the back of her head into his cock and keeps shoving his cock bar deep down her throat she gasps for air he keeps shoving his cock down her throat she coughs and splatters then keeps gagging as he fills her throat with come and she swallows and gulps coughing and splattering he keeps holding the back of her head and forcing his cock down her throat he steps off the lounge then pins her back of her knees to the lounge then shoves his cock up her arse hole then thrashes her and rams his cock up her arse hole ring she screams as he slides his shafts all up along her tight arse hole ring he feels his shafts sliding back and forth along her arse hole ring then fish hooks her then keeps sliding his shafts all along her arse hole back and forth along her arse hole ring she keeps screaming he keeps sliding his erection along her tight arse hole ring as she screams argh then comes he keeps sliding his cock along her arse hole ring then pumps his shafts back and forth along her arse hole ring he keeps shoving his shafts along her arse hole ring he keeps upwards then slams his cock down into her arse hole doing deep and hard down wards thrusts that pound his cock into her arse hole ring he keeps launching upwards then slamming his erection knob to her arse hole pounding her arse whole into the lounge slamming his cock down into her tight arse hole ring he thrusts upwards and slides his cock hard and fast up her arse hole she acc rems a argh then comes he leans forward then chokes her throat into the lounge his hand around her throat she makes a choking sound then he keeps doing down wards thrusts and sliding his shafts along her arse hole ring he scrapes her arse hole ring with his shafts sliding back and forth along her arse hole he thrusts upwards and smashes her arse hole then her whole body tenses and her eyes roll back and she comes he takes his hand off her throat then she gasps for air then keeps screaming as he re grabs the back of her knees and pins her to the lounge and thrashes her arse hole with hard and fast upwards heaves he slams his cock deep up her arse hole pumping her and pounding her arse hole she screams argh then comes he keeps sliding his erection up and down her arse hole ring and slides his shafts back and forth up along her arse hole he keeps sliding his shafts all along her tight arse hole then takes his cock out the comes on her he comes on her breasts and her neck then as he keeps pumping comes from his cock he hits her face and hair

Ivan watches as the queen makes breakfast at the wood cabin then after they eat the queen runs and jumps on the bed bouncing him and down on her back then sits up on her knees as Ivan walks forward then kisses her standing up she is kneeling the end of the bed then as his lips to duck hers he lays her back pinning her to the bed with his lips as he dives on top of her then starts humping her and sliding his cock in and out of her vagina ring as she screams he keeps pumping his cock up her vagina wildly with hard and fast upwards heaves smashing her vagina with his cock up the bed they end up at the top of the bedhead he is pounding her rough and slamming his erection up her with rapid deep thrust that keep her screaming argh argh argh with each upwards thrust he rams her into the bed and shoves his girth up her vagina ring his knob smashes up into her cervix as he uses his whole body to slide his shafts along her vagina ring she screams argh then comes as he keeps thrusting his body his stiff cock hammers up her vagina he feels his shafts sliding all along her tight vagina ring invigorating his cock keeps heaving his body upwards and his veiny top shaft scrapes her vagina ring as he slides it up into her vagina and keeps sliding it back and forth in and out his shafts especially the centre's grates her vagina ring she screams yes yes yes then comes he keeps sliding his shafts all along her vagina ring scraping grating and stretching her vagina ring she screams as he keeps sliding his shafts up and down her tight vagina as he goes into a set if seep upwards thrusts he launches his whole body upwards and stiffens his cock then feels her vagina stretch as he slams his shafts along her vagina ring then grabs onto the bedhead then slams her into the bed with pounding downwards thrust he keeps ramming her pussy into the bed his girth smashes her vagina ring into the mattress and she keeps screaming he re braces the bedhead then launches his stiff cock straight up her vagina slamming his girth up into her vagina ring as she screams argh then comes he keeps pounding her vagina ring with his shafts then falls forward onto her neck with both his hands and chokes her down into the mattress she makes a choking sound as he slides his veiny top shaft scraping her vagina ring as he pumps into her vagina ring with his shafts he slides his cock along her vagina ring his top shaft pleasuring her g spot he keeps sliding his shaft up her vagina ring he pounds and rams her vagina with hard and fast upwards heaves lunging upwards his cock slams her vagina he keeps smashing his cock up deep up into her vagina her eyes are rolling back in her head as she comes he lifts his hands of her throat and she gasps for air then screams as he slides his cock all along her vagina ring he pumps his cock back and forth along her vagina ring stiffening his shafts he slides them all along her vagina ring he shovels his cock up and around up into her upper roof of her vagina he feels his knob hitting her cervix he keeps sliding his cock up her vagina her then slams her pussy with hard and fast thrusts pounding his cock up her vagina he lunges upwards and stiffens his cock at the same time scraping and grating her tight vagina ring he keeps launching upwards with his erection pounding her vagina he pounds her vagina ring with erratic rough penetrative thrusts that keeps her screaming he is ramming and pumping her fast she keeps screaming her body bounces up from the impacts he re grabs the top of the bedhead then with all his strength launches upwards with his erection his girth smashes her vagina ring as he keeps thrusting up and down using his arms to slam his body into hers as his cock pounds her vagina with rapid intense rough upwards thrusts he keeps vertically impaling her tight vagina with his cock then slides his shafts back and forth along her vagina ring he feels his top shaft scraping her vagina ring he feels his shafts scraping all along her vagina ring as his slides it in and out his balls slap her arse cheeks as he pounds his cock deep up into her vagina his side shafts grate her vagina he keeps grabbing the bed head and does deep and powerful upwards thrusts slamming his cock up her pussy using his arms he throws his whole body up to wards the bedhead his cock ramming her pussy as she screams argh then comes he keeps pounding and hammering his cock deep up inside her vagina then slides his girth up her vagina ring she keeps screaming as he pumps her vagina with his cock he lifts her up then throws her into the bedhead she slams onto it then goes onto all fours then screams as he runs forward on his knees and plugs her vagina with his cock then holds her hips and thrashes her she is screaming as he pumps and rams her from biding he feels his body slamming into her arse cheeks as his cock slides up into her vagina he shoves his cock deep up her pussy slamming his girth up her vagina ring he slides his shafts up along her vagina ring he stiffens his cock as he slides it in and out if her and feels his shafts grate and thread her vagina as his cock slides up into her pussy he feels her vagina leak then slides his cock deeper and further up into her vagina his girth stretches her vagina ring as he slides his cock back and forth into her vagina he launches upwards and spears her vagina with his erection grabbing her by the hips he thrashes his cock deep up into her vagina ring and pounds her with rapid intense upwards strokes that keeps her screaming he drills his erection deep up inside her vagina doing vertical upwards strokes his cock slides vertically up into her vagina ring she keeps screaming he rams her pussy and makes a loud clapping sound as he pumps her vagina then feels his shafts sliding all along her vagina ring as she screams argh then comes he keeps pumping her then belts her arse cheek ouch she screams as he spanks her with his hand then keeps slamming and ramming her pussy pounding and pumping her vagina he re grabs her by the hips and drills her pussy with hard and fast intense upwards thrusts jamming her pussy with his erect pole his girth smashes into her vagina ring as she keeps screaming he keeps pumping her pussy with his cock then shoves his cock up her arse then grabs her hips and slides his cock hard and fast up her arse hole she screams he thrashes her pounding her arse hole with his cock he slides his cock back and forth along her arse hole ring them keeps pumping his cock up her arse hole she screams argh then comes he keeps sliding his shafts along her arse hole ring he balances on her hips then keeps sliding his shafts along her arse hole ring she keeps screaming as he slams his shafts into her arse hole then keeps plugging her arse hole with his shafts and sliding his shafts all along her arse hole ring he spits on her arse hole then slides his cock up her arse hole ring he keeps spitting then feels his shafts sliding back and forth along her arse hole she keeps screaming as he slides his cock up along her arse hole ring he keeps sliding his erect cock all along her arse hole ring he slides his cock back and forth all along her arse hole ring then pumps he smashes his cock up her arse and rams her from behind with upwards heaves and smashing upwards thrust he bangs and shoves his w re too straight up into her arse hole ring drilling her arse hole with his throbbing cock he pumps and rams her arse hole stiffening his cock he slams his girth into her arse hole ring spitting on her arse hole he pumps his cock up into her arse hole with hard and fast upwards thrust he pounds her arse hole with his cock then re braces her by the hips and smashes her arse hole with his stiff cock pounding into her arse hole ring shoving his cock no her arse hole he keeps pounding her with hard and fast upwards heaves he drills his cock up her arse she screams argh then comes he keeps pumping her and shoving his cock deep up her arse she keeps screaming he pushes her down and she falls on her stomach he lands on top of her then re shoves his cock into her arse hole ring she screams as he grabs the bedhead then shoves his cock up her arse as hard and fast as he can pounding her arse hole ring with upwards heaves he feels his cock harden then slides it deep and rough into her arse she screams as he downwards thrusts his erection into her arse hole and keeps ramming her arse hole into the bed using his arms to heave his body upwards his cock plugs her arse hole and his girth smashes into her arse hole ring as she screams argh then comes he thrashes her arse hole ring with his girth she keeps screaming as he pounds her arse hole into the bed spitting on her arse hole he slides his cock deep up her arse hole and re grabs the bedhead then pounds her arse hole his cock going deep up her arse hole ring he rams his erection hard and fast into her a se as she lay on her stomach screaming her face cheek on the mattress as he heaves his cock up her arse hole and shoves his cock deep up into her arse hole his girth smashes s her arse hole ring she screams argh then comes he keeps shoving his erection into her arse hole then grabs her throat and chokes her she makes a choking sound then he thrusts upwards and spears her arse hole with his erection going hard and fast up her arse hole he pounds her arse hole and shoves his whole cock deep up her arse hole ring as he keeps pounding her arse hole in he feels his cock tighten around his knob and shafts he keeps sliding his cock up her arse hole then slides his shafts back and forth along her arse hole ring then spits on her arse hole then keeps pumping his shafts into her arse hole ring he does hard and fast upwards thrust she comes he keeps pounding her arse he re grabs the bedhead then slams his cock into her arse hole pounding her with hard and fast upwards thrust he feels his cock explode then rams her with his whole body thrusting he pumps her rapidly then shoves his cock deep up into her arse as he comes he feels his cock spasm inside her arse as he is coming he rams her arse hole she is screaming and comes as he keeps pumping her with hard and fast upwards thrusts after he has come then slides his cock out from her arse then holds her right shoulder and flips her over then lays on top of her and kisses her his knee in the bed beside her as he puts his palm on the back of her neck and pages her with open mouth tongue kisses sliding his tongue down her throat

Then as the wood cabin is surrounded by Chinese Ivan takes the plasma canon to the window then starts pumping plasma blasts at them bang bang the whole if the windows shatter from machine gun fire then as a Chinese soldier comes towards the window Ivan quickly shoots him boom he flies back thru the air as Ivan looks back and sees the queen on the floor screaming he links it then with both arms aiming he keeps blasting boom boom he shoots soldiers as they keep running up then Ivan can see flames then he can see a dragon on the roof boom a Chinese comes thru the door then straight back out again he keeps blasting plasma bursts at soldiers as they start to man the rockets Ivan keeps shooting when whoosh Ivan tackles the queen as the rocket hits the side of the hut blowing a hole thru one side Ivan lifts up the table then as soldiers run in thru the side of the hut Ivan has to quickly shoot boom boom as soldiers run in thru the side he keeps blasting them then re aims at the cart boom he shoots it and it explodes whoosh the dragon is burning the other side of the hut Ivan quickly runs over then shoots up out if the window boom the dragon is hit and slides off the roof on fire Ivan can see a soldier about to go on the other side of the table Ivan runs then whack he throws his axe at him and he falls forward over the table the queen is screaming as Ivan quickly runs and slides in next to her then keeps firing over the table then as a soldier crashes thru a window then goes to shoot them Ivan gets up over the table then boom he shoots and the soldier hits the wall on fire as more soldiers gather outside Ivan slams the table up against the wall then keeps aiming at the soldiers and blasting boom boom he quickly shoots them then as they position a cart in front of the hole then go to shoot a rocket from it whoosh get down Ivan holds the queen down the quickly shoots up and over the table boom he hits the cart and it explodes Ivan quickly takes the queen out the back door he kicks it open then boom he fires a soldier steps out into the plasma burst then Ivan keeps firing at them boom boom he uses the table for cover then lifts his plasma canon up and shoots boom the cart explodes a soldier leaps from the side boom Ivan blasts him and he flies backwards hitting a crate on fire another soldier comes in front of the table boom Ivan shoots he catches fire a dragon runs from the treeline then comes towards the log cabin breathing fire whoosh boom Ivan quickly opens fire lifting his arms up and over the table he aims boom he hits the dragon with the plasma burst the dragon explodes he keeps firing plasma bursts at the soldiers as they come from the carts and keeps shooting machine guns into the table Ivan can see from the back door a soldier running thru the back door he kicks it in boom Ivan blasts him and he fly's back out the door Ivan grabs the queen then races with her out the back door then sees a soldier on a horse boom he shoots him off he backflips off the horse on fire Ivan runs and leaps on the horse then lifts the queen up they gallop towards the forest when a cart comes out in front of them boom boom Ivan shoots it kaboom it explodes and they swerve around it then Ivan can see the soldiers with machine guns running boom Ivan blasts them with his plasma canon then as a mythological beast is released Ivan blasts it with his plasma canon boom boom he hits it twice and it catches fire then keeps running towards them the queen screams boom Ivan shoots it again with the plasma and it explodes they make it to the forest when along the oath are more soldiers running and shooting them boom boom Ivan shoots and hits them boom they catch alight Ivan has to turn his body the other side soldier a come from everywhere shooting machine guns boom boom Ivan blasts them then gets to a bend he goes around it straight into a cart the cart shoots a rocket whoosh Ivan shoots it boom then keeps firing plasma bursts at the cart kaboom it explodes a dragon swoops onto them whack Ivan just it with his plasma canon them shoots it boom it hits the pilot as the dragon attacks Ivan's horse and bites it Ivan aims the plasma at the dragons head then boom he blows it off and it crashes into the road soldiers gather each side of the road shooting machines guns at them boom boom Ivan aims and blasts them a cart blocks the road whoosh they fire at them boom Ivan shoots the rocket it explodes then he swerves the explosion then boom he hits the cart and it explodes he swerves that as well then is forced off into the forest he gallops around trees and thru the bushes when he gets to the river he can see chokes soldiers behind him in a cart Ivan turns and aims at them boom he aims at the cart and it explodes the river has a dragon soaring across it towards them then whoosh it shoots a fireball directly towards Ivan boom Ivan shoots the dragon it hits and the dragon explodes Ivan gallops along the river

Then can see up ahead a dragon it's breathing fire at them Ivan pegs his axe at the pilot the pilot backflips off as it hits his head Ivan quickly goes up to the dragon then heaves the queen on then keeps onto the dragon as well they go to fly off when from the trees soldiers come and shoot them with machine guns boom boom Ivan shoots at the same time digs his heel I to the dragon whoosh it breathes fire at them kaboom the plasma and fireballs hit with accuracy and the soldiers erupt in flames and Ivan gets airborne the dragon ascends and takes off it soars across the lake then as Ivan follows the river he gets to a bridge on the bridge is the whole Chinese army with carts and dragons they see Ivan and open fire Ivan shoots his plasma canon boom boom he hits a dragon about to fly off the bed he them as the carts fire rockets Ivan blasts his plasma canon he shoots the bride and it catches on fire boom boom he keeps shooting the bridge a dragon swoops him he has to smash his plasma at it to stop it from biting them then Ivan blasts the dragon boom the dragon gets hit then crashes into the water Ivan keeps firing at the bridge then it starts to collapse and the carts and soldiers fall into the water Ivan flaps the dragons do he and it spears up over the collapsing beige and fly's into the sky whoosh whoosh carts fire rockets at him from the Ivan takes the queen to the river by canoe then a he rows her across he sees up her skirt and can see her vagina as he sits facing her and rowing backwards he watches her she wearing a summer dress and a frilly hat as they arrive she sees the picnic he set up on the river bank then he puts his hand out then lifts her up off into the shore they have a Beetroot hummus with Turkish toasts Tomato and bean bruschetta Streusel cake with candied citrus Lemon squash scones with mascarpone tomato and spinach muffins quiche Goat's cheese and fennel tart with polenta pastry and roasted peaches Pancake skewers They have lemonade to drink after Ivan takes her for a walk under the tree and she sees ropes she gets excited and danced and says are you going tie me up and spank me he lifts her dress off then gets a semi at her perky breasts and nipples and pussy he does her right wrist up then blindfolds her as he ties her left wrist up as well and as she stands there almost on her tippy toes he cracks the whip above her head and she screams and trembles he can see her crossing her legs and clenching her body with anticipation then as he whips her back she screams and thrusts upwards tightening her whole body he can see the grazes that the whip has left he whips her again on the back then she screams ouch that one hurt she tries to look around to see where he coming from panicking she looks nervously then screams as the whip hits her back again she lifts her body up and clenches her hands around the restraints then settles down breathing rapidly he can hear her taking deep breathes as she sucks back the pain argh that hurts she screams as he whips her arse cheeks she keeps screaming then he unleashes a heap of rough hard and fast whips that shred her arse cheeks with lines and tears from the lashes all across her are cheeks she just stands there facing away from him screaming argh stop it it hurts crack he whips her back argh he whips her arse cheeks she screams arrggh as he goes up to her and feels all along the abrasions he can feel her grazes with his palms as she thrusts her body away from him telling him to stop and get away that it hurts to stop it now please crack he whips her hard with a massive lash across her back that lifts her up off her feet screaming stop it it hurts crack ouch she screams as he whips her arse cheek and upper thigh with the lashes scratching lines across her beautiful skim he keeps whipping her argh then he thrashes her and keeps whipping her argh argh she screams argh it hurts stop it he tells her to shut up then crack he whips her back on top of the whip marks already there arghh she screams then turns her back left and right then tries to cover her back twisting her whole body from him he quickly whips her vagina and she screams and turns back around argh argh he whips her back twice then her arse cheeks as she screams stop it now that's enough argh it hurts crack he whips her arse cheeks and she screams argh you bastard argh he whips her again she keeps screaming as he walls up then squeezes her arse cheek with his hand arghh she screams and thrusts upwards as he keeps squeezing her arse cheek arghh she flicks her arse real quickly and his hand goes away smack he re grabs the other arse cheek and squeezes it she screams let it go ouch ouch it hurts arghh he squeezes it in his hand harder then she starts to scream louder aghh he lets it go then crack he whips her back argh she thrusts forward arching her back in pain screams argh stop it crack he whips the whip and hits her arse cheeks she screams ouch and lifts her body up and down screaming argh he gets the boat paddle then whack he smacks her arse cheeks with it arghh she screams he uses both hands on it then whack argh it bel he her arse cheeks and she screams argh he goes around to his back hand then lines her up whack he swings it and it hits her arse and she screams argh then throws it down picks up the whip then crack argh he whips her arse cheeks then keeps whipping her arse cheeks and back with hard deep whips he leaves shredded whip marks all across her back as she just thrusts there screaming argh he keeps whipping her then watches as she lifts her body up and down screaming argh stop it it hurts he keeps whipping her then walls up to her and unties her and takes her into the picnic blanket the gets her on all fours she is screaming in pain and is tensing her body blindfolded she keeps screaming he holds her side with his hands and when she feels him touch her hips she screams then he walks forward on his knees then spits on her arse then slides his cock up her arse then she screams ohh he feels his shafts slide all along her arse hole back and forth then he keeps sliding his shafts all along her arse hole ring then spits on her arse hole then keeps sliding his shafts along her arse hole and slams his girth into her arse hole ring and smashes his cock deep up her arse then spanks her arse cheek and re grabs her hips and thrashes her arse hole with his stiff cock he keeps belting her arse cheek and pumping his cock up into her arse hole shoving his girth into her arse hole ring he pounds her arse hole from behind with his shafts sliding all up and down along her tight arse hole ring he keeps pumping her and ramming his cock up her arse hole then whack ouch she screams as he spanks her grabs her hips then thrusts upwards and shoves his bonor deep up into her arse hole his girth smashes her arse hole ring he drills and tears her arse hole ring heaving his body upwards his cock goes vertically up into her arse hole he gets sensations all along his shafts as he slides them back and forth along her arse hole then buries his girth into her arse hole ring with hard and fast upwards thrusts that keep her screaming then as he grabs her with both hands on her hips and drills his cock up her arse she screams argh then comes he keeps pumping her and spanks her then keeps pumping her with hard and fast upwards heaves he feels his cock grating her arse hole ring then she screams argh then comes he keeps pumping her with rapid hard and fast upwards thrusts then pulls her knees out from her she drops on her stomach then he slams his cock downwards into her arse hole she screams argh as he keeps doing hard and fast downwards thrusts pinning her hips down with his hands he pounds his girth into her arse hole then keeps slamming his cock into her arse hole ring ramming her arse cheeks into the blanket she screams argh then comes he keeps sliding his cock vertically up her arse hole shoving his knob deep up inside her arse hole his girth pounds her arse hole ring then he holds her throat and chokes her then keeps sliding his cock deep up her arse hole at the same time she makes a choking sound he can feels his top shafts grating her arse hole ring he keeps sliding cock up her arse then spits on her arse e hole then feels his cock slide up into her arse hole his girth stretches her arse hole ring he keeps pounding her arse hole into the blanket then she comes he takes his hands off her throat and she gasps inhaling rapidly she then screams as he grabs her hips and pumps his cock up into her arse hole thrashing her arse hole with his shafts she keeps screaming he keeps pumping her then elevates her hips slightly in the middle then rams pounds and pumps his cock into her arse hole with rapid hard and fast thrusts he drills her arse hole ring with his bonor shoving it deep up inside her arse hole he starts to come then thrashes her pounding her arse hole ring he groans then flips her over she lands on her back then he runs up her body then shoves her cock in her mouth and comes he keeps groaning as his cock pumps come in her mouth as he is ejaculating she starts to gag as he sits up on his knees then shoves his hand sin the back of her head then slides his cock deeper down her throat all the way to the back of her throat as she coughs and keeps gagging he just holds her head there she keeps splattering as he forces his cock deep down the back of her throat she swallows then keeps coughing and splattering he keeps his cock deep down the back if her throat as she gulps he takes his cock out from her mouth and lets her head to she gasps for air and inhales he combs her hair back from her face then put his hand on the back of her neck and lifts her lips up to his and open mouth pashes her and tilts his head and slides his tongue down her throat then changes sides puts his lips on the other side of hers then keeps open mouth pashing her and sliding his tongue down her throat

Ivan walks into the bedroom angry then the queen turns around says what's wrong he grabs her by the hips and throws her on the bed she screams and goes to run off the other side he reaches Ivan and snatches her by the ankles then drags her across the bed then leaps onto her he pulls his pants down then lunges upwards and rams his cock into her vagina as she screams and thrusts about he pins her down by the throat then she makes a choking sound he pumps his cock up into her vagina with rapid hard and fast upwards thrusts he can hear her choking as he is pounding his cock into her pussy he can feel his veiny stiff top shafts scraping her tight vagina ring as he slides back and forth with his shafts along her vagina ring he keeps choking her into the mattress leaning forward and over her he applies pressure to her windpipe and keeps choking her with his hands out straight looking into her eyes as his cock pounds her pussy into the bed with slamming down wards thrusts he keeps sliding his pole back and forth along her wet tight vagina ring stimulating his shafts as they scrape her vagina ring he pumps his cock vertically into her pussy with penetrating downwards thrusts he slams her vagina into the bed pounding her with his thick cock he stretches her vagina ring as he feels her pussy leak his shafts slide back and forth all along her wet pussy walls he shovels his cock up and into her scooping his knob up and into her cervix he feels his side shafts threading her vagina ring as he slides his cock back and forth and up into her pussy he sees her eyes roll back and she orgasms she gasps for air then screams as he holds her hips and slides his shafts up her pussy he feels his top shaft grating her vagina ring she keeps screaming as he pumps her pussy hard and fast he takes his hands away then drills his cock up her pussy pumping her up the bed as he rams her pussy and keeps shoving his cock up into her vagina she keeps screaming argh argh argh underneath him he keeps looking down at her face then slams his cock down into her pussy lifting his arse up and smashing it back down his bonor plugs her pussy his shafts thread her vagina ring as she screams argh then comes he lunges upwards and heaves his erection deeper and harder up her tight wet vagina she is screaming as he keeps pounding her pussy with rapid hard and fast upwards thrusts that smash his girth into her vagina ring he lifts her up then pegs her into the bedhead she falls forward then gets up holding the bedhead with both hands then screams as he runs up behind her and shoves his pole up her vagina then pumps it in and out argh argh argh she is screaming as he is placing his hands on her hips and pounding her vagina with his cock then as he keeps sliding his cock up deep up into her pussy he pumps blood into his cock and stiffens his e section then grates and scrapes her vagina ring with his thick shafts she keeps screaming then he lunges up the bed his knob hits her cervix and he feels his whole cock slide deep up into her vagina he keeps heaving his cock up into her then does hard and fast thrusts that slide his cock back and forth along her vagina ring rapidly she is screaming as he keeps sliding his cock in and out of her pussy he feels his shafts scraping her pussy ring she keeps holding the bedhead and looking around screaming at him as he pounds his cock deeper up into her vagina she is screaming yes yes yes then comes he is sliding his shafts all along her vagina ring back and forth with rapid penetration and deep upwards thrusts he slams his girth into her vagina ring then feels it slamming her pussy lips he keeps pumping her and sliding his cock along her vagina ring ouch she screams as he spanks her arse cheek then keeps placing his hands on her hips and pumping his shafts back and forth along her tight vagina ring scraping it with his girth as he slides his whole cock deep up into her vagina he does rapid intense powerful upwards heaves that have his pole ramming her vagina as he stiffens his cock he shreds threads and grates her vagina ring then re braces her by the hips grabs them and bangs her pussy hard with his cock smashing her vagina she screams argh then comes as he is pounding whack ouch she screams as he belts her arse cheek with his hand then re stiffens his cock then vertically impales her pussy with it doing upwards thrusts he stabs her vagina with his pole sliding it deep up into her pussy re grabbing her hips he moves his body closer touching hers then drills and hammers her with rapid hard and fast pumps sliding his shafts back and forth along her vagina ring she is screaming then he snatches her throat and it goes silent he chokes her with his hands wrapped around her throat then thrusts upwards and keeps vertically impaling her pussy drilling his cock up her vagina he feels his knob hitting her cervix and his girth smashing her pussy lips then does hard upwards thrusts that have his erection deep up inside her vagina as he keeps sliding his shafts back and forth along her vagina ring she comes then he takes his hands off her throat then hears her gasp for air then cough he slides his shafts up into her vagina as she screams ah ah ah with each pump he keeps ramming and slamming her his cock pounds and pumps her pussy shoving his cock deep up into her vagina ring he grabs her hair then she screams ouch he re braces her by the hips holds her still then hangs his cock into her vagina making loud slapping sounds as he kneels there with her hips in his hands and uses her vagina to stimulate his cock and shafts by pounding his erection into her pussy lips and up her vagina his girth scrapes her vagina ring as he shoves it deep up inside her tight wet box he feels her hips in his hands and hears her screaming as he keeps holding her by the hips and drilling his pole up into her vagina his shafts thread her vagina ring as she keeps screaming he re grabs her hips and thrashes her pussy ring with his cock he stands up then whack he pounds his cock into her arse hole and drills his cock deep into her arse hole ring she screams as he grabs the bedhead with his hands then slams his pole into her arse hole she keeps screaming as he does hard and fast downwards thrusts that thread her arse hole ring and plug his cock into her arse he keeps squatting and shoving his erection deep into her arse hole banging her with hard and fast downwards thrusts that make her scream he drills and hammers his cock into her arse hole ring ouch she screams as he whacks her arse cheek then re grabs the bedhead and squats pounding her arse hole and plugging it with his whole cock jamming into her arse hole she screams argh then comes he lifts her up onto the bedhead then onto the wall she makes a loud thud then turns around and screams as he lunges into her then thrusts upwards shoving his cock vertically up into her tight arse hole ring arghh arghh she keeps screaming as he pumps her arse into the wall his cock sliding up her arsehole he keeps upwards and spears her arse hole with his erection and slams her into the wall making loud thuds as he pounds her arse hole ring with his cock ramming her arse hole and doing upwards thrusts that keep his cock spearing up into her arse hole his girth stretches her arse hole ring as he slides his shafts up and down along her arse hole ring he keeps doing hard and fast upwards heaves pounding her arse hole and sliding his shafts back and forth along her arse hole argh she screams as he slams her into the wall and shoves his cock vertically up deep up into her arse hole his girth stretchers her arse hole ring as he slides his cock up and down her arse hole whack he belts her arse cheek into the wall making a smack then thud sound she screams argh then he pounds her arse hole with his erection jamming it up into her arse hole ring he keeps plugging her arse hole with his cock she screams argh then comes he is drilling her with hard and fast upwards thrusts that keeps stretching her arse hole ring with his girth whack he belts her arse cheek argh she screams as he re grabs her by the hips then spears her arse hole and pounds her arse hole ring with his girth she screams argh then comes he keeps sliding his cock along her arse hole ring then kicks her ankle her legs spread wide then he pushes her into the wall she puts her palms up then is facing the wall screaming as he stands behind her grabbing her hips and sliding his shafts back and forth along her arse hole ring she is screaming argh argh argh with each upwards thrust he gets his cock up deep up and into her arse hole doing vertical upwards heaves he rockets his cock up her arse hole and feels his girth sliding back and forth along her arse hole ring he keeps pumping his erection up her arse hole she screams argh then comes he keeps sliding his cock up and into her arse hole ring then threads and scrapes her arse hole ring with his stiff pole sliding up and down her arse hole ring as she screams argh then comes he keeps pumping and sliding his cock up her arse hole then grabs her in a bear hug then impales her arse hole and shoves his cock hard and fast up her arse she is screaming argh argh argh as he keeps bear hugging her then leaping up and down sliding his shafts all along her arse hole ring he can feels his shafts sliding back and forth up into her arse hole as he keeps pumping his shafts into her arse hole ring he already had her in his arms then twists his body and turns around and slams her onto the bed landing on top of her he pins her hips to the bed prone boning her he slides his cock up her arse hole then thrashes her she is screaming as he slides his cock up her arse hole ring his shafts pumping her arse hole he re grabs her hips then launches upwards and slides his shafts along her arse hole ring pounding her arse into the bed he does upwards heaves and hard and fast thrusts that have his cock drilling hammering and plugging her arse hole as his shafts slide all along back and forth up into her arse hole she screams argh then comes he keeps sliding his cock up her arse then lifts the back of her knees up pitting her in a foetal position on her side his cock still inside her he pins her right arse cheek holds it down then pumps her arse hole and slides his cock up and down her arse hole ring she is screaming looking back over her right shoulder at him as he spanks her arse cheeks then keeps kneeling there sliding his shafts on and out of her arse hole ring he feels her tight arse hole ring on the top am bottom of his shafts as he keeps sliding his cock along her arse hole ring she is screaming he pumps his shafts along her arse hole ring sliding his cock along her tight arse hole then snatches her throat and chokes her with both hands she makes a choking sound his shafts slide all along her arse hole back and forth into her arse hole ring he keeps sliding and pumping his shafts into her arse hole then rams his cock up her arse pounding her and plugging his erection deep up her arse hole he shoves his cock hard and fast up her tight arse hole then keeps sliding his shafts back and forth along her arse hole ring plugging her arse hole with his cock he can see her eyes rolling back she comes then he releases his hands from her throat at the same time slides his cock up into her arse hole then as he keeps sliding his cock along her arse hole ring he comes he takes his cock out then straddles her pinning her under him he walks forward on his knees then shoves his cock in her mouth then grabs the back of her head with his hands then slides his cock deep down the back of her throat then comes he keeps pumping come into her throat as he holds her hair and head and forces his cock down her throat she gags and coughs groaning as he feels his cock spasm inside her mouth she keeps splattering and choking on his cock as she swallows and gulps he takes his hands off her head then slides his cock out from her lips them he puts his arms down beside her then pushes his body back and gets on top of her then holds then back of her neck with his right hand then brings her lips to his in a passionate tongue kiss he slides his tongue down her throat using his left elbow to pivot off and keep kissing her he open mouth pashes her changes sides then slides his tongue down her throat

Ivan gallops out from the castke straight ahead is a barbarian cart as it comes out in front of him boom he blasts it then watches as it explodes and Ivan swerves around it barbarian come from the forest one throws an axe Ivan ducks it then shoots him with the plasma canon as he is shooting him another barbarian with a sword steps out Ivan aims the plasma canon at him then pulls the trigger boom he blasts him across the ground rockets fly from the tree line as a cart can be seen in the forest Ivan gallops towards it shooting his plasma canon boom it explodes and as a barbarian leaps off it and runs at Ivan with his sword Ivan has to quickly use the plasma canon as a hockey stick and whack him in the chin lifting him up off the ground thru the trees as another barbarian cart is trotting parallel to Ivan thru the trees Ivan watches as they aim the rocket around at him boom Ivan shoots it first and it explodes then he has a dragon above him thru the trees it swoops down and attacks him face first like an eagle Ivan has to flick it off his face then aims the plasma canon at it then boom he blasts it then watches as it burns and crashes Ivan's horse gallops over it whoosh a rocket flies at Ivan he lifts his plasma up and shoots it boom then it causes a massive explosion Ivan covers his face to ride thru it then whack he is hit by a cart and nearly crashes into a tree he hangs on and re corrects his balance then aims his plasma at the cart quickly boom he shoots and it hits the front of the cart the barbarians at the back quickly fire a rocket whoosh Ivan shoots his plasma canon then kaboom the cart explodes he has to take cover around the trees as the rocket explodes around him Ivan can see a mythological creature Ivan lifts the plasma canon up then with one hand takes shots at it boom boom as he turns to go around it the plasma bursts hit it on the head and it catches alight then Ivan turns the horse back around then as it is burning with its head on fire swinging it's huge arms boom Ivan shoots it on the back and it falls on its face he gallops off into the forest only to be fired upon by dragons from behind him whoosh they shoot fire onto the back of his head he gallops faster whipping the reigns as the dragon catches up flapping it's wings Ivan turns back while galloping and shoots boom the dragon hits the ground on fire and crashes into the forest floor as the other one breathes fire at Ivan as well boom Ivan shoots ok and it hits a tree and explodes Ivan keeps galloping a barbarian on horseback with a bow and arrow is blocking the path aiming at him Ivan lifts the plasma canon up with both hands then aims and fires boom the plasma burst fly's towards the barbarians then kaboom it blows him off the horse Ivan has to quickly swerve the horse then a barbarian runs with a spear from the bushes and spears Ivan's horse and he crashes on the path and slides across the bushes he goes to get up when whoosh a rocket fly's above him he stays down then looks thru the forest for the cart arghh the barbarian with the spear runs at Ivan Ivan grabs it with his hand then throws him with it into a tree as he keeps looking around for the cart he can see it coming thru the trees straight at him shooting another rocket whoosh

Ivan runs and leaps behind a tree then gets up as the rocket goes past him and boom he shoots the cart kaboom it explodes then Ivan is surrounded by three dragons all around him boom he shoots the first one then he turns his body his plasma held down between his hip boom he shoots another one the next one bites his body and Ivan has to elbow it away then hits hit on the head with the butt of the plasma canon the pilot takes out his knife then tries to stab Ivan in the neck Ivan blocks it with his plasma canon then reaches up with his left hand and grabs his throat and tears him off the dragon as he is falling onto the ground the dragon turns and leans its head out and bites Ivan in the head Ivan quickly shoves the plasma canon in its mouth to stop him biting him then eye gouged it and pokes its eye out digging his thumb into its eye socket the dragon goes ballistic nearly biting his plasma canon in two Ivan heaves it out of its mouth then smashes it and he hits it over the head then quickly aims it under its head and blows it off a barbarian cart with a mytho-logical creature pulls up barbarians leap up onto the top of its cage then they open it boom Ivan quickly shoots it while it's still in th3 cage then runs up to it then boom he shoots it again and the barbarians above catch alight from the uprising flames Ivan watches as they run and leap off the top on fire boom boom he blasts them then as the creature burns in the cage a rocket gets fired at him whoosh Ivan can see another cart that has wolves on it they release the wolves at the same time shoot a rocket boom Ivan shoots the cart and the cart explodes then as he is shooting the cart the first wolf has bitten onto his shooting arm then as the second one leaps up and bites him in the face Ivan back fists it to the ground he shakes the other one off his right arm then gets his plasma up and boom he shoots one then turns boom he shoots the other one then as Ivan looks up there is a mythological beast that runs towards him then keeps up thru the air and pounces on him Ivan is tackled under it then lifts the plasma canon up boom he blasts it off him then as it is on flames he gets up then boom boom he blasts it into a tree the beast and the tree catches alight whoosh a cart fires rockets at

Ivan then he aims his plasma canon then boom he shoots it and it explodes a barbarian on horseback comes and hacks at Ivan with his sword Ivan has to lift out his axe and block it then boom Ivan blasts him off the horse he holsters the axe then gets up onto the horse then gallops towards the path then as a barbarian on horseback comes from behind him and swings his sword at him Ivan turns back then boom he blasts him another one comes and the barbarian on the back leaps off and tackles Ivan off his horse Ivan flicks him off and he catches onto the ground the other barbarian swerves into Ivan then boom Ivan blasts him with the plasma canon up ahead are wolves that run out onto the path then leap up and attack Ivan's horse and try to bite him Ivan quickly kicks one with his leg then stomps another off then boom he blasts one into the ground the other one has bitten the horses neck and is attacking it Ivan takes out his axe then reaches over and whack he hits it off the horse in the distance is a cart waiting for Ivan whoosh they fire a rocket at him boom Ivan fires his plasma canon at it and it explodes then the cart goes to fire another rocket Ivan lines it up and aims then boom kaboom the cart explodes then Ivan is swung into as a barbarian holds a rope then swings out in front of him he kicks Ivan off his horse and Ivan crashes in the bushes as he gets up the barbarian clubs him in the head and Ivan has to get his balance then left hooks him and right hooks him in the ribs he gets the plasma canon then aims it at him boom the barbarian clubs the plasma canon up in the air and it fires into the trees then Ivan front kicks him backwards then aims again and boom he blasts him he slides across the leaves then as another barbarian jumps from the tree onto Ivan and covers his eyes Ivan runs into a tree then tries to flick him off then at the same time he can hear another one running at him he throw a the one on his back towards the other one then looks up he threw him straight into his spear the barbarian throws the spear then takes out his knife and lunges at Ivan Ivan grabs his wrist then throws him into a tree then kicks him in the back into the tree them takes out his axe and cracks his skull open then has to quickly turn around as a barbarian on horse comes and slices him with a sword Ivan lifts up his axe and blocks him then boom he blasts the plasma canon up and he catches alight and is thrown from the horse Ivan can see a cart escaping then leaps onto the horse then gallops towards it he whips the reigns then hurdles over bushes and chases the cart swerving thru the trees they fire a rocket whoosh Ivan swerves it then it explodes in a tree Ivan catches up to the cart then leaps onto it from the horse then kicks the barbarian about to shoot a rocket in the chest and he flies off the cart as the driver and passenger turn around Ivan goes to aim his plasma and blasts them when they hit a bump in the road and Ivan plasma canon misfires and hits the trees above then the passenger with his sword slices Ivan's plasma canon Ivan swings the plasma canon back the other way and hits the passenger onto the driver and they both fall off the cart a cart comes from behind Ivan shooting rockets whoosh Ivan has to quickly manoeuvre the cart and whip the reigns and steers the cart left the rocket fly's straight past then Ivan slides the rocket and aims at the cart whoosh kaboom the cart explodes Ivan gets to a clearing overlooking the forest he can see on the road below a road block of carts and mythological beasts then whips the reighns and goes towards it then gets back on the rocket then whoosh whoosh he fires two rockets and watches as they fly towards the carts and explode then as the carts fire their rockets whoosh whoosh Ivan shoots back with plasma bursts then steers the cart around the rockets kaboom he hits their carts and they explode then he can see another cart firing rockets whoosh whoosh Ivan aims the plasma canon at then then boom the rockets explode as the barbarian run off the cart and come towards Ivan with weapons drawn Ivan aims his plasma at them boom he blasts one then aims on the other side and boom he blasts the other one then gets to the mythological beast it is on chains when the barbarians release it it runs at Ivan boom he shoots it with the plasma boom it hits it in the head as the barbarians throw spears at Ivan and shoots bows and arrows Ivan has to quickly fire at them boom he shoots one then boom he shoots the other one the mythological beasts on fire comes at Ivan then hits him off the horse Ivan gets up then aims his plasma canon at it the beasts knocks it out from his hands then Ivan takes his axe then pegs it at its head then as the beasts gets angry and swings it's paw at Ivan Ivan dodges it then looks for his plasma the beast is treading on it Ivan goes and shoulder barges it off his weapon then picks it up whack the beast hits Ivan and Ivan slides across the ground then shoots the beast the it gets angry then stomps on Ivan and Ivan has to roll from under it the beast keeps stomping on Ivan then traps his leg under his paw Ivan heaves his leg out then gets up and re aims his plasma canon at the beast and shoots whack the beast hits Ivan and the plasma canon fires the opposite way Ivan turns around then boom he shoots it in the head and it drops on its back Ivan is tackles from behind by a barbarian with a club Ivan's plasma canon goes sliding forwards the barbarian hits Ivan on the top of the head while sitting on him he keeps bashing the back of his head into the ground with the club Ivan reaches behind him then grabs him and throws him forward of him then gets up and stomps on him with his boot then gets the club whack Ivan is tackled by another barbarian he gets up with the club in his hand then hits it over the head of the barbarian that tackled him dropping him to the ground the other barbarian is picking up Ivan's plasma canon then Ivan puts his left foot forward then heaves the club at him pegging it at him it spins thru the air then whack it hits him in the head Ivan snatches the plasma canon back from his hands then elbows him into the ground with the plasma butt dropping him face first Ivan lifts the plasma canon up then boom he shoots him a pack of wolves run at Ivan and a cart shoots a rocket Ivan lifts his plasma canon up then with both are aims at the rocket boom it explodes then boom he shoots the cart then as the wolves attack him he blasts them too boom boom boom he creeps the plasma canon from right to left shooting each one of them individually than as the last one leaps onto Ivan and tackles him backwards then bites him in the face Ivan left hooks it off him it growls them leaps back on him biting him Ivan looks the plasma strap around its throat and chokes it then lifts it up and smashes it into a tree then runs with it and smashes it into another tree he takes the plasma canon then point blank executes it then whack he is tackled into the tree and loses his plasma canon he turns around to see a drop bear Ivan tackles it then smashes it into the ground then gets on top of it then right and left hook punches it into the ground he keeps punching it with both his arms smashing it's head into the ground it stops moving and Ivan keeps punching it in anger after it then looks up a cart runs over him and he feels his body getting trampled on by horses he rolls out from under it then a barbarian jumps on him from the cart Ivan gets up then ouch as him on the air dropping him into the ground grabs the side of the cart then stomps on his head and keeps stomping until one comes from behind him with a sword cornering Ivan between the cart and him Ivan front kicks him back then runs and punches him in the head knocking him back further he stumbles and slides onto his back Ivan does a drop knee into his ribs then punches him in the head takes his sword then goes to impale him when a barbarian on horseback gallops towards him Ivan gets up then clunk metals collide as Ivan swings his sword at him and the barbarian blocks it with his sword Ivan stabs him with his sword then runs in closer then pierces the sword into his chest he falls off the horse as Ivan goes to get on the horse a barbarian is pointing his plasma at him Ivan gallops the horse up then tramples on him with the horse and stomps him into the ground the horse keeps lifting up and down then Ivan can see it's hooves putting dints in his head Ivan Ivan sees a barbarian with a sword running from at him Ivan leaps onto a branch then with both feet kicks him in the head into the ground landing on top of him Ivan grabs his sword then with both hands on the grip he points it down then lifts it up then down and thrusts it into his heart then leaves the sword in goes to get his plasma canon when a barbarian with a crossbow jumps out in front of him and pops up Ivan grabs the crossbow and wrestle him with it up into the air then kicks him in the knee then he buckles to the left Ivan heaves the cross bow from his arms then points it to his forehead then pulls the lever the arrow goes halfway into his head at point blank range Ivan gets the plasma then has to shoot it at a cart coming towards him boom boom the plasma burst hits the cart and it explodes Ivan can see up ahead a barbarian compound then goes towards it he aims the plasma canon and runs with it at the same time from the barbarian fortress walls come the rockets whoosh whoosh Ivan keeps running forward and runs around them then boom he stops and aims at one kaboom it erupts in flames then as Ivan he looks up they are aiming the rocket at him whoosh they fire Ivan runs then leaps towards the wall then takes cover he looks up then as the re aim the rocket at him boom he blasts it then kaboom it explodes he runs along the wall then into an entryway only to be coat hangered by a massive Unic Ivan sweeps his feet and it does do anything to him he goes to get up and the univ kicks him into the wall Ivan his the wall then lifts up his plasma canon then boom he blasts him another one comes and ghetto kos Ivan from the side dropping him Ivan goes to get up then he kicks him in the guts Ivan is lifted up then falls back down as the univ goes to stomp on Ivan Ivan kicks him in the balls the univ laughs then stomps on Ivan Ivan gets up then jumps up and punches him it doesn't do nothing then as the unik goes to punch him Ivan ducks it then left and right punches him the unich just uppercuts Ivan and sends him flying backwards Ivan reaches for a cross bow then lifts it up and shoots him in the eye he screams the goes to remove it Ivan runs and tackles him then gets on top of him and ouch as him in the head washing his head onto the ground then takes the arrow out and shoves it in his other eye then gets up off him he lay screaming and blinded as he goes to get up Ivan kicks him back down then Ivan is tackled by a barbarian he is driven towards the wall in a tackle Ivan reverses the tackle then slams him into the wall then stomps on him between the wall and the ground then as he is knocked out Ivan takes his knife then as the unich is getting up Ivan runs and leaps up then stabs him in the throat whack Ivan is tackled and is on

his back on the ground the barbarian is sitting on top of him
with a knife in his hands his arms back over his head he drives it
into Ivan's skull Ivan moves his head then the barbarian stabs
again Ivan blocks it using both his arms to the him off at the
same time Ivan gets on top of him then takes the knife of him
and goes to stab him when he sees a barbarian holding his
plasma canon at him Ivan frisbees the knife at his head and it
hits him in the neck at the same time he fires boom Ivan ducks
and the plasma burst hits the wall behind him whack Ivan is
tackled onto the ground and a wrestling match starts Ivan gets
on top first then punches his fist into his head the barbarian tries
to kick Ivan off him Ivan keeps punching him in the head then a
wild comes and runs at him sprinting Ivan gets off the barbarian
then uses him as a shield the wolf tears into the barbarians neck
as the barbarian bleeds onto Ivan he pegs him forward then gets
up then boots the wolf in the head it growls and goes to come
back Ivan lines it up then grabs its body and snaps it's neck then
drops it Ivan kicks it again then sees a sword he keeps over picks
up the sword off the ground then baseball swings it and chops
it's head off from the wall above a barbarian runs along it then
leaps down onto Ivan

Then as he keeps down onto Ivan Ivan moves out if the way he
crashes on the ground then Ivan grabs him by the hair then
smashes his head into the wall then takes out his knife then as
he turns around he is attacked by a barbarian with a sword Ivan
blocks it with the knife then kicks him in the knee then as he
screams then goes to line Ivan up with a sword kill Ivan runs in
and shoves the knife into his heart then he yells Ivan twists the
knife around inside then takes his sword from him just as two
barbarians run at Ivan Ivan pegs the knife into one with an axe
them then one with a sword Ivan hits his sword into him clunk
clunk metals keeps colliding as Ivan goes right and left s wings
at him with the sword he defends them then Ivan runs at him
slides him he blocks it with his sword then Ivan elbows him
across the jaw he stumbles to the side Ivan lunges at him then

slides the sword thru his neck then takes at back out then chops his head off Ivan looks up a barbarian leaps off the wall onto him Ivan goes his knee them lifts the sword up and impales him he grabs his sword then turns around and as a barbarian runs at him with his sword Ivan blocks it with his left sword then stabs him with his right sword Ivan runs forward to the next one with a club he swings it at Ivan Ivan dodges the club then with both swords at once he shoves them up into his chest then heaves his sword back out then as a barbarian with a sword comes at him and another one with a club is besides him Ivan takes the one with the sword first and with his sword in his left hand he back hands it across his throat the one with the club hits Ivan in the shoulder as Ivan turns his body then he squares up and blocks the club with his sword then stabs him in the top of the head with the sword leaving it in a barbarian with a cross bow is on the wall pointing it at him Ivan throws the sword it spins thru the air then whack it hits him in the stomach he falls off the wall Ivan scoops up his plasma canon then goes on a rampage he blasts the plasma left and right a barbarian on the wall boom one running at him boom another one coming thru the walk-way boom he keeps blasting them then he can see a barbarian ride a horse up into the entry way then he leans over and tries to slice Ivan Ivan blocks the sword with his plasma canon then boom he shoots him Ivan gets to the stairs a barbarian leaps off the stairs at Ivan and swings his sword around and over his head in mid-air at Ivan Ivan dodges and he falls to the bottom of the stairs as he goes to turn around whack Ivan golf swings his head near off with the plasma canon then runs up the at its and turns straight into a dragon whoosh it breathes fire at Ivan holds its neck the other way and it breathes o to the wall a big flame Ivan grabs its neck under his arm and wrestles it then throws it down the stairs then walks down after it and keeps kicking it down the stairs then gets his plasma canon boom he blasts it and it splatters he goes to turn around and the pilot has a knife Ivan uses the barrel if the plasma to hit it from his hands then runs up the at its with the barrel then shoves it into his guts then lifts him up and throws him over his head with it he slams down the stairs and rolls down them Ivan keeps running up the stairs then two armed barbarians come to the top of them boom Ivan blasts his plasma at the one on the left then the one on the right stabs Ivan with his sword Ivan swings the plasma around and blocks it from hitting him in the head then lifts the plasma canon up with both hands and chokes him onto the wall with it lifting him off his feet and pinning him to the wall and choking him he kicks Ivan in the guts and Ivan drops him then as he goes to left punch Ivan Ivan lifts his left arm and blocks it then grabs him and throws him head first down the stairs he slides head first down them then turns around at the top of the stairs is a mythological beast that blocks the way up Ivan quickly grabs the sword then thrusts it into its heart then as it goes ballistic and hits Ivan Ivan ducks then grabs it by the back and slams it into the wall then trips it's leg and throws it down the stairs he goes to the top of the stairs then runs along the hall only to see two barbarians come around In front of him then they takes their swords up and go to swing at him he blocks one with the plasma then elbows him then smashes the sword from the other ones hands the first one with the sword lunges at Ivan Ivan quickly blocks it with the plasma then headbutts him back then backhand swings the plasma into the other one while aiming the plasma back up and blasting him up the hall the barbarian goes to tackle Ivan into the wall Ivan flicks him off then boom he shoots him Ivan runs up the hall then from above a dragon breathes fire at him whoosh Ivan runs under it then turn a around boom Ivan blasts the dragon then leaps running up the hall then turns he floods it along till he gets to a room full of dragons boom Ivan shoots and they all come after him boom boom Ivan shoots his plasma canon at them kaboom one explodes then as the other ones gather around him Ivan quickly lifts the plasma canon up in both hands then aims and shoots boom he keeps shooting them one runs at him and bites him Ivan blasts it in the head boom it explodes then as the other one bites his plasma Ivan misfires and just the wall boom he misfires again then as another dragon comes he aims at it boom he misfires into it killing it as he keeps wrestling with the other one whoosh they fire rockets from the wall at him Ivan is wrestling with the dragon kaboom the rocket hits the dragon then it explodes Ivan keeps firing his plasma at the dragons then he shoots up at the wall whoosh the fire a rocket boom Ivan fires back then kaboom the wall catches alight and a barbarian runs and jumps on Ivan Ivan is wrestling the dragon with the barbarian on his back Ivan runs forward then slams the dragon into the wall it releases his plasma then Ivan heaves the plasma over his shoulder and knocks the barbarian off then boom he shoots the dragon then takes off he sprints thru the fortress then can see all their weapons he quickly kick a the crates over then boom he burns them with the plasma then as he is doing that barbarian comes from behind him with a sword and swings it at Ivan Ivan hits him with the plasma on the neck and drops him to his knees Ivan lifts him up then heaves him one handed into the fire then leaves the weapons room he looks on the next room and can see all dragons everywhere young ones then as the passage way is blocked off by barbarians Ivan jumps on the cages then opens them the dragons run out to wards the barbarians and starts to bite and eat them Ivan waits for them then runs out between them and goes down the hall he looks back to see them all getting attacked from their own dragons Ivan runs along the wall then leaps onto crates then gets up onto the wall and runs along it from the top wall he can see the barbarians have the exit surrounded by carts then on the far roof is a rocket Ivan leaps over to it then whoosh he aims at the cart below kaboom it goes up in flames and explodes along the wall and rapidly descends he gets to another cart that aims it rocket at Ivan whoosh boom Ivan fires at it as well then kaboom the cart explodes Ivan runs down the wall then leaps across in mid-air and crashes into courtyard he runs towards the entry way then turns back boom he shoots a cart and it explodes from a plasma burst Ivan runs out towards the forest then looks back only to be lifted up by a dragon and pilot Ivan's feet go off the ground as the dragon drops him to the ground Ivan slides back and hits the ground hard then goes to get back up the dragon stomps on him Ivan smashes the plasma canon into its feet and legs keeping its claws and talons away from piercing his body he keeps wrestling with his the dragon breathes fire at Ivan then boom Ivan blasts it with his plasma canon then the pilot leaps onto Ivan and tackles him Ivan gets up then with the side of the plasma canon slams it across his head then again he keeps smashing him with the plasma canon then stomps on him whack Ivan is tackled by a unich and a wrestling match erupts Ivan gets on top of him then with the plasma canon butt slams it into his face then with the plasma in both hands he lifts it straight up then smashes him in the head the unich knees Ivan off if him and Ivan goes flying as he goes to get up and turn around

As he goes up to turn around and attack him Ivan is lifted up by another one and hurled thru the air he gets up then goes to fire his plasma one kicks his plasma away then Ivan touches him in the stomach it doesn't do anything the unich punches Ivan and he drops he gets back up then Ivan tackles him and drops him onto the ground then with the plasma canon belts it into his head and keeps smashing him he stops moving then Ivan gets up the other one is running at him Ivan runs at him then with the plasma canon as a baseball bat he slams it into his side arghh he yells Ivan lifts the plasma up over his head then whack he belts his knee then as he is buckled to one side Ivan upper cuts the plasma up into his head then drops him Ivan lunges at him then with his plasma canon up over his head he keeps whacking him in the face with it then stands up he can see the forest the fortress burns in the background he runs off into the forest then whack a barbarian with a club stands out onto the path a hits him Ivan lifts the p plasma canon up and blocks it then front kicks him away he falls in the bushes Ivan executes him as another barbarian leaps over bushes running at him with a sword Ivan blocks it then with both hands uppercuts the plasma barrel into his guts then elbows him then smashes him with the plasma canon a barbarian on horse with a pet dragon on his shoulder releases it at Ivan it fly's at him and Ivan is tackled by it Ivan grabs it then runs with it into a tree and smashes it into the tree then as it drops he stomps on it and keeps stomping on it the barbarian on the horse takes out his cross bow then fires it at Ivan Ivan uses the tree as cover then runs out and leaps up grabs the cross bow then heaves him off the horse then smashes him with the cross bow knocking him out he keeps onto the horse then gallops off into the forest after some time he sees company from behind him on horseback are several barbarian that have weapons Ivan has to ride and shoot at the same time boom he looks back as the plasma blasts hits a barbarian on horseback he explodes then as Ivan keeps galloping and aiming backwards boom he aims at a barbarian about to spear him he catches alight from the plasma bursts then hits a tree Ivan quickly looks back and forward then as the oath turns up ahead he quickly takes an eight hand then as the barbarians go left they can be seen thru the trees Ivan shoots the trees boom the plasma blasts hits the barbarians direct and it explodes then Ivan looks ahead a barbarian with a bow and arrow comes out into the path and goes to fire boom Ivan quickly fires first then turns his head as the arrows quickly scrapes past him he swerves the flaming corpse then whips the reigns then as the oath goes back into two a barbarian on horseback gallops at Ivan with his sword and swerves into him Ivan back hands the plasma canon into his sword and disarms him then Ivan swerves into him and whack he back hands the plasma into his head smashing him off the horse then as the other barbarian gallops into Ivan boom he quickly turns around blasting him then he explodes Ivan takes up the path and then gets back to the road towards the kingdom when a cart of barbarians comes from behind him shooting rockets whoosh boom Ivan shoots back kaboom the rocket his Ivan's horse an she is doing off the road and slides off into the bushes then down the slope as be goes to get up and run up and shoot them they are already off and are running at him with weapons he leans to the right then whips the plasma canon into a barbarians head smashing him to the ground then juggles his plasma canon up into his arm to shoot it one handed across at a barbarians running at him with a sword boom he aims and shoots and blasts the barbarian he swerves the burning cart then keeps galloping after some time he gets back to the castle then runs upstairs then the queen is in the bath when he walks in her dripping wet from the bath kissing her at the same time he takes her from the bathroom she grabs a towel from a hanger on the way and quickly fires herself on his shoulder before he throws her on the bed then gets on top of her then parts her legs open then with his fingers spreads her vagina lips then licks her clit he uses his top of his tongue to slide up her clit then back down over it then keeps licking her clit up and down then as she moans he keeps licking her clit and re parts her pussy lips then uses his tongue to slide up and down her clit she keeps moaning as he puts her clit between his lips then licks the top of it with his tongue then re parts her pussy lips spreading them then licks her clit up and down she keeps moaning the starts to move her body and does jolts he can see her body shake then she moans he keeps licking her clit then shoves his tongue up her vagina then twists and turns his tongue up inside her pussy shoving his tongue up her vagina as far as he can before re parting her pussy lips and licking her clit he slides his tongue up and down her clit then can see how wet her pussy is as she keeps moaning and he licks her clit with his tongue he keeps licking her enflamed clit re parting her vagina lips he pulls them right back then her clit pops out he licks it with his tongue up and down as she lets out a loud passionate moan he licks her clit with his tongue then she thrusts around and lets out a scream he has to hold her down by her legs with his hands and arms as she keeps moving and moaning he slides his tongue up and down then she lets out a scream then he licks her clit up and down till she screams argh then comes he keeps licking her clit up and down after she has come then she keeps screaming he gets up on top of her quickly then slides his stiff cock up her wet pussy and can feel his cock go boiling hot from her hot juicy pussy he feels his knob almost burn off from his hot her vagina is inside then as he pumps his cock upwards into her wet vagina he feels his shafts sliding along her tight vagina ring his cock feels like he scraping her vagina ring she keeps screaming he uses his hips to pump his cock in and out of her vagina he keeps sliding his shafts all along her vagina ring then pounds his cock up deep up into her vagina thrusting upwards he stiffens his cock then grates and tears her vagina ring as he thrashes her she screams argh then comes he slides his shafts all back and forth along her vagina ring then rams her pussy into the bed with hard and fast upwards heaves he feels his girth pounding her vagina ring and his knob smacking her cervix she keeps screaming then he grabs her hips and smashes his cock up her vagina pumping his shafts back and forth along her vagina ring he keeps pounding her pussy with his cock she keeps screaming oh my god he is plugging her vagina with upwards heaves his cock slides up into her pussy he can feel her vagina leak then his cock glides back and forth along her vagina ring he keeps pumping his cock up her vagina he lunges upwards and his cock slides deep up inside her vagina he keeps slamming his cock up her pussy she screams argh then comes he keeps banging her pussy his shafts sliding all along her vagina ring back and forth as she keeps screaming he does hard and fast upwards thrusts and rams her pussy into the bed he grabs her hips then smashes his cock up her vagina then pumps his shafts hard and fast along her vagina ring launching upwards he spears her vagina with his pole sliding his shafts back and forth along her pussy ring she screams argh then comes he feels his shafts sliding and scraping her vagina ring he turns her over then she goes on all fours and is screaming as he kneels there and slides his cock up into her vagina he feels his top shafts sliding in and out of her vagina as he keeps pumping his cock up into her vagina from behind spanking her she screams ouch then he places his hands on her hips then slides his cock in deep up into her tight wet vagina his girth sliding back and forth along her vagina ring she screams argh then comes he is sliding his shafts back and forth along her vagina ring then spanks her again making a loud slapping sound as she screams ouch he keeps sliding his cock up her vagina with hard and fast upwards heaves he plugs his stiff cock up her vagina then pumps her hard and fast with rapid intense upwards heaves that smash his girth into her pussy ring she screams as he keeps ploughing her from behind and sliding his shafts along her vagina ring feels his side shafts threading and grating her vagina as his erect cock slams in and out of her vagina ring he pumps blood into his cock then feels his shafts expand and stretch her vagina ring as she screams argh then comes whack ouch she screams as he spanks her arse cheek then holds her hips and pumps his cock up into her vagina sliding his shafts back and forth along her vagina ring he slides his cock deep up inside her pussy she keeps screaming then he steps off the bed and slides her across the side by her hips then holds her hips while he slams his cock into her arse hole then slides his shafts back and forth along her arse hole ring he keeps sliding his cock up her arse hole ring and feels his girth sliding back and forth along her arse hole ring he keeps sliding his shafts up into her tight arse hole he can feel his shafts sliding back and forth along her arse hole ring he keeps pumping her then grabs her hips and thrashes her arse hole ring with his bonor slamming his whole cock deep up into her tight arse hole and pumping her arse hole with hard and fast upwards thrusts jamming his cock deep up inside her arse hole he belts her arse cheek with his hand then re grabs her and punishes her arse hole ring with his girth pounding her arse hole with hard and fast upwards thrusts rammimg her with his cock going deep up inside her tight arse hole ring he drills his cock up her arse hole and keeps pumping his cock deep into her arse hole ring he slides his shafts all back and firth along her arse hole and lunges upwards and pumps his cock deep and hard up her arse hole ring she screams argh then comes he keeps sliding his shafts all along her arse hole ring and rams her arse hole with deep upwards thrusts he lunges his whole cock deep up into her tight arse hole she keeps screaming he pounds her arse hole ring with his shafts then slides his girth back and forth along her arse hole ring whack he belts her arse then keeps sliding his cock back and forth along her arse hole ring with hard and fast upwards thrusts he rams slams and bangs her tight arse hole ring then slides his cock back and forth all along her arse hole she screams argh argh argh as he kneels there his hands on her hips sliding his cock hard and fast along her arse hole ring with rapid intense slides he pumps his cock up her arse hole she screams argh then comes he keeps sliding his shafts long her arse hole ring then puts his hand on her right arse cheeks then pushes her onto her back then chokes her into the bed then slides his cock up her arse hole then keeps sliding his shafts back and forth along her arse hole ring as he chokes her and she makes a choking sound he feels his cock sliding along her arse hole ring he keeps pounding his cock into her arse hole and slamming his erection deep up into her arse hole ring pumping her arse hole into the bed with rapid hard and fast downwards thrusts slamming his cock up her arse hole and sliding his shafts back and forth along her arse hole ring her eyes roll back as she comes he takes his hands off her throat as she gasps for air then he slides his cock up her arse with hard and fast penetrative thrust she screams as he keeps pumping his cock up her arse he holds her hips and thrashes her arse hole ring with his shafts she keeps screaming as he pins her down to the bed and is pumping her arse hole with his cock sliding his cock back and forth along her arse hole ring then he slams his girth I to her arse hole she scram then he pins her back into the bed holding the back of her knees with his hands then drills his cock into her arse hole scraping her arse hole ring as his girth slams deep into her arse hole he pumps his cock hard and fast up her tight arse hole she keeps screaming as he does downwards thrusts and shoves his cock deep into her are whole sliding his shafts back and forth along her arse hole ring he keeps plugging her arse hole with his shafts sliding them back and forth along her whole arse hole ring she screams then he snatches her throat and chokes her into the bed then keeps pounding his cock into her arse hole she is choking as his hands are around her throat as he pins her down to the bed and slides his shafts back and forth along her arse hole ring then feels his cock slides deep up into her arse hole ring her eyes roll back and she comes he takes his hand off her throat then she gasps for air inhaling as he holds her hips and slides his cock back and forth along her arse hole ring he keeps sliding his shafts all along her tight arse hole ring then takes his cock out and comes on her face and neck

The queen is being annoying and demanding Ivan's attention while he reading maps she throws a tantrum then he links it he gets up out from the bed and runs over to her she runs away he grabs her under her arm then drags her across the room kicking and screaming she keeps bitch slapping him all over his head and body as he holds her up to the end of the bed then gets the ropes ready she sprints off and he looks the rope around her neck and clotheslines her then drags her back across the floor choking her he keeps his hand around the rope on her neck in his left hand while with his right he undies the knot she is on her arse choking up against his leg he looks down it her hand on her neck trying to loosen it he releases his hand quickly and she gasps for air then he keeps rope around her neck as she screams and tries to get up and run he holds her under his arm then gets her wrist and with great difficulty he snatches her wrist lifts her up in the air then ties her up she upper cuts him in the stomach with her other hand he does feel it then gets her other wrist then ties that up to the beam then let's her go she is hanging by the arms backwards facing the bed tied up to the top of the bed frame screaming and yelling he walks up to her then puts a blindfold on her then cringes at her ear piercing wails then gags her mouth as well can still hear her screaming thru the gag he lifts her up on his arms then runs her clit then holds her up by her legs and keeps rubbing her clit hard and rough with up down slides of his fingers he does it real going she is screaming as he keeps running her clit up and down while holding her up she thrusts and starts to orgasm he slides his fingers and runs her clit up and down with his index and middle fingers she keeps thrust-ing and orgasming in his arms then he can hear her screaming thru the gag as he runs her clit to organs she keeps thrusting and screaming her whole body tenses as she comes he leaves her then goes to the draw then crack he whips her back he keeps whipping her back and can hear her muffled screams as he whips her arse cheeks her back and her upper thighs with the whip she dangles around screaming he walks up to her then takes the gag off argh she's screaming he lifts the whip back over his head then throws his arm forward crack arghh she screams he keeps whipping her and she keeps screaming her whole back purple and red she has lines everywhere as she keeps screaming he feels her lines and with his palms feels all the abrasions the whip has left she is screaming kicking and thrusting trying to kick him where she is then he grabs her legs then ties them up near the ceiling to the top of the bed frame them holds the whip under hand then whips her back doing fast little uppercuts that have the whip cracking on her back and arse cheek then whips it around and up into her pussy she screams argh that hurts stop it he keeps whipping her pussy and she screams and thrusts around screaming no stop it it hurts be just keeps doing it and listens to her screaming argh argh argh with each upwards whip he flicks his hand as the whip goes straight up into her vagina between her open legs he whips her pussy she keeps screaming then he unties her arse and she falls down her legs and ankles tied to the bed frame as she lay hanging upside down facing away from the bed he takes her blindfold told off she is screaming looking at him upside down hanging he is looking at her fresh skin and how he wants to turn it purple and scratched she is screaming let me go and trying to free herself and is thrusting and wiggling to get free from the rope bindings he watches her try her best then whips her breasts then she screams as he leaves a massive set my if lash marks straight across her breasts and nipples she is screaming argh argh argh the whole time and starts thrusting and moving saying release me argh it hurts he walls up to her then looks at the whip marks she spits on him then screams let me go he looks down at her and she looks down at him by the look in his eyes she can tell it's no use and just goes back to screaming and trying to free herself from the bindings he steps back then quickly whips her breasts argh argh she screams argh she keeps screaming argh then he whips her again argh she thrusts around screaming arghh it hurts stop it please stop it he pulls her up by the hair then tongue kisses her and shoves his tongue down her throat he feels a sharp pain as she bites his tongue he lets go of her head and she swings backwards and slams her head on the mattress he whip a h we straight away and goes off lifting his arm back he throws it forward and the whip hits her breasts and she screams stop it argh it hurts please stop it argh she screams as he whips her breasts with the whip then listens as she screams the castle down he can see her breasts he left red abstract all over them stretches and lines everywhere she is screaming and thrusting up and down the while time constantly screaming argh he whips her argh he keeps whipping her and she screams argh argh argh with each whip he tells her to shut up then keeps whipping her breasts she screams louder argh then he walks over to her then squats and looks at her then tells her this is her fault that she did this to herself she spits at him then he chokes her then spits at her his bloodied mouth from her biting his lip leaves a red slime and spit across her face he wipes it off using her hair then tells her to be quite she is annoying then whips her vagina with the whip argh she screams that hurts he looks and then does it again ouch she screams not there anywhere b argh he whips her before she could finish dictating to him he keeps whipping her vagina lifting his arm back over his head he slams the whip down and whips her vagina leaving lashes all around her set pussy he can see the scratches on her vagina the whip left as she just scream the whole time argh argh argh after every whip she screams he keeps whipping her then squats down beside her on the other side and talks to her he tells her if she doesn't stop screaming everytime he whips her he will never stop then asks her is she understands she nods her head back and forth in appliance he whips her hard and right on the pussy she screams he shakes his head at her then whips her again argh she screams he keeps whipping her then she makes muffled screams as he is whipping her he can see her closing her mouth and holding back the pain as he keeps whipping her she makes more muffled screams then he whips her harder on the breasts and she screams he shakes his head at her then just keeps whipping her hard and fast across her breasts she is screaming and he keeps telling her with each whip crack argh what crack argh her whips her again did he tells her then crack he whips her again tell you then whips her hard and she screams argh her screams muffle and she doesn't make any noise he keeps whipping her only can hear her holding her breath he whips her vagina then her breasts she holds her breath and he can hear her holding back the screams crack he whips her breasts and he looks at her she is holding back the screams she is looking at him saying please stop it it hurts he is humming at the same time thinking about some barbarian dragon that got away and is taking it out on her he looks down at her while he is still whipping her she has stopped screaming as he started to whip her softly not paying attention he whips her properly argh she screams and she just starts screaming again he whips her vagina argh she screams he whips her breasts argh it hurts please stop he keeps whipping her arse she keeps screaming them he walks over to her and tells her one more time I explain it to you you dumb fucken snob queen cunt he grabs her by the hair the pulls her ear up to talk into it then tells her make it simple stops fucken making noise the more noise you make the more it's going to hurt you i got all the time in the world then he drops her head re picks her up by the hair then kisses her then goes back and starts to whip her again he starts off extremely hard crack argh he hits her vagina and she screams arghh he keeps whipping her then and shaking his head at her as she screams in pain he whips her vagina with hard and fast whips the whip cracking on her vagina making red lash marks and lines all across her pretty vagina she stops screaming and naked a muffled held back whining sound holding back her scream he nods his head to her like good girl then crack he whips the whip and cracks her vagina then can't hear her screaming only a whining sound he whips her again crack he whips her hard then looks at her still no screams he whips her breast argh she screams loudly he shakes his head at her then keeps whipping her breasts argh argh she screams then he puts his left foot forward and with all his strength he thrusts the whip into her breasts she doesn't scream he does it again as hard as he can front foot forward lays onto her crack she holds back the screams sounding like a boiling kettle he keeps whipping her then she is shaking and holding back the screams good girl he thinks to himself on the way to the her down he can see the relief in her eyes as he walks over then he can't resist he leans forward with his left foot then throws his arm back them forward and whips her again hard and deep crack them looks at her face she doesn't say anything he walks over to her then unties her then she goes into the bed he places her in front of him as if he were setting a table her legs spread then leaps up into her with his erection then lunges upwards up the bed his knob smashes into her wet pussy lips and his shafts slides up her vagina as his knob slams into her cervix he keeps launching upwards and is lifting her gradually to the top of the bed by pounding her up the bed he is heaving his cock deep up inside her vagina she is screaming he is humping her rough with deep pounding thrusts he lifts her up further up the bed using his girth to stretch her vagina ring and lift her towards the bed head he keeps thrusting his cock up her vagina and can feel his Cam feel how boiling hot and wet she is his cock almost making a splash as he plugs it into her dripping wet vagina he keeps smashing his erection deep into her tight pussy and pounding her arse cheeks with his body and slamming them into the bed he can see the bedhead then lifts her up a bit more with his cock thrusting up inside her at the same time lifting her up the bed then grabs the bedhead then smiles at her she is screaming looking up at him he heaves his whole body forward using the bedhead to force g is cock deep and hard up into her vagina smashing his shafts and firth into her vagina ring by slamming his stiff cock deep up inside her wet vagina he feels her leak and then as she screams ah ah ah he stiffens his cock then thrashes her she orgasms then he keeps pumping his pole up her vagina then re grabs the bedhead then rams her wildly thrusting his whole body he thrashes his cock up deep and rough into her vagina she keeps screaming then he lets go of the bed head then drops his arms and hands around her throat and chokes her into the bed then looks at her making a choking sound then down wards thrusts and pounds he slams his erection deep and hard into her pussy she is shuddering her whole body with each down wards thrust he pounds her pussy into the bed then changes angle a and slides his shafts upwards along her vagina ring slamming his shafts deep up into her vagina he keeps his arms out straight and around her throat choking her into the mattress as he keeps drilling pounding and plugging her tight wet pussy with his stiff cock he slides his shafts all back and forth along her vagina ring then she tenses her whole body and comes he takes his arms and hands off her throat then puts his palm behind the back of her neck then lifts her lisp up to his and open mouth kisses her passionately at the same time he grabs her in a bear hug then drills his cock into her vagina he scrapes his veiny top shaft all up and down her upper vagina ring she is screaming as he shoves his top shaft back and forth up and down grating her vagina ring then keeps being rough and slamming his cock deep up inside her pussy with upwards heaves he slams his girth into her vagina ring and she screams argh then comes then keeps sliding his shafts all up along her vagina ring pounding her pussy into the bed he shoves his cock hard and fast up her pussy she is screaming then he lifts her up and throws her into the bedhead she lands holding the bedhead then braces herself argh she screams as he shoves his pole up her arse then slides his shafts back and forth along her arse hole ring she keeps screaming as his kneels there sliding his shafts all up and down along her arse hole ring he feels his shaft threading on and out of her arse hole as he vibrates his cock back and forth rapidly all up and down her arse hole ring then slams his girth up her arse hole and she screams he slides his girth back and forth into her arse hole then hold a her hips and slides his shafts all up and down along her arse hole then slides his whole cock from knob to shafts to girth along her arse hole ring back he feels his shafts sliding up her arse hole she keeps screaming as he just a kneels there and keeps sliding his cock and shafts up her arse hole he stands up as she goes down onto her forearms and elbows he grabs the bedhead then diagonally spears her arse hole with his cock jamming his pole deep into her arse hole he pounds her arse hole ring and keeps slamming his whole cock deep into her arse hole she is screaming looking up over her shoulder as he slams her into the bed she puts her palms up on the bedhead and holds on screaming as he slams his erection diagonally into her arse hole ring and does hard and fast thrusts his balls slapping on her pussy as he slams her arse hole with his girth plugging her arse hole ring with his cock he keeps smashing her arse hole with his shafts and girth pounding her into the bedhead she is screaming her head down he keeps his cock pumping her arse hole then as he stiffens his erection he threads grates and scrapes her tight arse hole ring with his veiny throbbing cock he slides his shafts back and forth into her arse hole she screams argh then comes he keeps drilling and pumping her arse hole then lifts her up in a headlock and slams her into the wall and chokes her then keeps shoving his cock up into her arse hole ring she is making a choking sound as he keeps his firearm wrapped around her throat and is sliding his cock up her arse hole ring he thrusts upwards and shoves his cock deep up into her arse hole with hard and fast upwards heaves he launches his girth into her arse hole ring pounding her arse hole with his cock then slides his shafts all up along her arse hole he feels his girth pounding her arse hole as he keeps sliding his cock up her arse hole she comes he pulls his arm away and she gasps for air inhaling then screaming as he pushes her body into the wall with both his hands then holds her hips then shoves his cock up her arse hole he feels his shafts sliding up into her arse hole and keeps pumping his cock up her arse hole as she screams he slides his shafts up along her arse hole then keeps pumping and sliding his cock up into her arse hole ring he shoves his cock straight up her arse e hole then re grabs her hips and thrashes her arse hole ring his shafts sliding up her arse hole he keeps spitting on her arse hole then slides his shafts up and down deep up her arse hole with upwards heaves he slides his cock up her arse hole then she comes he keeps pumping her arse hole with hard and fast upwards heaves then slides his shafts all along her arse hole ring he lifts her up then turns around with her then falls straight on top of her onto the bed argh she screams as he slides his cock all up along her arse hole ring then pumps his cock up her arse hole and pounds her arse hole into the bed ramming his cock deep and hard up her arse she keeps screaming he thrusts up and down his cock drilling her arse hole he keeps prone boning her and sliding his cock up her arse hole then pounds and slams his cock straight up her arse hole ring she screams argh then comes he keeps pumping his shafts along her arse hole ring them slides his shafts back and forth along her arse hole stimulating his knob and shafts he puts her up into doggy then heaves his cock up her arse hole and thrusts back and forth his cock drilling her arse hole from behind then as he thrashes her and rams her with hard and fast up the arse pumps he takes his cock out then comes on her back and on her arse hole he pushes her onto her back then gets on top of her then holds her by the cheeks and shoves his tongue down her throat and kisses her then puts his hand behind the back of her neck pulls her lips to his and slides his tongue down her throat and kisses her passionately as she huffs and puffs panting he keeps kissing her with open mouth tongue kisses then gets her by the back of the neck then she down outs her head into his cock then he lays back and feels her mouth suck on his cock his cock stays hard then as she keeps sucking his cock he grabs her hips and throws her body into the bed then gets on top of her pints his bonor down then slides it up her arse then holds her by the back of her knees then pumps her he starts of hard and fast slamming his cock into her arse hole and pounding her arse hole ring then goes vertical upwards heaves and slides his cock all up and down along her arse hole she keeps screaming as he keeps sliding his cock up and along her arse hole ring he keeps pumping her arse hole then chokes her into the bed she makes a choking sound then he holds her down with his arms out and straight his hands around her neck as he slides his cock up into her arse hole he thrusts upwards and shoves his cock deep and hard up her arse hole then keeps plugging his cock up her arse hole thrashing her arse hole ring with his stiff cock hammering deep up her arse hole he stuffs his erection up her arse then keeps sliding his shafts along her arse hole her eyes roll back and she comes then he take his hands off her throat and she gasps for air then screams as he keeps pumping his cock up her arse sliding his cock up her arse hole ring with back and forth pumps he keeps sliding his cock up her arse hole she screams argh then comes he keeps sliding his cock up her arse hole then uses his shafts to slide all up and down her arse hole he shoves his cock deep up her are whole then thrashes her pounding her arse hole sliding his shafts all along her arse hole ring then he takes his cock out then shoves it in her mouth she gags then he holds her by the back of the head and slides his cock deep down the back if her throat and comes she keeps gagging and coughing splattering as he shoots and pumps come into her mouth then keeps forcing his cock down the back of her throat she swallows then coughs then splatters he keeps his hands on the back of her head forcing his cock deep down her throat as she gulps he takes his hands off her head then gets on top of her and kisses her and open mouth pashes her sliding his tongue down her throat he puts his hand on the back of her neck and keeps open mouth tongue kissing her then changes side and slides his tongue in her throat and keeps groping her

Ivan hears the queen making noise again then runs into the bathroom then drags her by the hair across the room she is kicking and screaming as he throws her onto the lounge then whacks her arse cheek with his hand she screams as he keeps belting her arse cheek and lifting his arm back and then swinging it forward and spanking her he can see the red blush marks it leaves them keeps spanking her she is screaming saying stop argh he hits her harder he keeps spanking her arse cheek then she screams stop it stop it please stop whack he hits her argh she screams as she doesn't get to finish before he wraps his hand across her arse cheek then he pushes her down over the top of the lounge then whack he spanks her arse she screams stop it Ivan please stop it it hurts whack he keeps spanking her then she screams ouch he gets her by the hair then pulls her head down then whack he spanks her arse cheek and she screams he keeps pulling her by the hair and spanking her then grabs her roots then holds her there then whack he belts her arse cheek then he gets a huge book then whacks her with it argh she screams as he keeps smacking her with the book then just gets the whip and lifts her dress up and over off her head grabs the belt and ties her wrist up to the corner post if the bed she stands there as he whips her back she thrusts into the pole screaming them crack he whips her back again she is thrusting up and down screaming argh it hurts and stops it please stop it it hurts crack he whips her arse and she jumps up clenching her arse cheeks together screaming ouch it hurts stop it as she tries to look around she can't she is tied up to the corner post screaming her head off argh argh she screams as he keeps whipping her he walks up to her then puts his palm on her cuts and lashes then slides his hand on it feeling it she is screaming and trying to punch and kick him away using all her strength to thrust left and right and try and break the corner post she screams argh with each whip he puts lashes all across her back then puts the whip up over his head then steps forward and whips her with all his strength she screams no stop it please it hurts crack argh she keeps screaming as he whips her arse and back to shreds red lines criss cross her whole backside and back as he walks up to her then locks her ankle out her legs open wide as he bends his legs gets his cock up and under her vagina then vertically slides his cock up into her vagina then as she screams he holds her hips and slides his shafts up into her pussy then pumps her with his shafts sliding all along her vagina she is screaming tied to the corner post of the bed frame he is sliding his shafts back and forward up into her vagina with rapid hard and fast pumps he get a his cock to slide along her vagina ring he keeps pumping his shafts up into her pussy then feels her vagina leak and a warm sensation comes over his knob and shafts as her pussy juices flow around his cock and he slides his cock faster up into her vagina she keeps screaming as his shaft goes vertically up her vagina and slides back and forth along her vagina ring stimulating his cock he feels his shafts scraping her vagina ring and grating and threading her vagina walls he keeps stiffening his cock then as his cock throbs and gets harder he feels it stretch her vagina ring she screams as he slides his stiff shafts up into her vagina ring then pumps his cock back and forth along her vagina ring she is screaming ah ah ah with each vertical pump he slides his cock all along her vagina ring she keeps screaming then as he keeps rocking his shafts back and forth along her vagina ring she screams argh then comes he slides his shafts up her vagina then holds her hips and thrashes her pounding his cock deep and hard up her tight wet vagina he pumps his cock deeper and harder vertically up her pussy she is screaming as he rams his cock deep up into her vagina he feels his cock threading her vagina as his girth pounds into her vagina ring he shoves his whole cock straight up into her vagina she screams argh then comes he keeps sliding his shafts all up and along her pussy then launches his erection deep up into her pussy with hard and fast upwards heaves he buries his cock up her pussy then lunges upwards and heaves his stiff pole up deep into her vagina she keeps screaming as he slides his shafts up onto her pussy then he thrashes her smashing her from behind be pounds his cock vertically up her tight vagina she scream argh then comes he keeps ramming her pussy lifting her left leg up he gets up and under her then vertically thrusts his cock deep up her vagina she screams as he keeps pounding her pussy with his cock and shoves his erection hard and fast up her arse into her vagina he slides his shafts up her vagina then pounds her pussy with upwards heaves he plugs her vagina with his stiff hard cock then launches upwards and slides his shafts all along her vagina ring as she screams argh then comes he keeps sliding his shafts up her pussy then whack ouch he belts her arse cheek then holds her hips and pumps his cock up her vagina with hard and fast upwards heaves he rams his cock up her vagina he re grabs her hips and thrashes her she is screaming argh argh argh as he smashes his cock up her pussy she keeps and her vagina wettens then he glides his shafts along her vagina ring and slams his cock up deep up into her vagina as she screams argh then comes he keeps sliding his shafts up into her vagina as she screams oh my god he slides his shafts up into her vagina then keeps sliding his shafts all along and up her pussy ring he unties her hands then pushes her onto the bed she gets up on all fours then he holds her hips then slides his shaft back and forth up into her pussy he keeps thrusting and pounding hammering his cock deep up inside her vagina as she screams he feels his knob hitting her cervix as he holds her by the hips then pounds his cock up her pussy and slides his shafts up onto her wet tight vagina he keeps pumping his cock up her vagina then lunges upwards and spears her vagina she screams argh argh argh then argh as she comes he keeps pounding her vagina his girth smashes into her vagina ring and his cock slides up her vagina she keeps screaming then he grabs her hips and thrashes his cock up her pussy with deep upwards heaves he plugs her vagina with his cock ouch she screams as he spanks her then keeps pumping her pussy with his shafts sliding up into her vagina ring he heaves her legs off the bed and she falls on her knees over the side of the mattress then he slides his cock up her arse then pumps his shafts in and out of her arse hole ring she screams argh then he keeps sliding his cock up her arse and shoves his girth into her arse hole ring argh she screams as he slides his shaft up her arse hole then holds her hips and thrashes her arse hole ring with his cock his girth pounds her arse hole ring and he feels his shafts slide all along her arse hole ring as she screams argh the comes he is pounding her arse hole ring with his girth then heaves his erection straight up her tight arse hole with hard and fast upwards heaves he shoves his cock deep up into her arse hole drilling his cock up her arse hole ring she screams argh argh argh with each upwards heave and hard and fast upwards thrust he slams his shafts up her arse hole she keeps screaming he pounds his cock up into her arse hole ramming her with hard and fast deep upwards thrusts then chokes her with his hands around her throat she makes a choking sound as he pounds her arse hole ring with his girth and keeps thrashing her with hard and fast upwards heaves that slide his cock deep up into her arse hole he keeps sliding his shafts up her arse hole then he feels his girth stretch her arse hole ring as he does vertical upwards heaves that have his girth pounding her arse hole ring she comes then he lets go of her throat and she gasps for air coughs then she screams as he slides his shafts back and forth along her arse hole ring then keeps plugging her arse hole with his cock he lifts her up then throws her into the bed and he hold a her hips then slides his shafts back and forth along her arse hole then spits on her arse and keeps sliding his shafts all along her arse hole ring with hard and fast upward heaves he plugs his cock up her arse hole she keels screaming as he slides his shafts up into her arse hole she screams argh then comes he feels his cock sliding back and forth along her arse hole then lunges upwards and stiffens his erection the tears her arse hole ring with his cock sliding straight up her arse hole he keeps pumping her then runs and heaves his cock straight up her tight arse hole as she screams yes oh yes he thrashes her pumping his cock up her arse hole he slams his bonor deep up into her arse hole then does rapid hard and fast upwards heaves then spanks her arse cheek with his hand then re braces her by the hips and thrashes her with hard and fast upwards heaves he plugs her arse hole ring with his cock and keeps pumping her arse hole with deep upwards heaves he throws her to the window then as she stands there and poses lifting her hands up and opening her legs he runs up and shoves his cock straight back up her arse she screams as he holds her hips then pounds her she is screaming as his cock slides all along her arse hole ring he keeps pumping her with hard and fast up-wards thrusts then feels his cock go deep up inside her arse hole she screams argh argh argh as she puts her palms on the window and he stands behind her pumping his cock up her arse hole she screams argh then comes he keeps sliding his cock up her arse hole then shoves his girth deep up her arse hole and rams his cock up her arse then grabs her in a headlock and chokes her with his forearm across her throat she makes a choking sound as he slides his shafts in and out of her arse hole then heaves his cock up her with hard and fast thrusts he smashes his erection up her arse hole then keeps pounding her arse hole ring with his cock sliding his shafts all along her arse hole ring she comes then he stops choking her she gasps for air then screams as he holds her hips then slides his shafts along her arse hole she screams as he keeps pumping his cock up her arse then spits and feels his shafts sliding along her tight arse hole ring as he slams his cock up deep up her arse hole then grabs her hips and thrashes his cock hard and fast up her tight arse hole she screams as he slides his shafts all along her arse hole ring she screams argh them comes he keeps sliding his shafts along her arse hole ring then turns her around then lifts her up and shoves his cock up her arse vertically he keeps lifting her up his cock sliding up her arse hole as she bounces up and down off his cock he keeps lifting her up and sliding his cock up into her arse hole with hard and fast upwards heaves sliding his whole cock deep up into her arse hole slapping her arse cheek he spanks her then keeps lifting her up and plugging his cock in her arse hole then slides his girth along her arse hole ring then pins her throat into the wall and chokes her at the same time pumps his shafts up her arse with hard and fast upwards heaves his cock slides deep and hard up her arse hole pumping his shafts along her arse hole ring his shafts slides up into her arse hole he keep choking her into the wall with his hands then feels his shafts sliding up along her arse hole ring her eyes roll back as she comes he pins her to the wall and keeps sliding his cock up into her arse hole he slides his cock back and forth up her arse hole then keeps sliding his shafts all along her arse hole ring he sees her eyes roll back as she comes he takes his hands off her throat and stops choking her as she inhales he re catches her hips and side then slams her into the walls and keeps sliding his cock up her arse she screams as he hammer and drill his cock up her plugging her arse hole with his girth he slides his shafts back and forth along her arse hole ring then heaves his cock deep up her arse she screams argh then comes he keeps pumping his shafts along her arse hole ring and sliding his cock up her arse he slams her into the wall making a thud then slides his cock up her arse hole with hard and fast upwards heaves he smashes her tight arse hole drilling her and shoving his cock deep up into her arse hole as she screams argh then comes he keeps pounding her arse hole with his cock then take a her on the bed then leaps with her onto the bed and slides his cock up her arse hole then keeps sliding his shafts all along her arse hole ring she screams as he keeps sliding his shafts up her arse hole pounding her and ramming her arse hole into the bed sliding his shafts all along her arse hole she screams argh argh argh in a echoing tone as he slides his shafts up her arse hole ring then as he is pumping her arse hole missionary he thrusts upwards and rams his girth into her arse hole ring and stretches her arse hole she screams argh then comes as he pounds her arse hole ring into the mattress with hard and fast down wards thrusts he keeps pounding her arse hole into the bed sliding his shafts up along her arse hole as she screams argh then comes he keeps pumping his shafts along her arse hole ring as she screams he feels his top shaft scraping her arse hole ring and sliding back and forth as she keeps screaming he gets her by the throat and chokes her into the mattress then with his hands around her throat he pounds her arse hole into the bed with his stiff cock he slides his shafts all along her arse hole ring then keeps pumping her the pounds his cock into her arse hole and rams her arse hole into the bed as he is drilling his cock up her arse he stiffens his erection then shoves it deep up her tight arse hole ring then slides his shafts along her arse hole her eyes roll back and she comes he takes his hand soft her throat then rams and smashes her arse hole with his cock and hammer his cock deep up into her arse hole ring pumping his shafts along her tight arse hole as she screams ah ah ah as he drills her arse hole with his shafts sliding along her tight arse hole ring he lifts her up then throws her on her stomach then slide his shafts up and into her arse hole she keeps screaming as he thrashes her pounding her with deep up-wards heaves he stiffens his cock then slides it up her arse hole then keeps sliding his shafts up along her arse hole ring he feels his girth pounding her arse hole as she screams argh then comes he keeps sliding his cock up her arse hole then scrapes her arse hole ring with his shafts sliding along her tight arse hole ring then heaves his cock up deep up into her arse hole as she scream argh then comes he keeps pumping her then reaches his hand around and chokes her she makes a choking sound then he slides his cock harder and faster up her arse hole he slides his shafts up her arse hole then pumps his cock up her arse he rams and slams her arse hole into the bed then slides his shafts all along her arse hole ring as he chokes her from behind prone boning her he slides his shafts all up and along her arse hole ring he keeps spit-ting then spits again and slides his cock along her arse hole ring he pumps his shafts up into her arse hole as she comes he takes his hands off her throat then keeps sliding his shafts up along her arse hole she screams argh as he pounds her arse hole into the bed ramming her with upwards thrust he heaves his cock deep and hard up her arse hole ring then slides his shafts up into her arse hole she screams argh then comes he feels his shafts sliding all up along her arse hole ring then takes his cock out then turns her over then slides his cock in her mouth as he groans and comes he lifts the back of her head up with his hands then kneel-ing there over her body he forces her mouth onto his cock then shoves his cock deep down her throat as he keeps shooting come into the back of her throat he hears her gag and cough splattering on his cock choking on his come she swallows then gulps keeps coughing and splattering as he forces her mouth onto his girth he slides his cock out of her mouth making a plug-ging sound then takes her up from between his legs with his hands then kisses her and tilts his head and open mouth pashes her sliding his tongue down her throat he changes sides and open mouth pashes her then keeps sliding his tongue down her throat and kissing her

Ivan sees the queen sitting on a chair in the study when he walks in she bed a tease then turns around in it then tells him to come and take her he walks over taking his shafts odd then pants by the time he gets to her he got a hardon then pulls her undies down then leaves them at her knees then straddles her legs then puts his cock up her vagina then starts pumping vigorously as she is screaming he slides his cock vertically up her vagina she is kneeling in the chair her knees to the back of it as he straddles her legs closed together then feels his shafts sliding in and out of her vagina ring as she screams he keeps holding her by the hips and sliding his shafts back and forth along her vagina ring then feels her vagina leak then become warner inside he keeps plugging her vagina with his cock then slide his cock deeper and further up into her vagina she keeps screaming as he steps forward then plugs her vagina with his girth then slides his shafts back and forth as he is pumping her his cock triples in hardness and he feels his shafts slide all along her vagina ring then keeps sliding his cock all along her vagina ring as she screams argh then comes he feels his cock sliding all along her vagina ring then re grabs her hips and thrashes her pounding his cock hard and fast straight up into her vagina he rams her pussy with pounding upward thrusts and penetrating heaves his cock slides all up along her vagima ring as he spanks her arse cheek and spanks her then re grabs her hips and hammers his cock up her vagina then stuffs his whole cock deep up into her tight pussy plugging her vagina with his girth he slides his shafts all up along her vagima ring as she screams argh then comes he is thrashing her smashing his cock vertically up deep up her vagina then keeps pumping his shafts all up along her pussy ring he feels his cock grate tear and thread her vagina his body slamming her muscly arse cheeks as he grabs her hips and pounds her with rapid hard and fast upwards heaves lunging his cock up her vagina he launches his erection up her pussy his shafts sliding all up along her vagina ring as she scenes argh then comes he keeps sliding his cock up her vagina then holds his shaft then lifts his cock up his knob slides into her arse hole ring then as he pushes his cock up her arse she screams and he slides his shafts up all along her arse hole ring them as she keeps screaming and holding onto the back of the chair he stands there pounding her arse hole ring with hard and fast upwards heaves that smash his girth into her arse hole ring he keeps ramming her and plugging his cock up her arse as she screams ah ah ah with each thrust he keeps sliding his shafts all up along her arse hole ring them pumps his cock up her arse hole with vertical upwards thrusts he buries his erection up her tight arse hole and hammers his cock up her arse hole ring as she screams argh then comes he keeps pumping her with hard and fast upwards heaves then slides his shafts all up and along her arse hole ring pounding her arse cheeks forward his shafts slide up along her arse hole as she screams oh my god he holds her hips then pounds her with deep upwards thrusts ramming his cock up her arse then re bracing her by the hips and pounding her arse hole with his girth sliding his shafts all up and along her arse hole she screams argh the comes he keeps sliding his shafts all up along her arse hole then chokes her she makes a choking sound he pulls her throat back and her body then rams his cock up her arse pumping her with rapid hard and fast thrusts he drills her arse hole with his cock pounding her with intense rough deep upwards heaves he smashes her arse hole ring with his girth then slides his shafts all up along her arse hole then keeps pumping his shafts up her arse hole then keeps holding onto her throat with his hands at the same time is pounding his cock up her arse hole and sliding his shafts all up along her arse e hole ring she comes then he takes his hands off her throat then slides his cock up her arse hole he feels his shafts slide all up along her arse hole ring then spits on her arse hole then keeps spitting then smashes his girth into her arse hole and pounds his cock deep and hard up her arse he keeps sliding his shafts all up along her arse hole then pounds her arse hole ring with his erection going deep up inside her arse hole she keeps s reaming as he drills and smashes her arse hole ring with his cock sliding his shafts all up along her arse hole ring he keeps pumping her with hard and fast upwards thrusts heaving his erection vertically up her arse as she screams argh then comes he keeps sliding his cock all up along her arse hole then grabs her hips and smashes her she is screaming as he is coming his cock explodes he keeps grabbing her hips and is hammering her arse hole she screams as he keeps sliding his cock all up along her arse hole after he has come pumping her arse hole he slides his cock out then lifts her up in his arm then kisses her sliding his tongue down her throat he tilts his head then keeps sliding his tongue deep into her throat and open mouth pashing her

Ivan walks into the bedroom the queen is sitting by the windowsill in lingerie with her hands on her knees and her legs spread looking at him he walks over to her then kisses her sideways onto the windowsill then with both hands he puts his fingers under her undies then peels them down to take them off quickly then keeps kissing her and tilting his head and sliding his tongue down her throat he pulls down his pants then gets on top of her then puts his arms on the windowsill then heaves his body up his cock slides up her vagina as she screams he keeps sliding his shafts up all along her vagina ring and kissing her on both sides of her mouth as his top shafts scrapes her vagina ring as it slides up her pussy she keeps screaming as he pounds his girth up into her vagina ring and he heaves his whole body upwards and jams his cock up her vagina he threads grates and tears her vagina ring with rapid hard and fast upwards lunges that keeps his shafts sliding all up along her tight vagina ring as he feels her vagina leak warm juice he keeps sliding his cock all up and along her vagina ring his knob rams into her cervix she keeps screaming passionately argh argh argh with each upwards heave and hard and fast pump he feels his veiny top shaft pleasuring her g spot as he rocks his cock up along her upper roof of her vagina she screams argh then comes as he keeps sliding his shafts all up along her vagina ring he chokes her she makes a choking sound as he wraps his hands around her throat and slides his shafts back and forth up along her pussy ring he can see the face she make of panic as he keeps pumping his cock up her pussy with hard and fast upwards thrusts he plugs her vagina and his shafts slide all up and down her vagina ring as he keeps shoving his cock deep up inside her vagina he keeps his arms out straight and his back up as his hips gyrate and his shafts slides all along her pussy ring her eyes roll back as she comes he takes he hands from her throat then she gasps for air and inhales then keeps screaming as his cock slams up into her pussy and shoves his girth back and forth along her vagina ring he slides his shafts all up along her pussy she screams ah ah ah with every pump he slides his cock vertically up her vagina his girth stretching her vagina ring he lifts her up from the window sill keeps rooting her and stands up and slides his cock up into her vagina and she bounces high up and down off his cock as he gets right up and under her and vertically impales her with his cock sliding straight up into her pussy her breasts are bouncing as she looks her arms around his shoulders and holds in screaming as he keeps pumping his cock up her he feels his whole cock going vertically up her tight pussy and his shafts sliding all up along her vagina ring making a slapping sound as his cock pounds up into her vagina and she screams argh then comes he keeps doing rapid upwards heaves and hard and fast lunges he feels his shafts sliding all up along her vagina ring as he has his arms around her lifting her up and down slamming her with his cock she keeps screaming as he stands there by the windowsill sliding his shafts all up along her vagina ring as she screams argh argh argh with each upwards pump he re braces her curvy arse and smooth legs in his arms lifting her up properly then keeps sliding his shafts all up and down along her vagina ring he feels his cock stiffen then his shafts expand threading her vagina as he pumps his cock up into it he spanks her arse cheek from behind whacking her making a crisp smack sound she is screaming looking at him as he keeps pumping her up and down off his cock his shafts sliding vertically up and down along her tight vagina ring as he smashes his knob into her cervix with a heap of rough upwards heaves he does energetic upwards thrusts that keep his cock drilling up her pussy he slides his shafts all up and down along her tight pussy ring as she screams argh then comes he keeps pounding her pussy and pumping her up and down all along his vertical pole as he keeps sliding his shafts all up along her vagina ring she is screaming he kisses her then slams her into the wall and keeps sliding his shafts all up along her pussy as he ravishes her and keeps sliding his cock up along her vagina she keeps screaming he keeps pumping his cock up her then heaves his whole body upwards his veiny top shaft slides all up along her pussy as she screams argh then comes he slams her up into the wall again as she scream argh and makes a loud thud he slides his cock up into her pussy and pumps his shafts up all along her vagina he feels his cock hammering upwards sliding vertically straight up her vagina as he gets up and under her his girth stretching her vagina ring as he slides his shafts up along her vagina he chokes her into the wall then slides his cock up her arse she makes a choking sound then he rams his cock up her with hard and fast upwards heaves he plugs her arse hole with his cock then slides his shafts all up along her arse hole ring he feels his shafts threading her arse hole as he pumps his cock up and up further along her arse hole ring he keeps choking her into the wall his hands around her throat as his cock drills up her arse hole he feels a tight sensation all along his knob and shafts as they scrape her arse hole ring he keeps pumping his shafts up along her arse hole ring and feels them sliding up her arse hole he keeps pounding her and thrashing her arse hole with his girth stretching her arse hole ring as he shoves it up her then as he keeps sliding his shafts all up along her arse hole ring she comes he takes his hands off her throat as she gasps for air he keeps sliding his shafts up along her tight arse hole ring then lifts her off the wall then holds her up and pumps his cock up her arse sliding his cock vertically up her arse hole he keeps pumping her standing up his arms around her legs and arse as his cock bounces her up and down in the air he sees her breasts bouncing as she holds onto his neck looping her arms around his body and screaming as his cock drills up her arse hole with hard and fast upwards heaves he keeps pumping his cock up into her arse hole she keeps screaming his shafts sliding all up along her arse hole he keeps pumping his shafts up along her arse hole his body males a loud slamming sound as it slams into hers as his cock hammers up into her arse hole he feels his cock stiffen and his shafts expand then she screams louder as his cock stretches her arse hole ring and he slides his shafts all up along her arse hole he keeps pumping his cock up her arse and re braces her properly lifting her back up he slides his shafts all up along her arse hole shoving and pumping his girth into her arse hole ring as she keeps screaming he keeps sliding his shafts all up along her arse hole he puts her back on the top of the lounge then slides his shafts all up along her arse hole rocking his shafts along her arse hole ring he watches as she screams she holds onto the back of the lounge with her arms as he slides his shafts all up along her arse hole ring she screams as he hammers her arse hole and shoves his cock deep and fast up her arse thrashing her arse hole sliding his shafts up along her arse hole ring he rocks his shafts back and forth along her arse hole ring then spanks her arse cheek from up and under her then makes a loud clap as he palm connects with her arse cheek then he slides his shafts all up along her arse hole then smashes her arse hole with his girth slamming it into her arse hole ring he stretches her arse hole ring pounding his cock up into her arse hole and shoving his erection deep up her arse hole ring he keeps sliding his shafts all up and down her arse hole then slams his cock straight up into her arse hole she is screaming as he slides his shafts all up along her arse hole then spits and pounds her arse hole smashing his girth up into her arse hole ring he stretches it then keeps pumping his shafts all up along her arse hole he belts her arse cheek again then slides his shafts all along her arse hole he drops her down off the lounge as she falls on her arse he shoves his cock in her mouth then comes he pins her between the back of the lounge and his cock forcing his cock down the back of her throat as he grabs the back of the lounge then shoves his cock deep down the back if her throat and comes he shoots come into the back of her throat and she splatters and gags choking on his come she gags then swallows as he keeps his cock down the back of her throat she gulps then he heaves her up then she sits with her arse cheeks that little bit on the lounge that makes them look sexy then he tilts his head and open mouth pashes her sliding his hand onto the back of her neck he pulls her lips forward onto his and keeps sliding his tongue down her throat and kissing her

Ivan walks up the hall the queen is walking the opposite way with a sexy runway walk where she looks like a runway model she has heels on as he puts her into the wall lifts up her dress then shoves his cock up her vagina then starts pounding her with hard and fast upwards heaves she is screaming as he attacks her with deep upwards thrusts of his cock he hits her pussy hard with his cock smashing it deep up her he feels his knob hitting her cervix as his shafts thread grates and tears her vagina ring he keeps pounding his cock up her pussy hammering his cock up deep inside her vagina he keeps smashing his cock up her pussy she screams as he reaches around then slides his hand all over her breasts while doing vertical upwards heaves with his cock he keeps rubbing her breasts with his hands and gently squeezes them while his shafts slide hard and fast all along her vagina ring he feels his shafts grating her vagina and his girth threading her pussy ring as he launches upwards he stiffens his cock and the shafts scrape her vagina ring and stretches it he can feel it especially around the top section of his girth he keeps slamming his girth into her vagina ring stimulating his shafts she is screaming bent over in the hall her elbows and forearms against the wall she is making a kettle boiling sound as he thrashes her and pounds her pussy with his cock smashing his cock deep up inside her vagina almost lifts her arse and legs up in the air as he gets right up under her with hard and rough upwards heaves shoving his girth up her pussy lips as she screams argh then comes he keeps sliding his shafts all up and along her vagina ring then feels a warm feeling around his knob as her vagina leaks it becomes more slippery and he slides his shafts quicker all up and along her wet pussy his cock slides deeper and further I to her wet pussy his girth pounds her vagina ring as he keeps launching his whole body upwards and stiffening his cock and impaling her vagina he slides his shafts all up along her vagina ring and pumps his cock up her pussy then rams and slams her with rapid intense upwards strokes he ravishes her pussy and keeps sliding his shafts all up along her vagina ring as she screams argh then comes he holds her hips then keeps sliding his shafts all up along her vagina ring then pins her body to the wall and slams his cock into her vagina and pounds her pussy into the wall she keeps screaming as he kisses her and tilts his head and pashes her as he slides his shafts up all along her vagina ring as he goes faster and harder she braces herself holding the wall with both palms screaming looking back at him as he slides his shafts all up along her vagina ring he she screams as he spanks her then keeps sliding his cock up her pussy with vertical up-wards heaves he stiffens his cock as it slides in then it expands and grates her vagina on the way in she screams as he feels his girth scraping her vagina ring he keeps launching his pole verti-cally up into her vagina he feels his cock going straight in and out up and down hammering his cock up her vagina he keeps sliding his shafts all along her vagina ring then kicks her ankle out as her legs open wider she screams as he shoves his cock harder and deeper up her pussy his shafts sliding all up and along her vagina ring she screams as he pulls her hair then keeps pumping his cock up her vagina he turns her around then as he kisses her into the wall with his lips he lifts her up then keeps pumping his cock up her vagina and sliding his shafts all up along her vagina ring he feels his cock throb and go harder his shafts expand inside her then he grates threads and scrapes her vagina ring as his cock squeezes up into her tight vagina he keeps sliding his shafts all up along her vagina he keeps pump-ing his cock up her vagina then puts his hands around her throat he hears her make a choking sound then he slides his shafts all up along her arse hole ring then keeps slamming her pussy with his cock and drilling his cock up her vagina with hard and fast upwards heaves she rams her pussy with his shafts then keeps sliding his cock all up along her pussy then he thrashes her pounding her he vertically impales her pussy her eyes roll back and she comes he takes his hands off her throat then she gasps for air inhaling he keeps grating her vagina ring with his shafts and sliding them all up along her pussy then keeps pumping her cock up her then he rams and drills his cock straight up her vagina heaving himself upwards his erect cock spears her pussy and he pounds her pussy into the wall thrusting forwards he keeps sliding his shafts all up along her vagina then does rapid intense rough upwards thrusts that have his cock slamming her pussy he lifts her up from the wall then keeps pumping his cock up and under her shoving his cock deep up inside her vagina she is bouncing her breasts going up and down as he holds her there pumping his cock vertically up and under her vagina getting right up and inside her with hard and fast upwards thrusts then slides his cock up her arse then as she screams louder he keeps sliding his shafts all up along her arse hole ring and pumps his cock up into her arse hole he keeps spitting on her arse hole then does vertical upwards heaves that have his cock pumping her arse hole and his shafts sliding all up along her arse hole ring as he is pumping her she is screaming ah ah ah with each upwards thrust he feels his shafts sliding all up along her arse hole ring then re braces her getting his arms under the back of her knees then lifts her up drilling his cock up into her arse hole he slides his shafts all up along her arse hole then launches upwards and spears her arse hole with his cock vertically impaling her tight arse as he shoves his cock up her he stiffens it then it scrapes and threads her tight arse hole ring he keeps sliding his shafts all up along her arse hole then as he thrashes her and pounds her arse hole ring with his shafts she screams argh then comes he keeps sliding his shafts all up along her arse hole then belts her arse spanking her it makes a loud clap sound as is palm hits her arse cheek he re braces her lifting her back up then slides his shafts all up along her arse hole ring he feels her tight arse hole ring going up and down all along his shafts as he keeps pumping his cock up her arse she screams argh then comes he slides his shafts all along her arse hole ring then slams her into the wall and chokes her then as she makes a choking sound and he is pinning her to the wall choking her with his arms out straight he feels his cock stiffen then grate and thread her arse hole as he shoves his girth into her arse hole ring and pounds her arse hole into the wall then he slides his shafts all up along her arse hole ring then keeps pumping her and sliding his shafts all up along her arse hole ring she comes then he takes his hands away she gasps for air then screams as his shafts keep sliding all up along her arse hole he keeps pumping his cock up her arse hole ring then slams her into the wall and shoves his cock straight up her arse hole vertically impaling her with hard and fast upwards heaves he feels his shafts sliding all up along her arse hole ring he lifts her up off the wall then keeps stroking his cock up her arse hole and pumping her with hard and fast upwards lunges he keeps her bouncing up and down off his cock she is screaming argh argh argh with each vertical thrust his shaft slides all up along her arse hole ring he feels his girth stretching her arse hole ring as he shoves his cock deep up her arse and drills it up her she keeps screaming as he slides his shafts all up along her arse hole ring he puts her down then he hears her knees drop on the floor he holds the back of her head then slams her head onto his cock and comes he groans then feels his cock spasm inside her mouth as he pumps and shoots come into the back of her throat she keeps deep throating him as he hears her gag and cough choking on his come she splatters then keeps gagging as he forces her mouth onto his girth she keeps gagging then swallows as he hears her gulp and splatter he has filled her throat up with come